D1607995

A LAWLESS MOUNTAIN TOWN BORN OF GOLD AND BUILT BY
GREED IS BESET BY ANCIENT HORROR

CLAW
EMERGENCE BOOK 2
INTO DAYLIGHT

KATIE BERRY

Copyright © 2023 Katie Berry

All rights reserved.

ASIN: B0C9XQ9RT8

Print ISBN-13: 9798850772949

No portions of this book may be reproduced without permission from the publisher, except as permitted by Canadian copyright law.

Published by Fuzzy Bean Books

Cover Art Copyright © 2023 Katie Berry

This is a work of fiction. Names, characters, businesses, places, events, locales, and incidents are either the products of the author's imagination or used in a fictitious manner. Any resemblance to actual persons, living or dead, or actual events is purely coincidental.

ENTER TO WIN!

Become a Katie Berry Books Insider; you'll be glad you did. By simply sharing your email address*, you will be entered into the monthly draws! That's right, draws, plural.

Each month there will be two draws: one for a free digital download of one of my audiobooks and the other for a free autographed copy of one of my novels delivered right to your mailbox.

There will be other contests, chapter previews, short stories, and more coming soon, so don't miss out!

Join today at:

https://katieberry.ca/become-a-katie-berry-books-insider-and-win/

*Your email address will not be sold, traded, or given away. It will be kept strictly confidential and will only be used by Katie Berry Books to notify you of new content (or perhaps that you're another lucky winner of the monthly draws).

PREFACE

Writing a book is always challenging, as you can imagine, but it can be even more so when facing unexpected surprises. That was the case with the book you currently hold in your hands, and I had several obstacles that delayed its production.

One of the biggest challenges was my hip replacement surgery and recovery. It was quite painful at times and hard to get comfortable and find the right position in which to write for many months. I must admit, it was great for research since I had to hop around on crutches as Caleb does in the story.

Just as I entered post-production on the novel, my lovely little cat, Mimsie, went missing. It was quite distressing, and I found it hard to focus on writing for any length of time or even find the motivation some days. Mimsie was like a little daughter to me, my sweet little soul, as I called her, and it is truly heart-wrenching to have her in my life no longer. As of this writing, she has yet to come home, and I feel such a hole in my heart some days. However, when I hear stories of people whose cats return out of the blue after several months, I still hold some hope, but it fades a little more with each passing day.

It is ironic that I have been writing about monster ants in the novel since I have been having some real-life issues of my own with some of the tiniest ants I have ever seen. Just mother nature providing me with some free inspiration, I suppose, so that's always appreciated.

That's about all for now, so I will leave you to read this tall tale of friendship, courage, greed and monsters. In it, you will find more of the characters you've come to love, more desperate situations, more thrills and chills, and hopefully, more laughter as well.

But before I go, I want to thank you again for your support. Writing is my only job and the only one I want. It fills my days with challenge, creativity and satisfaction. I am so very grateful to have you along for this journey and hope as you read this, it gives you some of the joy I had while writing it. I will see you at the back of the book. Enjoy!

-Katie Berry

July 1st, 2023

For Mimsie

Thank you for your companionship, your love and the joy you bring to my soul whenever I think of you.

CHAPTER ONE

The monstrous spider scuttled closer to Caleb and the doctor and then paused. Behind it, the swarm of spiderlings from the produce bins crawled overtop of each other in their eagerness to catch up to their mother.

Shaking his head in disbelief at the approaching arachnids, Brown said, "This is fascinating. I wouldn't have thought they could operate at such a high level in the confines of this frigid environment."

"Fascinatin' isn't the word I would've used, Doc," Caleb said, his eyes wide, his breath coming in short gasps. The spiders were now getting dangerously close. Mama was in the lead, the spiderlings fanning out behind her in a small regiment of eight-legged death. She paused again to let out another low, barely audible hiss, then continued to advance on them.

Fortunately, these arachnids were not moving as quickly as the one he'd had the displeasure of meeting up in the cavern. Despite dropping to the floor from the silken web over the produce bins with some alacrity a moment earlier, most of that seemed caused by gravity. And though Caleb was pleased to see the cold had slowed them somewhat, it wasn't enough by half, as far as he was concerned.

Caleb looked from the advancing spiders to Brown, who still held the brass pump sprayer, and said, "Were you goin' to use that little mister of yours any time soon, Doc, or were you just goin' to show it to them?"

Finally seeming to recall what he held in his hands, Brown said, "Yes, my boy. Sorry, I was taken by surprise by the sheer number of these creatures." He handed Caleb the long-handled scoop net, which he'd also been holding, saying, "Take this for me, would you?"

Backing up slightly, Caleb wedged both crutches under one arm and took the net. "I'll do my best, but I'm not a juggler."

Adjusting the nozzle on the front of the sprayer, Brown said, "I think I need a bit more reach." With that done, he aimed at the mama spider and let loose a sputtering stream of the acidic spray.

Droplets rained down on the spiders in a heavy mist, and thankfully, they had the desired effect. As the first burning drops touched Mama, she let out another faint hiss and dodged sideways and slightly backward. Due to her speed, she only received a small spattering of spray. And though it seemed to cause the animal some discomfort, it had minimal effect, no doubt due to the thickness of the spider's skin and its larger size.

The smaller spiders were not as lucky, and they spasmed for a moment as the solution coated them, then curled up their legs into little balls as they died. This cleared a path for the two men, and they were able to move back toward the tool room and away from the locked doors at their backs.

Cornelius let out a small whoop of delight and said excitedly, "It works just as I'd hoped!" He pumped the sprayer several more times, and more of the burning mist settled over a larger portion of the spiderlings. Almost immediately, they curled up into small death balls, twitching and spasming as the acetic acid in the solution penetrated their thin, newborn skin. Mama Spider hissed again and tried to circle around the men, her surviving offspring fanning out behind.

Caleb nodded toward the spiders, saying, "I'm glad it works, but let's not count your spiders before they're all dead, Doc."

The doctor's earlier comment about the animals not being acclimatised to the cold reminded Caleb of his experiences in the sweltering South African heat during the Boer War. Their heavy wool uniforms had not been conducive to hot climates such as Africa, and the troops had fought as much against their apparel as they had against the Boers. Thankfully, the army had introduced khaki uniforms shortly after his arrival in South Africa, so he hadn't suffered from the heat for too long. He was quite certain that if the temperature had been any warmer in this ice house, the pair of them would already be paralysed and in the process of having eggs laid in their bodies.

As they backed through the doorway to the tool room, more thoughts of his time in Africa swam through Caleb's head. At first, he couldn't figure out why, but it became clearer as they passed through the tool room. The Boer's guerilla tactics had been quite effective against the regimented actions of Her Majesty's Fifth. Caleb had seen many army mates succumb to the Boer's short, highly focused, and violent attacks. Sometimes they seemed to appear out of nowhere and later vanish just as quickly. The Dutch settlers used the rugged, mountainous landscape's steep hills and valleys to their advantage. They would swoop down and ambush the condensed columns of soldiers whose actions were constrained by the narrow geography. And when not pouncing on the British in the mountains, the Boers would stalk their enemy unseen using the long grass of the veldt for cover.

These thoughts of Africa's varied terrain caused Caleb to say, "I think we need to retreat further; I have an idea." He nodded toward the door that led to the catwalk over the pit, keeping his eyes on the spiders at all times. He hoped the spiders might be even slower when out over the ice since it was much cooler there. And it might be easier to defend their position since the spiders could only come from one direction and not fan out to surround them as they were seemingly attempting to do. And so, just as the Boers had taken advantage of the local terrain to launch their attacks, Caleb hoped to use the ice house's layout as a defensive strategy to spare their lives.

The doctor pumped his sprayer again at the remaining spiders, and this time they dispersed as he did, avoiding most of the mist, and only a small portion curled up in the throes of death. Seeing the creatures avoiding the spray as they did, Brown remarked, "It appears they're learning."

They backed from the tool room and edged onto the catwalk, Caleb slapping at the spiders with the net as Brown sprayed them again and again. Soon, they'd crossed most of the catwalk and were nearing the entrance. The chill of the ice blocks below penetrated Caleb's winter jacket, and he wondered how the spiders liked it. Watching their erratic and somewhat slower movements, he gave a small grin, happy to see they didn't. Mama Spider was now at the back of the pack, herding her offspring forward to attack the men as they retreated.

Cornelius continued to pump as they backed up the remaining distance, Caleb swatting what the doctor missed. Unfortunately, many of the baby spiders had now moved off to the edges of the catwalk, attempting to crawl underneath and overtop to avoid the deadly mist and, at the same time, sneak around behind them.

Suddenly, the sprayer gave a sputtering wheeze as it spat out the last of the acidic solution. Shaking his head, the doctor said, "Well, that's it, my boy. Our deterrent is no longer a viable option."

"What d'ya mean, Doc?"

"We're out of juice and on our own."

"I was afraid that's what you meant."

As they continued to back up, Caleb removed the jacket from his shoulders and flung it toward the approaching spiders saying, "Here you go, something to warm you up." It flopped overtop some of them, and others scattered in panic, falling to the ice below as they did.

Moments later, they were in the vestibule, the single hanging lantern bathing the small room's walls with sinuous shadows. Despite the lack of sunlight, it was noticeably warmer here.

Giving another small hiss, Mama scuttled into the vestibule just as Caleb reached the front door. He handed the net to the doctor, saying, "You can probably handle this better than me."

"Capital idea, my boy." Brown hung the sprayer on his belt and took the long-handled net in both hands.

Still several feet away, the large spider paused and trembled momentarily, and Caleb wondered if it was cold. Then, all at once, he saw the tremble for what it was, preparation, and the spider suddenly launched into the air.

Fortunately, Brown had been paying attention, and he whisked the net out, deftly catching the creature inside. "Gotcha!" he said triumphantly.

"These things can leap now?" Caleb said in amazement. He wondered how things could get any worse and added, "Well, at least they can't fly."

"That would be fascinating to see but highly doubtful."

With the spider's pointed, hairy legs now tangled in the net's webbing, the doctor gave it a couple of twirls to seal the creature inside, and he said to it with glee, "Now, you're all mine, my pretty."

Spiderlings that had been hanging back behind their now-captured mother began scuttling toward them en masse. Despite the number of spiders Caleb had seen curl up and die thanks to the doctor's spray, these things just kept coming, and there seemed no end to them. With a shudder, he felt his anxiety ratchet up to new levels.

"Now would be an excellent time to depart these premises," the doctor observed.

"You read my mind, Doc." Almost backed against the thick cedar entrance door, Caleb turned slightly, about to reach for the handle. His heart skipped a beat, and he felt suddenly glad he'd looked instead of blindly grabbing behind his back. One of the larger spiderlings had clambered onto the doorknob only inches from his fingers. He jerked his arm back and grabbed the small crowbar, which he just remembered was hanging from his belt. Face filled with disgust, Caleb stabbed the spider with the crowbar's tip, impaling the creature. It dropped to the ground, its green innards leaking onto the rough-cut wooden floor.

With the spider dead and no more in sight of the handle, Caleb turned it with panicked fingers and almost fell out the door. He hopped out into the welcoming heat of the late June afternoon.

Brown backed out next, stomping on any of the small spiders that approached the doorway as he went. "Hold our friend here for a moment, would you?" He handed the net to Caleb, who took it with a reluctant grimace, and Brown slammed the door shut.

Caleb held the wriggling spider out as far in front of

himself as he could and looked with loathing at the squirming, hissing thing. "What are you going to do with this, Doc? Keep it as a pet? And what about the rest of them? We didn't kill them all, you know. There were still quite a few left."

"That is an excellent question, my boy. There is always the hope that without their mother to guide them, the rest of her little family will wither away and die."

"Or perhaps freeze to death," Caleb suggested.

Shaking his head, Brown replied, "The temperature is not quite cold enough in there for that, and since we can't rely on hope to solve our problem, we'll have to come back soon with a better arsenal to clean them out." Brown reached into a tan leather satchel slung over one shoulder and withdrew a piece of string. While Caleb continued to hold the spider, the doctor tied off the top of the net so the oversized arachnid couldn't escape.

With that done, Cornelius returned to his satchel, rummaged around for a moment, then gave an "Aha!" and withdrew a piece of paper. He unfolded it and positioned it on the door with several thumbtacks also drawn from the satchel, saying, "You just never know when you might need one of these."

Hand-Printed in large block letters, the sign read, 'QUARANTINED! DO NOT ENTER.'

Brown took the net from Caleb and helped him climb aboard Emily. The mule had become a bit skittish after seeing the spider in the net, and she snorted in agitation as Caleb climbed aboard. Once he was in the saddle, he scruffed her mane to comfort her, looking at the arachnid as he did. "Yes, it's a horrible ugly thing, isn't it, Emily."

The mule whinnied in seeming agreement.

As they began their journey back to town, the doctor commented, "Aesthetics are all in the eye of the beholder, my boy. And whatever you and your mule may think of this beast, bear in mind we just might need its assistance in the very near future."

CHAPTER TWO

Thomas Sinclair raised his glass and sipped some of the whisky inside, his eyes trained on the woman before him.

Across his massive mahogany desk sat Kitty Welch. All she could see of the Scotsman over his glass were his bushy eyebrows and tumultuous tuft of kinky red hair. After being escorted into the room by Angeline and Lucias, she'd been directed to sit in a chair across the desk from Thomas.

Though it was a beautiful sunny day outside, the thick velveteen drapes to Sinclair's office were drawn tight, and no light from the outside world could enter. Despite the heat of the summer afternoon outside, the room remained chilly, almost cold, in fact. Kitty shivered and pulled her thin shawl tighter around her slender shoulders.

With a small sigh, Sinclair placed his glass back on a cork coaster in the centre of his shining desk. "So, lassie, what did you overhear of our little conversation?" As he spoke, Thomas gave a slight nod toward Lucias, who stood off to one side and slightly behind him, shrouded in shadows.

Giving a small shake of her head, Kitty replied, "Nothin', really. Only that you wanted Lucias to change people's minds if they had any reservations and that he and Angeline should take care of that other business; that's all I heard."

Sinclair tented his fingers and replied, "Well, we don't have to worry about that then."

This was encouraging news, Kitty thought. With hope rising in her heart, she said, "Really?"

"Yes, really. Because that other business just happens to be you," Angeline said from her place on the scttee, a wicked gleam in her eyes.

Kitty's heart skipped a beat at this pronouncement, her eyes widening in surprise, and she asked, "Business with me?"

"Aye, it's something I've been meaning to tend to for a while now." Sinclair removed a cigar from a nearby box and amputated one end with his small guillotine cigar cutter. With a solid thunk, the cigar's tip fell into a miniature basket on the other side. Kitty shuddered slightly as she watched this, envisioning what may have happened to her if she'd stayed in Aberdeen instead of fleeing the country as she had. Although she didn't believe she would have received the death penalty for her actions back home, the sight of the diminutive device of death on the desk nonetheless brought back some unwanted memories.

Sinclair lit the cigar and leaned back in his thickly-padded leather chair, then took a long drag and blew several smoke rings. His chair was on small castor wheels, which allowed him to roll around the room's polished hardwood floors without standing. Puffing his pruned Panatela like a potbellied locomotive, he sat upright, chugged over to the bookcase next to his display cabinet, and withdrew what looked like a ledger. He rolled back to his desk, opened the ledger and pulled out several pieces of yellow paper which looked alarmingly like telegrams. This was not a good sign, Kitty realised.

Sinclair shuffled through the telegrams for a moment, then held one up and asked, "What d'ya know of the events in

Newhaven?"

Kitty shook her head and said nothing, her eyes growing even wider. It seemed that Thomas Sinclair knew much more of her past than he'd ever let on.

Sinclair sorted through the telegrams again and held up another, asking, "And what of Tullibody?"

Her shoulders sagging, Kitty shook her head again, but with much less conviction, then said, "Hardly anything."

Angeline said from her seat across the room, "That's not what you told your friends."

Kitty glared at the woman but said nothing. She knew this to be untrue, and though she'd shared some vague details with Lucy, it had not been more than that. How had Thomas learned of Newhaven and Tullibody, she wondered. It was something which she would never share with anyone and never had so far, even in her most soul-searching admissions to Lucy. And yet, for whatever reason, her employer seemed to have more information on her than she could have ever imagined, information which delved more deeply into her background than she could ever have wanted, and it all seemed thanks to Angeline.

Looking to another telegram in the ledger, Thomas said, "Ya might want to do a wee bit of talkin', lassie, if ya know what's good for ya. I have friends inside the Yard, and I'm sure they would be more than happy to know I have some information regardin' both of those unsolved burglaries and more."

This was everything Kitty had hoped would never happen. Her second-floor shenanigans here in this nameless western town were bad enough, but the thought that her past had now caught up with her and that she might be arrested and shipped back to Aberdeen to answer for it was something she just couldn't bear.

William McLeod had been the boy who'd gotten her into the burglary business when she'd only been a wide-eyed girl of sixteen. His good looks and gentlemanly ways, not to mention the money he lavished upon her, were too much for her to resist, and she'd been smitten by his charms. He always seemed to have the money to take her somewhere or treat her to a meal in one of Aberdeen's more upscale restaurants, and it had only been after going out with the boy for a little while that she'd learned of his more wayward ways.

Through mendacious means, William had managed to talk her into helping him in a small 'job'. And thanks to her own dalliances with petty theft in an attempt to aid her ailing father and dear mother, she'd admitted she knew something of liberating other people of excess valuables. It was something she'd confessed in a moment of passion and regretted as soon as it had been loosed from her lips. And though William had not outright threatened to turn her in, he had used the information to his advantage, playing on her fears of being jailed for life in Craiginches prison. Eventually, William was arrested and questioned by the Yard. However, he hadn't been charged with any crime since they'd had no evidence. But that hadn't stopped William from trying to implicate Kitty in the crime.

Her decision to aid William had led to her doing two 'jobs', which Thomas Sinclair seemed to know all about. But still, she wondered, how? Her mind turned briefly to Angeline across the room. There was something about that woman that always struck Kitty as odd. It was as if Angeline's penetrating hazel eyes were boring into Kitty's very soul whenever she had the misfortune to run into her. In a brief flash, Kitty recalled the time Angeline had seemed to lift the very thoughts from her mind as she'd passed by her in the corridor to the storage room and office. Could this woman actually read minds, she now wondered.

Kitty and the other girls had long surmised that Angeline and Thomas were romantically involved. It was part of the reason they thought he never made any advances toward them, though he most certainly could have, being their employer and a generous one at that. No, she was fairly certain that whatever influence Angeline had over Thomas, it was more than just her apparent mind-reading talents and elegant good looks. In fact, the man seemed to trust Angeline even more than his hired gun, Lucias.

Taking another sip of his scotch, Sinclair placed his glass back on a cork coaster, studied her for another moment, and then looked down at the telegrams again. "Something you may not know about me, lassie, is that I know many people from my business dealings back home as well as over here in North America, along with just about every other continent on this planet." He looked up at Kitty with cold eyes and added, "Joseph Tully was an acquaintance of mine back in Scotland, with whom I did a wee bit of business at his jewellery store. He was, and is, a man that knows his gems and has helped me identify several stones I now prize very highly. And I am more than sure he would like to talk with someone who knew where his four-thousand pounds Sterling worth of jewellery went."

"But I don't know what happened to them," Kitty replied, which was quite true. After she had entered through a second-floor window over the jewellery shop, she'd let William MacLeod and the rest of his hooligan gang into the building to rob it. William had quickly fenced the jewels via his connections throughout the west of Scotland, then shared the fruits of their larceny with his gang members. Unfortunately, he had never gotten as far as sharing any of the money with Kitty before he'd been arrested and tried to finger her for the crime.

With all this information at Sinclair's disposal, Kitty knew it would be a simple affair for him to cable the bobbies at the Yard and have them contact the North-West Mounted Police. Then, they would have her extradited to Aberdeen, where her worst fears would come true, and she would live out the rest of her life behind bars in Craiginches. With resignation, she said, "But I never saw any of the money and only climbed through a second-floor window and unlocked the door for them!" Still dealing with her current case of nerves, Kitty came close to laughing aloud as the irony struck her—she was still a second-floor girl here at the saloon but looking after things in a completely different manner than she had back in Aberdeen

Thomas continued, "Nonetheless, you were involved in the jewellery's disappearance, and since no one was ever formally charged in that burglary, you'd make a fine substitute because they already have you listed as a prime suspect. And I'm sure the Yard would be more than happy to have someone to indict for that crime after having it open on their books for the last seven years."

Kitty tilted her head forward in resignation, her voice breaking with emotion, and she said, "What do you want from me?"

"Very little, actually," Thomas said as he leaned back in his chair and puffed his Panatela for a moment longer. "It's not about what I want from you, but rather, what you can do for me."

CHAPTER THREE

Jesús Oritz moved faster than he ever had in his entire life. His sense of self-preservation was quite strong, and as soon as he'd seen the overwhelming number of monstrous ants, he'd known that the adage of 'he who runs away, lives to fight another day' was more than apropos to his current situation.

When he was only yards from the tree where he'd tied his horse, the panicked beast snapped its reins and galloped away, whinnying in fear, leaving Jesús mountless. He would have taken Antonio's ride, but it, too, had broken free just before his own horse had arrived at the same conclusion.

Shaking his fist at his receding mount, he called, "You useless burro!" He now had no choice but to jog down the path behind it. Unfortunately, he was not used to such physical exertion and, until this point in his life, had mostly relied on horses to get him to wherever he needed to go, and walking, or God forbid, running, was something he'd kept to a bare minimum.

Oritz pounded down the path in pursuit of his horse, his breath beginning to catch in his lungs, his heart hammering painfully in his chest. His predilection for cigars was always something that he loved and loathed at the same time. He enjoyed their taste and the act of smoking, but he despised the hacking cough he had as a result of them. He was not a stupid man and knew that they were not good for him, and he mentally made a deal with himself that if he got out of his current predicament alive, he would give them up before his lungs gave up on him.

Something rapidly approached at his back, moving toward him at a much faster rate than his own short legs would allow. Not wanting to risk a backward glance lest it slowed his progress, he felt some small relief when he heard a voice faintly at his back and realised it was Antonio following his lead and fleeing the scene of the ant attack.

"Boss! Wait up!" Antonio called.

But Jesús was unwilling to slow his pace, determined to put as much distance between himself and the monstrous insects as possible. Antonio was younger and taller, and he was sure the man would catch up with him eventually.

Puffing and wheezing, Jesús rounded a corner in the path and saw Cookie up ahead. The man was sitting in the same spot he'd been kicked to earlier. He was now rocking back and forth, his eyes still wide, arms locked around his knees.

Seeing Jesús approach, Cookie said, "See? I told you you'd be sorry!"

Jesús stumbled to a halt near the cook and said, "Madre de Dios! What in the name of hell are those things?"

"They're big buggerin' ants from hell, from what I can tell," Cookie replied, a smug and frightened look playing across his face all at once, as if unsure how he should be feeling right now.

Stumbling to a halt near the two men, Antonio said, "Not...like... any damned ants... I've ever seen," he wheezed.

Jesús shook his head. How had this simple vacation across

the border into the territory of these trusting, friendly and easily robbed Canadians turned into this monstrous maelstrom of madness? In all his years of robbing, murdering, raping and plundering, he'd never lost so many men all at once, and he was angry and terrified, both at the same time. Here he was, an important member of one of the most notorious gangs in the Western World, and his band of blood-thirsty brigands had just been reduced from twelve angry men to one sycophantic right-hand man and the kitchen help.

"What're we gonna do now?" Cookie asked.

"Yeah... this ain't good," Antonio gasped. He'd been leaning forward with his hands on his knees and now stood upright and held one hand to his side, a pained expression on his face.

Sure that his sarcasm was lost on the man, Jesús shook his head and said, "Thank you for pointing out the obvious, Antonio; I had not noticed." But still, it begged the question, what would they do now? As far as Jesús knew, the rest of his company had been either eaten alive or fled into the hills. If he were a betting man, which he was, he'd lay his money on the former rather than the latter.

The town was not far, and laying low there would be the safest course of action for the time being. However, at some point, they would need to return to the encampment and try to retrieve some of the supplies they'd purchased in town, namely the ammunition they'd picked up at the hardware store. As Jesús had beat his feet and fled from the overrun camp, he'd seen the horse to which the ammo had been attached brought down by the enormous ants—One Ear's horse, if he recalled correctly. In any event, he was fairly sure the creatures would not have found brass-encased cylinders of lead and gunpowder to their liking and was confident that the sacks of ammo would still be usable.

But for now, they would head to town and regroup before venturing back to camp. Hopefully, a day or so of absence from the voracious red creatures would allow them to settle down and get back to doing whatever it was they did when they weren't in the middle of devouring every living thing in sight.

Cookie looked back down the path toward the river and seemed as if able to read Jesús's mind, saying, "I sure would like to get my pots and pans back."

Antonio laughed, saying, "After we lose almost the entire gang, you're worried about your cookware?"

Shaking his head, Cookie said, "An army travels on its stomach, and without something to cook in, we ain't eatin' nothin'."

Jesús nodded in agreement. "We will go back and get our belongings once those vile creatures have calmed down. Returning too soon could mean our ending up eaten as well, and rather than travelling on our stomachs, we would do so *inside* the bellies of those diablos rojo instead."

CHAPTER FOUR

"How're you doing, Sandy? Holding up okay?"

"It's all good over here, Mr. Cochrane." Changing his grip slightly, Sandy sighed. It was not from the effort of holding the rear corner of the wagon up as the blacksmith replaced the wheel he'd just mended. No, his sigh was from boredom.

Sandy was currently at his other job as a blacksmith's assistant. When he wasn't spending time guarding the front door of the Nugget Saloon, he worked a few hours a day helping Angus Cochrane at the smithy. Today, he was functioning as a two-legged human jack. Most days, he started work here at his half-job at six in the morning, then worked until just a little before ten when he went to his full-time position at the saloon. He was currently on a late afternoon break from the Nugget and had agreed to help Angus briefly during his unpaid hour off.

This half-a-job was helping to pay for his new passion, reading, all thanks to Miss Kitty's encouragement. She'd recommended several authors for him to check out and seemed to know just what he'd enjoy, saying it was thanks to her six brothers and trying to keep them entertained by reading stories to them over the years. Unfortunately, books didn't come cheap, and there were so many that he wanted to read that he didn't think he'd ever be bored again, as long as he had money to buy them.

Through Kitty's suggestions, he'd recently discovered the writings of Jules Verne, and he'd found several of the man's novels at Vicker's Five and Ten. After buying Journey to the Centre of the Earth and falling in love with the story, he'd been on a mission to buy each of the man's great works but needed to save up between paycheques. Vicker's also had some cheaper dime novels and penny dreadfuls, which he might look into in the future, but for now, he was focussing on buying Verne's hardcover works one by one for the exorbitant price of three dollars each. He liked to proudly display them on the small shelf in his shed like a hunter would his trophies, knowing he had actually read each and every one of them, some several times over.

He was hankering to get back to the latest novel he'd bought last week, this one about a mysterious island, also by Jules Verne. He was very close to the end, and the protagonists (a word Miss Kitty had taught him) had just discovered a mysterious cave, making him think of Mr. Caleb. Though he'd already lent several books to the man, Sandy thought this one would also be good for his memory. Judging by what had washed out of that mysterious cavern in the hills along with Caleb, it seemed real life was as fantastical as anything he'd read in Mr. Verne's adventures.

"Okay, Sandy, you can put her down now."

"Sure enough, Mr. Cochrane." Sandy gently placed the wagon back on the ground, flexing his hand temporarily. It had stiffened up a bit, holding the wagon's edge for so long, but his arms weren't tired—it took a lot more than a wagon to do that.

Rufus lay nearby, watching Sandy with eagle eyes. Seeing Sandy had his hands free again, the Irish Wolfhound thumped its tail, stirring up a small cloud of dust. Sandy bent down and scratched the dog's ear, then scruffed the top of its head, and it grunted in pleasure at the attention. Since Farley's death, the dog had been living part-time with Angus during the daytime and spending the nights with Sandy, so he was being well looked after until they could find the large dog a permanent home. He was growing rather fond of the animal and figured he might just be the person who would eventually welcome the orphaned dog into his life on a full-time basis.

Angus had seen Sandy flexing his hand and asked, "Was the wagon getting a bit hard to hold?"

Sandy shook his head, saying, "No, sir. Just a little tiring on the hand. I think I might wear a pair of gloves next time."

Angus nodded at the thick leather gloves near the forge and laughed, saying, "That's what they're there for."

"Yessir," Sandy said with a nod. The wagon in question was the water pumper from the local volunteer fire department, of which Angus Cochrane was the chief. The smithy was also the temporary firehall until the official building was finished construction in the next few months. On a recent call out, one of the wagon's wheels had been damaged. And so, in addition to his duties as chief of the fire department and seeing as he was the local blacksmith, it had fallen on Angus to fix the wheel.

Sandy had been at that particular callout, his first, actually. The excitement, action and satisfaction were things that Sandy had discovered he quite enjoyed. Their most recent callout hadn't been life and death; it had merely been a young girl's cat that had run up a tree. Sandy had volunteered to climb the ladder, but once it had been extended, they discovered its two-story reach was insufficient to get to the small, frightened kitten. But that hadn't mattered, Sandy had merely reached his arm out and gently called to the trembling creature, and it had come willingly into his outstretched hand. It was something he got from his gram-gram (or so his mother said). Most animals, no matter what their stripe, came to him willingly for some reason.

Seeing no more head scratches were forthcoming, the dog stood and ambled over to the feeding trough and looked inside for some food. That dog ate almost as much as he did, Sandy thought with a shake of his head. He'd fed the animal some meaty scraps Maggie had given him from the Nugget's kitchen this morning, but that seemingly had not been enough to satisfy the animal for long.

Cochrane nodded toward the dog poking its nose into the feeding trough and said, "That reminds me of your friend's mule the other day. She's a feisty little thing. When she wandered in here, she acted like she owned the place! Pushed right in there next to the other animals and started chowing down."

"Yessir, Emily is a mule with a mind of her own, that's for sure."

"Speaking of your friend Caleb, just what was it he found up there in the mountains?"

"Something that could do a whole lot of good and other things that can do a whole lot of harm." Sandy would say no more. Caleb had mentioned that if he ever found the cavern again, he would share some of the wealth inside as thanks to his new friends for the assistance they had selflessly provided him. However, Sandy wasn't a man who went around talking about another man's business, not without his express permission, which he hadn't yet received from Caleb.

Sandy was just about to tell Angus his dinner hour was up and that he needed to get back to the Nugget when he spied something that made him stop in his tracks. It was Goldie and a couple of his gang members, but they were on foot, and that was very strange. He'd expected the man to have his two large enforcers with him and to also be on horseback. But instead, it was only him and his scar-faced friend. Following along behind them was a scraggly-haired oldster, currently muttering something about his pots and pans.

The trio of men moved through the alley next to the smithy. As they passed, the smaller gold-toothed man in the round hat looked Sandy's way and gave him a fierce scowl. But that had been all, and they'd walked on by, saying nothing.

But where were their horses, and the rest of their men, Sandy wondered. He watched as they made a beeline for the telegraph office. Whoever they were going to contact, it couldn't be anyone good. After a brief moment, the three men exited the telegraph office and entered the Kootenay Saloon a few doors down. It also provided rooms for rent, and Sandy wondered if they would check in to wait for whoever they'd telegraphed to arrive, just as the man in the red flannel had done last week before becoming fish food in the river.

Just as he digested all of the information his eyes had taken in, who else should he see coming up the street other than Mr. Caleb. He was riding his mule with the Doc at his side, a troubled look on both their faces. Sandy felt fairly certain by the time he got a chance to share the news of the bandits' return, and once the Doc and Caleb shared the outcome of their visit to the ice house, they would all, without a doubt, be wearing the same worried expression.

CHAPTER FIVE

Thrusting the scoop net toward Thomas Sinclair's face, Doctor Brown said, "This is what you need to deal with before concerning yourself with any of Caleb's gold!" He shook the net for emphasis and added, "And you need to worry about this creature's offspring as well because we could be in serious trouble."

As the spider struggled, a small hiss emanated from it, the sound as repulsive as the rest of it. Its mottled, spiky-haired grey and black legs poked through the holes in the netting. They wriggled back and forth almost rhythmically, as if keeping limber and ready should something, or someone, get close enough so it could reach out and enfold them in its loving embrace.

Caleb scowled at the spider dangling in the scoop net in front of Sinclair, his hate for the creature almost as strong as his disgust. Anger in his voice, he added, "Aye, and we found another body as well. Just a young boy." He shook his head as he thought of the poor lad they'd discovered in the produce bins at the ice house and how he must have suffered.

Sinclair nodded. "That'd be that delivery boy, Teddy Malone, that Sandy told me had gone missin'."

The man had just been informed that another of his

employees had been found dead, and he acted as if the news was no more important than a passing conversation about the weather.

"That's all you have to say about it?" Caleb asked incredulously.

Sinclair rolled his eyes slightly and replied, "And I'll have the undertaker drop by and pick him up so we can give him a proper burial. How's that?"

"But there's still some spiders in there," Caleb said with concern.

"He should be fine," Sinclair said, then looked to Brown. "After all, you said you'd killed most of the spiders with your spray anyway."

Brown responded, "Yes, a substantial number of them. But there were still quite a few that got away. We should still return and give it another spray, just to be sure."

Thomas said, "I'll tell Ezra to keep an eye out for any of the little buggers when he's there."

Caleb shook his head sadly once again. "If he's not careful, he might end up havin' to bury himself."

Brown said, "I really should examine the boy's cadaver in more detail."

"Why?" Sinclair asked. "From what you told me, it was the same thing happened to him as happened to Jones. I'm sure one victim of these beasts looks very much like the next."

"Not this one!" Caleb said. "Those monsters had longer with that poor boy than they did with Farley, and they ate him alive!" His anger surged back, temporarily replacing the anxiety he'd experienced when the doctor had spoken of returning to check the ice house.

In addition to having no conscience or compassion, it seemed Sinclair had very little fear of the creeping horrors either, judging by his reaction to the spider so far. Though the beast was on full display before the Scotsman, he didn't flinch. He'd regarded the monstrous spider with mild interest and only a slight grimace of disgust, but there had been no fear that Caleb could see, and he said, "You seem hardly surprised by the size of that thing."

Sinclair shrugged and said, "The doctor already informed me that you'd encountered spiders, which were the cause of Farley's demise, so I'm not surprised you found more."

"But not this big! Those were babies. This is one of the adults. The kind that lays its eggs inside your lungs!"

Behind Thomas, Lucias's spurred heels jangled slightly as he moved back a pace at this news, the shadows helping to hide his obvious discomfort.

Sinclair waved the spider away.

Brown stepped back from Sinclair, saying, "My point is, if these things are allowed to breed, they could affect every biosystem in the region. They're like an apex predator."

Caleb added, "And with the speed that these things can breed, we need to organise a search throughout the town to verify there are no more of them."

Sinclair looked to Caleb as if he'd suddenly sprouted a second head. "How d'ya think I'm going to sound if I run around shouting about killer spiders, especially just before the Dominion Day holiday coming up this weekend? That's big business, and I don't plan on missing any!"

"Forget about your business for once! If you won't help,

we'll go to some other people in town, like the fire chief and the police chief and talk them into helping."

Sinclair laughed, saying, "The only other people of any influence in this town are in my back pocket already, all beholden to me in one way or another, and I want to keep it that way. And besides, they'd say the same as me and not want to panic anyone and scare away business or cause unnecessary worry."

The doctor held the twitching spider up before his eyes allowing it to dangle in the net. He chuckled, saying, "I think we're already well past that point."

Shaking his head, Sinclair said, "You can have Sandy help you if you need him. Go about it low-key, checking any likely spots, but not panicking anyone in the process."

"Likely spots? Where are they?" Caleb wondered aloud. He was appalled that this man cared more about his profit from the upcoming holiday than he did of the thousands of people currently residing in this small town.

Sinclair waved his hand dismissively at Brown and the spider, saying, "I'm sure the doctor will be able to figure out where. In the meantime, have you had any success with your recollections?"

Caleb shook his head and said, "No, I've had some flashes of memory, but nothing too much to go on, just rock, trees and a flash of gold." All this was true. But he'd had another, separate flash that he didn't mention, the one he'd had when reunited with Emily. The flash had involved tying the mule to a tree so she wouldn't roll downhill for some reason.

Angeline spoke, saying, "Rock and trees? That could be anywhere around here."

"Ya got that right," Caleb said with a doleful shake of his

head. But as he did, another mental flash went off, this one the spark of a plan, and he mentally fanned it as he spoke.

"Perhaps you need somethin' to jog your memory," Sinclair offered.

"Perhaps," Caleb agreed, still fanning his plan. "In the meantime, what would you suggest?"

Thomas's eyes narrowed slightly, and he said, "I want to show you somethin' that might help jog your memory." Turning to the doctor, Sinclair added, "You can come along, too, Brown." He gestured at the net, "And you can bring your little friend there too." The spider was now slung over Brown's shoulders, dangling at the end of the pole like a hobo's bindle—but instead of holding all of Brown's worldly possessions, the only thing it contained was certain death.

**

In his time at the Golden Nugget Saloon, Caleb had only experienced the basement gambling den from the perspective of his little hidden room behind the secondary bar's storage room shelves. But now, as part of Thomas Sinclair's entourage, they had entered the room to the left of Caleb's. It was just the four men now. Angeline had stayed upstairs to keep an eye on things while Thomas gave his tour.

Lucias held the door as they entered the other room. Sinclair went first, lighting a lantern as he moved across the threshold. "I'm goin' to get electricity to this valley soon. Just have to get the damned dam built first. I've been closely followin' Tesla's work at his new powerhouse in Niagara Falls and plan on implementin' some of his ideas."

Caleb nodded, wondering what kind of money it would take to build your own dam. More than he'd ever see in a hundred lifetimes, he was sure. In the growing light of the lantern, it appeared the other half certainly lived a different life compared to his hidden room on the other side. Dark oak panelling gleamed on the walls, and a rich brocade carpet in the centre sported intricate designs that, to Caleb's eye, looked akin to symbols of some sort rather than just a fancy pattern. This inner sanctum had no windows behind its closed red velvet drapes. Along the walls were even more curio cabinets, containing even stranger-looking items than the ones upstairs.

In keeping with the hidden spaces of which Sinclair seemed so fond, when Lucias twisted a bust of what looked like Genghis Khan, a bookcase against the wall opened outward, revealing something behind.

"What in heaven's name is that?" Caleb wondered. A wrought-iron gate lay across a small, darkened space beyond.

"An elevator?" Brown queried incredulously.

"Hydraulic," Thomas said proudly. "This was originally a natural shaft."

Lucias opened the cast iron accordion-style gate, and Thomas boarded first, followed by Brown and the spider, with Caleb hopping behind. After stepping aboard, Lucias rattled the gate closed and threw a lever. With a small clunk, they slowly descended into the bowels of the earth.

They arrived at the bottom of the shaft after several long, claustrophobic moments, and the doors opened to a large cavern. One that looked very much like it had been formed in the same way as Caleb's cavern somewhere up in the hills, at least from what he could tell in the dimness of the oil lantern's limited light.

But Lucias soon remedied that problem. Picking up a different style of lamp, he added some greyish pellets to a small metal tank on the bottom, then poured water drawn from a nearby bucket into a reservoir on the lamp's top. With everything tightened and properly set, he turned a valve which started dripping water into the pellets below. He gave a look that might have passed for a smile and said, "Calcium carbide is the only way to go when you're mining." He pulled a match from a safe withdrawn from his duster, struck it on the cavern wall and touched its flaring light to a small nozzle in front of a concave mirror on the lamp.

As the lamp flared to life, the area around them brightened immensely, allowing them to see much more of the cavern—and it was immense. A high ceiling dotted with stalactites arched overhead, barely illuminated by the new lamp.

"I could have used one of those where I was," Caleb said with an appreciative nod.

"Should you remember where it is, we'll make sure to outfit you with plenty," Sinclair replied.

As they moved further into the cavern, Lucias took the lead, the lantern's light dancing over the closest walls. Despite its brilliance, it did little to illuminate much of the large space. Gesturing into the receding darkness, Sinclair asked, "Does any of this look familiar to ya, Mr. Cantrill?"

Caleb nodded and said, "Aye, that it does." It did indeed look similar. However, instead of an underground lake, a river rushed darkly through one dim corner of the subterranean chamber. The stones which covered the floor looked very familiar as well, and he could have sworn he was back up in his cavern, except for one thing.

"You see what's missin'?" Sinclair queried.

"Gold," Caleb said and toed at several of the smooth round stones with the tip of his good foot. In his cavern, intermixed with these stones, had been gold nugget after gold nugget. But here, there were none.

"Correct," Sinclair said with a nod. "And from what you've

told me, that cavern you found sounds very much like what I found down here, and the reason I built my trading post and then my hotel over the very top of it."

"How much did you pull out of here," Brown inquired.

"Close to one ton of solid gold nuggets."

Caleb laughed, "There are a hundred times that up there, at least from everything I saw when I dropped into the business."

"Astounding," Brown said.

Caleb nodded and added, "And that doesn't include the veins of gold that swirl through the cavern walls."

Sinclair's eyes widened at this news, and he asked, "Veins of gold, you say?"

"As in plural?" Lucias inquired.

"Many different veins," Caleb said with a nod. I saw them running throughout almost every cavern I stumbled across. Must have been a half-dozen at least."

Brown shook his head in wonder. "To have one cavern like that would be incredible, but to have so many, it boggles the mind!"

"You go on keepin' boggled, Doctor Brown, but I have a pretty good idea what it might be worth," Sinclair replied.

The adding machine inside Thomas Sinclair's brain had begun binging and ringing as it tallied up the potential value of the gold find against the expenses of hauling it out. At least, that's what Caleb imagined was going on between the man's ears. There was a monumental amount of gold up in his mountainous cavern, but how much would they ever extract from it if he ever found it again? And if just three kinds of creatures he'd encountered up there were causing this much grief, what other grievous hellspawn had he yet to discover, and what sort of formidable resistance might it give? All of this was separate from the growing surety that if and when he ever found the cavern, Sinclair would, without a doubt, usurp his half of the partnership.

They made their way to the edge of the rushing river. A rather precarious-looking wood and rope bridge ran only a few feet above the water's swift darkness. Across this expanse lay another cavern. Caleb nodded toward it and said to Sinclair, "What's over there?"

Lucias replied, "Several more caverns, but they dead-end at a flooded chamber. There are also a few deep pits along the way just before the flooded one. Damned things look bottomless."

Sinclair finished, saying, "And since I don't currently have access to a deep-sea diving suit or a way to drain that flooded cavern, that's as far as we've been in that direction."

"And no sign of gold?" Brown asked.

Shaking his head, Lucias said, "No nuggets and no veins in any of the test spots we tried digging or blasting in."

Thinking of the lake in the cavern and the black beast that had followed him down, Caleb asked, "Was there anything in the water in that cavern?"

Lucias answered, "Not that we could see from the water's edge, only some blind fish is all."

"Did they glow in the dark by any chance?" Caleb queried.

Sinclair gave him that 'grown a second head' look again and asked, "Glow in the dark? Not that I saw. Lucias, did you see any?"

"No, sir. Just the same as you."

Caleb wondered at that. Although this cavern had some gold similar to his, it had many differences. And it seemed whatever life swam in the bottomless black lake up in his mountain monster retreat was truly unique in more ways than one.

"However," Sinclair added, "There is the small matter of the voices."

"Voices?"

"Aye. D'ya not have any of them up in yours?"

"No, it's as silent as sin."

Sinclair nodded toward his bodyguard and said, "Lucias?"

The terse gunslinger nodded and spoke, "I don't know what it was exactly, but I was sure I heard something down one of those bottomless tubes. Sounded like someone whispering to someone else. Never could make out the words, though."

"Was there someone else there?" Brown asked.

"No. I shone my lantern down as best I could but didn't see anyone, or anything."

"Did it happen again?" Caleb asked.

"Couple of times, but only when I was alone over there. Since then, I always felt kind of uneasy, like I was being watched."

That was something that Caleb hadn't felt when he was in his cavern and something for which he was quite thankful. The thought of voices whispering in the dark around him as he moved by those bottomless pits would have been almost too much to bear.

Since arriving near the river's edge, the spider had become increasingly agitated and suddenly began hissing again.

Caleb looked to the doctor and asked, "What's got its knickers in a twist all of a sudden?"

Brown said, "I don't know, but I think it's reacting to whatever is over in that cavern."

"And you say you saw no ants or spiders either over there?"

"Nothing like that," Sinclair said, shaking his head as he scowled at the spider.

They began moving back toward the elevator, and as they did, the spider quieted its manic movements.

"Well, as familiar as this looks, it hasn't triggered any more memories yet," Caleb said.

"Then I'd suggest you try rememberin' harder," Thomas replied.

"Or?"

"Or else next time, Lucias might not be there to save your Irish arse when your past comes looking for you."

"If I die, you'll never find the place," Caleb countered.

"Perhaps not," Sinclair responded. "But searching for it would be an engaging and energising project. And in the meantime, I'll continue to fleece the sourdoughs out of their money here at this little den of iniquity and wait until some other hapless vagabond like yourself comes across that cavern."

That stung, but Caleb knew the man wasn't far wrong. Sinclair would merely have to keep his ear to the ground, and when some other unsuspecting sourdough stumbled across the cavern, Sinclair would partner up with them and do to them, what he suspected Sinclair would do to him, if and when he ever found the cavern. "I suppose that's something you can always hope for."

Thomas smiled slightly and said, "In the meantime, if there's anything you need to help you remember, let me know."

Caleb still wanted to keep things mysterious for as long as he could until he was more certain of where he needed to look. This cavern had many similarities to his own but with much less gold and creatures involved. Thinking these cavernous thoughts, another popped into his head as he boarded the elevator. "There is somethin' I might want."

"What's that?" Sinclair asked.

"Well, since you have those fancy calcium lamps, I was wonderin' if you might also happen to have any nitroglycerin?"

CHAPTER SIX

Kitty's face rested in her palms as she wept silently. Her visit with Sinclair had ended in a less than satisfactory manner. Not that she was expecting a positive outcome after them discovering her peeping at the door. When Sinclair had been done with her, she marched right up here and locked the door, sat down and began to cry. That had been several hours ago, and she was supposed to be downstairs helping the sourdoughs buy overpriced alcohol and invite them upstairs to have fun, but she just couldn't face anyone right now. Once again, her friends were covering for her, with Lucy from London picking up most of the slack and Monique and Carla helping as well. She cried even harder when she realised how fortunate she was to have friends like that.

She was heartbroken. Despite her closeness with the other girls and the good pay provided at the Nugget, Kitty didn't think she could continue working here under these new circumstances. With Thomas Sinclair now lording her less-than-stellar past over her and using it to blackmail her into spying on Caleb, she was at her wit's end. According to Thomas, she was supposed to monitor Caleb and ensure he wasn't holding anything back or trying to back out of their deal.

But Kitty knew that spying on Caleb was out of the question because of how she was beginning to feel about him.

He was a scoundrel, most certainly, but he was a handsome and relatively honest one as things went. By his own account, he'd only ever been involved in some midnight bank burglaries over the years, and she took him at his word that was all, or at least nothing more troublesome or violent than that.

Just before their job together, Caleb had told the gang if anything happened that involved shooting at another human being, he would be out of there. And so, he'd kept his word and fled from Red Deer after things went wrong and the shooting started. The fact that his horse had been laden with most of the gold was an unfortunate coincidence, to be sure. Not only did poor Caleb have to contend with those men looking for their missing gold, but he also had Sinclair sniffing after what he'd found up in the cavern. And now, thanks to her employer's request to betray Caleb's confidence and spy on him, it had created a conflict between her job and her growing affection for her new Irish friend.

At this point, Kitty wasn't sure if what she was feeling was actually love, but felt certain she was bordering on the emotion. Since William McLeod's betrayal, she'd been careful not to get too close to anyone and had not sought out any further romantic partners. One part of it had been from the hurt and betrayal she'd felt, and the other had been due to her profession.

After a long day on her back, pleasing members of the opposite sex, the last thing she wanted was to have another man to please when she got home. But since getting to know this roguish, cute and funny Irishman that had washed ashore into her heart, Kitty knew she couldn't betray him. And although she didn't know how he felt about her, she had her suspicions. After all these years out in the world, she had become a fairly good judge of character and thought, or at least hoped Caleb also felt the same way.

And so now, she cried. Scared, alone, conflicted and unsure

who to trust. If Thomas Sinclair had his talons into her, she had to wonder about the rest of his employees. Did he have similar arrangements with them as well? Could she even trust any of them anymore? And what would Sinclair do if he discovered she hadn't been honouring his request? Most likely, just as he'd said he would do, and follow through on his threat to contact Scotland Yard and have her deported.

Taking several deep, heaving sobs, Kitty felt empty of tears, at least for a little while. She took a deep breath, feeling she knew what to do. Whatever the consequences of her decision, it appeared she had no alternative.

***

During his time in Africa, Caleb had seen many atrocities committed in the name of Her Majesty's Fifth, not only toward the Boers and the Zulu but also toward members of the regiment itself. After his time in the army, he'd experienced many bandits and other ne'er-do-wells out in the world, most wanting to steal what little he had, and not caring if they killed him in the process.

The world was cruel and unjust, and Caleb tried not to add to it. If he could find a verbal way out of a tense situation, then that was the way he always tried to go if he could. No, he was done with violence and had told Kitty as such. But now he had been dragged back into it anyway—the Hole-in-the-Wall Gang had seen to that. As of right now, he'd seen more than enough brutality and horror to last a lifetime, which, in light of upcoming events, might not be that long. His twenty-four hours were up tomorrow at noon, and then the gang would be back wanting their gold, and he sincerely hoped he would have another memory flash by then.

The only time he would ever consider violence these days was to save his own life in self-defence or in defending someone else's life, namely someone like Kitty Welch. He was on his best behaviour since meeting her. Despite her current situation, he knew it wasn't who she was, just as she knew that his being a gold-thieving bank robber was only a temporary position for him.

Whenever he thought about that woman, something funny seemed to happen with his heart, almost like he was a sufferer of arrhythmia having palpitations. More likely, it was fear, but a different kind than he'd experienced in the war and up in the cavern. This fear was of commitment—one of the unknown things in life which he'd never experienced or explored before.

Though he wanted to tell Kitty how he felt about her, he feared what she might say. But since he had some free time at the moment, he figured now might be a good time to find out, especially in light of everything else that was going on. The good doctor had departed with the disgusting spider from hell in search of other accommodations for it besides the scoop net. He breathed a sigh of relief, just glad to be away from the horrible thing for a little while.

Dominion Day was the day after tomorrow, and the whole town would be out to celebrate. Apparently, Canada becoming a confederation in 1867 and the beginning of its journey towards greater independence was a big thing around these parts. It was also supposed to be the day to name this lawless little backwoods town.

Personally, Caleb liked the name of the glacier in the mountains at the other end of the valley, Natánik. It was also the town's unofficial name. And so, he had entered it as his suggestion in the contest. Naming the place after one of its geographical features, which also honoured the area's aboriginal heritage, seemed a very good idea, and they should make the unofficial official.

His visit with Thomas in the cavern beneath the saloon had just ended, and he had several things now on his mind to discuss with Kitty. He hoped to invite her to the upcoming holiday festivities in the city park. If he was lucky enough to win the contest, he wanted to have her there with him. The prize of a train ride and hotel stay sounded like the ideal thing to further their blossoming relationship.

And now, he was in search of the woman in question. It was fairly busy in the saloon at the moment, with quite a few revellers already starting to celebrate Canada's birthday party a little early. Across the room, Sandy gestured for Caleb to join him near the batwing doors, and he hopped over in that direction.

On their way back from the ice house, Caleb and the Doc had stopped briefly at the smithy and shown Sandy and Angus the captured spider. However, they hadn't had much chance to talk since the boy had been preparing to return to his job as doorman at the Nugget.

"Hey, Sandy. Have you seen Miss Kitty?"

The blonde boy nodded, a serious expression on his face. "That I have."

With a slight smile, Caleb added, "Could you tell me where she might be?"

"Sure enough, Mr. Caleb." Sandy looked both ways in an apparent check to ensure they weren't being overheard and said, "But first, I need to tell ya somethin' else. I didn't get a chance at the smithy since by the time you told me about the spiders you found, I had to rush back here to work."

Caleb leaned forward on his crutches and said, "All right. I'm all ears."

"It's about those Holy Gang guys."

"What about them?"

"When I was workin' with Angus Cochrane on my break

from the Nugget, I saw them come back into town just before you and Doc Brown came by."

"That's strange; they were supposed to give me twenty-four hours before returnin'."

"Well, they didn't go to the Nugget."

"Where did they go?"

"They went to the telegraph office next to the Bank of Montreal, but they weren't there long, and then they went into the Kootenay Saloon across the street."

"That is kind of strange."

Sandy leaned closer to Caleb and said in a conspiratorial voice, "But things get even stranger."

"How so?"

"They weren't ridin' their horses and were on foot instead. And it was just Goldie and his skinny, scarred buddy, plus some older guy goin' on about his pots and pans."

"That is strange. Did you see where they came from?"

"From direction of the river."

"Okay, thanks very much, Sandy."

Sandy nodded and smiled slightly, seeming pleased he had shared his secret.

"Miss Kitty?" Caleb gently queried.

"Oh, right, sorry. She's upstairs in her room. Been there for a few hours now. Hasn't been takin' any gentleman callers at the moment, either. And when she went up there, it looked like she was about to burst into tears for some reason."

"Thanks again, Sandy." Caleb hobbled toward the stairs, now needing to see Kitty more than ever. This was big news. The Hole-in-the-Wall Gang had supposedly departed town and were to give him twenty-four hours. Why were they back so soon? And why only three of them? It seemed obvious they would have camped outside the town, but not too far away and down at the river made sense. And since he was familiar with how they operated, this change gave him new cause for concern. Had one or more of the creatures he'd brought down the mountain had some sort of engagement with the gang at their camp? And if only three had returned, and horseless to boot, there had to be something to Sandy's strange tales. Unfortunately, he had more than a sneaking suspicion he knew exactly what it was.

CHAPTER SEVEN

"You're quite the little chatterbox, aren't you?" Cornelius Brown squinted his eyes as he peered more closely at the outsized arachnid. It now resided in a small but ornate bird cage that he'd picked up at Vicker's Five and Ten and charged to Sinclair's business account. He tapped the cage with a tongue depressor, and the spider gave another small hiss as if the air were escaping from a puncture inside of it somewhere.

But checking this creature for air leaks was not on his agenda at the moment. As much as he wanted to dissect this animal, he didn't want to do so prematurely since observing it was of the utmost importance right now. That was a large part of why he wanted to keep the creature alive when he'd captured it in the net at the ice house.

Brown poked the tongue depressor into the creature's side through a gap in the cage's bars, eliciting another hiss. "Oh, just you hush now, Mama. I'm checking your solidity."

Although the arachnid looked a bit like a wolf spider, as Caleb thought, perhaps because of its mottled grey and black patches, Brown could clearly see this was not the case. In fact, with its bulbous lower body, the arachnid seemed more akin to a black widow in its general build and appearance.

He tapped the probe against one of the spider's legs, and they all twitched closed with a clatter, and it hissed at him again. The appendages seemed quite sturdy and, no doubt, had relatively strong gripping power, looking easily able to wrap around someone's head. However, he wasn't about to get his hand or anything else close enough to the cage to find out how strong they actually were.

Holding the cage slightly higher, the doctor probed the depressor through the thin bars at the bottom. He'd removed the tray meant to capture avian excrement and was now provided with an excellent view of the creature's undercarriage. Its slightly bulbous underside was much softer and less protected by chitin than its upper half, which was quite hard and almost crab-like. A small slit dimpled the spider's underbelly, looking to be of a reproductive nature. Needing verification, Brown prodded the spider's slit, eliciting another hiss, and this time, a physical reaction as well. A small ribbed tube with a claw-like tip slid partway out. It snaked back and forth for a moment, perhaps looking for an orifice to enter, then withdrew into the spider's abdomen once more.

Brown's heart went out to his friend Farley, and a shudder passed through him as he imagined this animal pressed against his own face and the violation of having its sex organ thrust into his mouth as it laid its eggs around his lungs.

He looked speculatively at the arachnid and scratched his grizzled chin. It was more resistant to acetic acid than its offspring, which was understandable. Their thin, newborn exoskeletons were much more permeable than the thicker chitinous covering on the mother spider before him and thus more easily penetrated by the acetic acid.

Narrowing his eyes at the creature, he said, "I think I'm going to have to up the level of acetic acid in my next batch of spray." Though the spider didn't respond, its numerous dark eyes regarded Brown intently as if listening to his plans.

Cornelius had recently been evaluating a new process of extracting gold from crushed ore using a combination of acetic acid and sodium cyanide. Fortunately, he had brought in the necessary chemicals with which to experiment just over a month ago. In use, the acetic acid helped stabilise the cyanide so it didn't release any harmful gasses during the gold extraction process. Without it, the procedure would be an almost impossible and highly hazardous task.

He had been reluctant to include the cyanide in his initial batch of spray due to the risk it could pose to public health if he ran around misting people's houses and property with the stuff. And that was the way he was going to keep it for now. If he increased the strength of the acid solution slightly, it would still kill the spiderlings and possibly the larger arachnids as well.

Marvelling at the arachnid's size, he realised he'd almost forgotten about the equally large ants, which were also part of Caleb Cantrill's grand adventure. He knew that regular ants couldn't stand vinegar since it affected their route-finding abilities, amongst other things. Hopefully, his more acidic solution might work against the larger ants and confuse or at least dissuade them from approaching.

However, there was something that he still didn't understand. If this spider were indeed the same kind Caleb found in the cavern, how had it multiplied so fast? He knew some spiders could lay multiple egg sacs throughout the year, just as this creature seemed to have done. But this beast, if it was the same, only had a few days for its babies to mature enough to come forth from Farley. And though the creatures at the ice house may have had a day or two longer to develop, no matter how he looked at it, these animals had an exceptionally accelerated growth cycle.

Were the metabolisms of these animals so accelerated that something which should have taken at least two weeks or more had taken less than a half-dozen days? If this creature, or one like it, had laid eggs in other unfortunates around town, that would mean many more broods hatching soon and wandering freely about the valley, looking for hosts of their own.

Thinking of offspring, Cornelius recalled the thing which had tried to take a bite out of Caleb, the same animal responsible for the demise of a gentleman known as the Red Flannel Man. Kitty said she'd seen some babies of that creature down at the river when she'd found Caleb. Were the black thing's offspring growing just as quickly as the spiders? He shook his head sadly—just another complication they would need to address. If all these creatures had accelerated growth and breeding, this valley could become overrun if they didn't do something drastic about their populations very soon.

To aid that cause, Brown knew he needed a better way to disperse the acetic acid. Atomising a solution even more concentrated than its current level was out of the question. And he wanted something a bit bigger than a rose mister since he needed more capacity and more of a stream than a mist. This would be especially important if he had to deal with hundreds or perhaps thousands more spiders and an equal number of ants. After a moment, Brown gave a small smile and nodded, pleased that the perfect answer had suddenly ignited within his mind.

CHAPTER EIGHT

"And like I was telling Antonio, if somethin's happened to them, and I need to get more, I don't know what I'll do, since the other pots and pans were so well seasoned. I'm sure the stores around this town don't have anythin' suitable to my needs. And then..." Cookie trailed off when Jesús slapped his hand overtop his mouth, stifling any further words.

His eyes drilling into the cook's, his hand still firmly across the man's mouth, Jesús said in a low, cold voice, "The next time you open your mouth with any talk of pots, pans, griddles or any other kitchen implements, I will stuff both a pot and a pan down your throat. Do you understand me?"

With wide eyes, Cookie nodded slightly, and Jesús slowly removed his hand. Despite his cautionary words just now, the cook looked about to say something more. Jesús raised his hand once again, but this time rather than placing it over the cook's mouth, he held up his index finger in a 'better mind what I just said' gesture and the cook's mouth snapped shut.

Jesús shook his head slowly back and forth, still unable to believe he was down to only two lackeys. He'd been hoping that some of his other henchmen might have escaped the fate of Three Fingers and One Ear, but none had shown up so far.

Stationed at a table near the front door of the Kootenay

Saloon, Antonio kept an eye out for any gang members that might wander back into town. His other eye was on the Golden Nugget across the street, which the Irishman currently called home.

When they'd returned to town, they'd gone to the telegraph office, wanting to request more manpower from south of the border. Unfortunately, that hadn't gotten very far. The clerk had ever so politely informed him that the telegraph lines had recently gone down and might be out for at least a couple of days until they could find and repair the damage.

At the time, he'd been frustrated, but strangely, now that he'd had a chance to think about it, Jesús was glad he hadn't been able to get a message through. He wondered what he would have said anyway, that his tough outlaw gang had just been assaulted and eaten by giant ants and black river beasts? Not very likely. Cookie had told him of Webb's demise and the creature in the river that had taken him out. Despite seeing the monstrous ants, it still seemed almost too fantastical to believe. And it wasn't like he could visit Johnny Law and tell them about it. They would think him crazy or drunk, or both and no doubt lock the whole gang up and throw away the key.

Though he still wanted to return to the encampment, Jesús figured there was no rush and felt more than sure that Cookie's pots and pans and the ammunition would go unharmed for a day or so. Anyone unfortunate enough to wander through that neck of the woods would be in for an unpleasant surprise if they weren't paying attention and disturbed the nest of those diablos rojo. He felt it was an appropriate name since they seemed to come from the very maw of hell itself.

And so, that left him sitting here with the last of his battalion of blood-thirsty bastards, and not the pick of the litter either. As much as he'd like to, he wasn't quite ready to go back to the Golden Nugget, guns blazing. With basically no gang to back him up, it changed things for several reasons.

Thanks to the disfiguring scar affecting the right side of Antonio's face, he couldn't shoot worth a damn unless he was point-blank in front of his target. And the last time the cook had fired a sidearm was likely during the American Civil War. Jesús realised that it left just him, and though he was an excellent shot, he was only one man. What he really needed was someone good with a sidearm to back him up, not a half-blind sidekick and an ancient dinner cook.

Most importantly, they didn't know how many other enforcers Sinclair had at the Golden Nugget Saloon. Though he knew the Irishman wasn't armed, he didn't know who else inside that saloon might be. He recalled the man in black who had appeared at their table in the basement when they were having some fun with the Scottish Senorita. The way that gringo had appeared out of nowhere and flashed his Colt Lightning against the side of One Ear's head, he looked as dangerous with his sidearm as he was fast. If several men like that were employed there, they might have a problem.

Before he returned to the Nugget for the gold tomorrow, he hoped to dredge up a few extra hands here in the Kootenay Saloon. From the looks of the clientele, this establishment was not as upscale as across the road, and things were considerably less expensive here. Not cheap by any means since this was still a gold mining town, but more affordable than the Golden Nugget and its exorbitant prices. Yes, the men who frequented this bar looked more his kind: unkempt, unshaven, and unemployed.

This coming evening would be a time of rest, relaxation, and a chance to mourn the dead. They had secured rooms in the back of this saloon for the next couple of days. According to a sign posted near the front door, the day after tomorrow was a federal holiday here in Canada. There was to be a celebration in the town's park with food, drink and aquatic competitions, with the evening ending in fireworks. Perhaps, once they got their gold, they might stick around for the festivities and spend some time robbing the drunken revellers.

But Jesús realised he was getting ahead of himself. He sipped some sherry from the small glass before him and had an amusing thought. When they headed back to the Nugget to hold their Irish friend to account, if the man didn't have the gold, then perhaps they would introduce him to the diablos rojo in the forest. After all, those creatures seemed continually hungry for their next meal. Maybe, Jesús thought with a sudden smile, they'd enjoy some nice fresh Irish stew.

CHAPTER NINE

Issac Ableman shook his head as he studied the leaning telegraph pole up ahead. It had been put in the ground not more than a year ago, and yet, here it was, tilting over at a drunken angle as if it had recently imbibed in a few too many. From what he could see, it appeared otherwise undamaged and hadn't been vandalised, with no sign of an axe attempting to bring it down.

That had actually happened over in Greenwood, according to George at the office there. Perhaps it was thanks to a disgruntled customer or some Luddite who didn't fully embrace the future as much as the telegraph company; whoever had been responsible, they'd felled four poles before tiring of the job. But that didn't seem to be the case here since everything above ground looked fine, and the tall, red cedar pole appeared fully intact, except for the drunken lean.

The problem appeared to be the ground where the pole had been laid, but again, there was no sign of sabotage there either. The soil hadn't been dug away with a shovel but seemed to have given way, which had caused it to tilt at an almost thirty-degree angle.

As Issac got closer, he could see the actual culprit was nothing more than a small sinkhole a little over a foot in diameter. Whatever had caused the hole must also have affected where the pole had been seated.

Ableman was both surprised and pleased to find the problem so quickly. When he'd left the office, he'd told Ned that he might be gone for a day or two, depending on how far he had to go to find the downed section of line. But this was good news, and it hadn't taken long at all.

But what had undermined that pole? The telegraph line ran along the valley past the river at several points, but there was no sign that any water had been up this far during the recent surge that coursed through the river basin last week. Perhaps an aquifer or hot spring had loosened the soil around the pole somehow? It was a possibility since there were plenty of both under the ground around these parts.

Unfortunately, there was no way he would be able to right this pole on his own. That would be something for tomorrow with an extra pair of hands. Right now, he needed to address the problem with the telegraph wire itself. When the pole had tilted sideways, it had snapped the wire at the same time. And so, his primary job today was to get the line spliced back together and working; then, they could at least send and receive telegrams again.

The first order of business was getting some wire, which resided on a spool attached to the bed of a small utility wagon hitched behind his horse, Nettie. The ageing animal was tethered to a nearby tree, contentedly nibbling some long grass near its base. As he approached, the horse looked up and snorted in greeting.

"Looks like we've got ourselves a wobbly wood, old girl." The horse chuffed and nodded as if in understanding. He stroked its ear for a moment, and the horse whinnied in pleasure. "We shouldn't be too long."

Issac pulled off a short length of wire from the spool and stripped the insulation from the tip. Leaving the horse where she was, he slowly trudged toward the end of the downed line, pulling cable from the spool as he went. His next step would be to climb the neighbouring pole and splice his wire to the one attached to the pole's top. Thankfully, he never went on a call without his climbing spikes. He quickly strapped them on and shimmied up the pole.

At the top, Isaac looked up and down the telegraph line. From this bird's eye view, things ran straight and true; no other poles looked affected, and their problem seemed to be a singular one.

With one end now spliced, he descended the pole and pulled a bit more wire off the spool, cutting the cable when he had sufficient length. With a sigh, he returned to the cart behind Nettie and began to reel the excess line back onto the spool.

Before he connected the second splice, he wanted a closer look at the little sinkhole. He ambled over and crouched down, trying to discern more of the pole's situation below the surface but saw only rocks, dirt and darkness. Upon closer inspection, the hole was just over a foot in diameter and looked like a marmot may have burrowed down there and undermined things. If the pole's base hadn't been compromised, it would be easy enough to reseat it in a new hole just a few feet the other way.

With a plan for the next day now forming in his head and eager to get things over and done with, Issac stood quickly—a little too quickly, in fact. A brief wave of vertigo gave his head a bit of a spin, and he had to lean heavily on the canted pole to stop from falling.

And that, apparently, was all that was needed, and gravity did the rest. The base of the pole suddenly kicked up and out of the dirt while the top slammed into the ground with a reverberating thud which vibrated through Ableman's bones.

Ableman called over to his horse with a laugh, "Son of a gun, that'll jiggle your jelly, Nettie!"

But Nettie wasn't laughing and instead seemed quite agitated, despite the falling post's one-time-only noise-making event.

"It's okay, girl. It's all over." He laughed again, adding, "That pole's only goin' to fall once, girl."

But Nettie would have none of it and whinnied in fear. She strained at her tether, her already large, dark eyes filled with fear.

"What is it, girl? What else is spookin' you?" Issac glanced about the immediate area but saw nothing that could cause the horse such distress.

And then he heard it, something which the horse's more acute hearing had picked up well before his own, though it was farther away. At first, it had been so faint, he'd mistaken it for the sibilant rush of the nearby river. But this was not the hiss of white water; no, this was harsher and much higher frequency, and whatever was making the noise was getting closer. He tilted his head toward the sound, mesmerised as he tried to figure it out. What was causing it?

Straining at her tether, Nettie bleated in fear, sounding almost human. She reared up and snapped the leather strap, then galloped off into the forest, the cart with the spool of wire bouncing along behind.

But Issac saw none of that, his attention fixed solely on the hole near his feet. He began backing away, a feeling of unease coming over him as the noise grew louder and louder. So entranced and unsettled by the sound, he practically bumped into the next telegraph pole, not realising he'd backed up so far.

The noise now seemed anything but entrancing and felt more like it was trying to crawl under his skin, striking at something deep within his primal core. It was alien and unheard by modern ears, something ancient, something deadly.

As the creature poked its head from the hole, Ableman couldn't comprehend what he saw. It seemed too large to be what he thought. In fact, it couldn't be. So he must be hallucinating, and it was a result of standing too quickly.

Issac blinked several times, but the thing had not gone away, so he couldn't be seeing things. Not big enough to be a marmot; perhaps it was a deformed gopher instead? But then, another and another and another popped their respective heads out of the same hole, and Issac realised he had been correct with his first guess.

Monstrous ants the size of rats scuttled from the hole. Fierce red, they keened and snapped their pincers, skittering here and there as they looked about for the cause of the resounding crash above their heads.

But how could creatures this size have existed around these parts, and no one had ever seen them before? Issac shook his head in disbelief.

Ultimately, whether the creatures had existed without being seen mattered not because they now saw him and did more than just turn their shiny red heads his way.

As one, they scrambled in a single direction, his.

Issac turned and almost ran face-first into the telegraph pole at his back. Luckily, he hadn't removed his spikes, and he began to climb, part of him thinking that someplace off the ground seemed like a great idea.

Not taking time to fasten his safety harness, he scrambled

up the pole in record time, his cleats digging deeply into the firm wood of the cedar. Up and up and up he went until suddenly he was at the very top and could go no further. Despite being covered in sweat and gasping for breath, he now felt a little better, far above the red mass of death that swarmed toward the pole. He almost laughed until he looked directly down, then screamed instead.

In his haste to be anyplace but where he was, Issac Ableman had made a snap decision that he now regretted. For whatever reason, he hadn't considered the option that the ants could climb the telegraph pole as well.

But climb they could, and soon they were climbing him as well, biting, scratching, and cutting into him with their shear-like mandibles. They clambered up his legs, his chest, his arms and then his head. They sliced into his cheeks, severed his ears, and tore at his eyelids. With a shriek, he could take no more and let go of the pole.

Some of the ants biting and tearing at him mercifully dropped away in the fall, giving him momentary relief as he plummeted to the ground. As he fell, he saw the cedar pole now covered in scuttling red bodies, the rapidly approaching earth below also filled with writhing, crawling crimson.

But ultimately, Issac Ableman was afforded instant relief not only of his most immediate and pressing pains but also all of his worldly worries. With a grinding crunch, every vertebra in his neck fractured as one as he landed in a broken heap at the bottom of the pole.

The ants that had fallen with him, those which hadn't been crushed, continued to dissect their prey, seeming undeterred by their fifty-foot free-fall. And now, working together, the group efficiently did their jobs, turning this latest threat into a benefit to the colony, allowing it to not only feast but flourish.

CHAPTER TEN

There was a sudden knock, and Kitty looked toward the door in surprise. Wiping her eyes on the corner of her dress sleeve, she said, "Who is it?"

"It's Caleb. May I come in?"

"Of course, just a moment," Kitty said. She stood and gave a sniff to clear her runny nose, then unlocked the door. That done, she wiped at her eyes a moment, then moved back to the bed to sit down.

The door opened slightly, and Caleb peeked his head inside. "Are ya sure it's okay?"

Kitty nodded and said with a small smile, "Always."

Closing the door behind him, Caleb hobbled further into the room. He nodded to the spot on the bed next to Kitty and asked, "Can I join you?"

With a smile, Kitty scooched over a little and patted the bed. Caleb leaned his crutches against the wall, then hopped over and sat with a sigh beside her, saying, "That was quite a climb all the way up from the basement to here. I feel like a regular mountaineer."

"At least you're gettin' your exercise." A hopeful smile played across Kitty's lips, and she added, "How did it go at the ice house?"

Caleb broke down what had happened after he and the Doc had arrived at the ice house and their dramatic confrontation with the spiders. He then detailed showing the captured spider to Thomas and the man's subsequent reveal of the mining operation beneath the saloon. He ended his little tale by saying, "And Sandy said you came out of the corridor to Sinclair's office a short while ago looking like your best friend had died."

With a sad shake of her head, Kitty said, "It almost feels that way. I had a run-in with Angeline and then Thomas in his office."

"That's almost as bad," Caleb said as he placed a gentle hand on Kitty's shoulder. "Did you want to tell me what happened, lass?"

After a moment of consideration, Kitty began to nod but suddenly changed it to a shake of her head and said, "But I really don't know if I should."

"Why not, lass?"

"Because of what Mr. Sinclair said."

"What did he say?"

"That I can't tell anyone what he asked me to do."

"Why not?"

Kitty gave a shuddering sigh, her eyes still moist with tears. "Because you're the person I'm not supposed to tell."

Caleb put his arm gently around Kitty's shoulder and said,

"Can I make a guess what it was about?"

Kitty nodded and wiped at her eyes with a handkerchief pulled from her décolletage.

"Sinclair said he wanted you to keep an eye on me, and keep him informed if I remembered anythin', and to try and pry the location of the gold from me, just in case I was actually holdin' out on him."

With a sniff, Kitty said, "Why, that's right!"

Nodding, Caleb gave a small smile and said, "I would have been surprised if he didn't try somethin' like that. And I do appreciate your candour." He rubbed her shoulder gently and added, "And now, since I guessed correctly and you didn't have to tell me outright, you no longer have to worry about that little problem."

Kitty reached around Caleb and hugged him, saying, "Thank you. That is a load off my mind."

"My pleasure, lass. And might I ask, what was he goin' to do if you refused?"

"He said he would turn me over to the police and have me deported to Scotland. He has telegrams and everythin', and says Scotland Yard will be wantin' to talk with me."

"Well, isn't that a fine how-do-you-do?" He shook his head. Here he was, having agreed to share the gold with Thomas Sinclair if he remembered its location, only to have his 'partner' force someone close to him to spy on him. And for the Scotsman to dangle her past misdeeds over her head to get her to cooperate was unconscionable. Not only was Sinclair greedy, but he seemed to have no moral boundaries. Shaking his head, Caleb now wished that he'd never found the cursed golden cavern in the first place. To have this woman that he felt so strongly about being made to inform on him was too much, especially because of all the emotional distress it seemed to be causing her.

"But I have to ask," Kitty said in a small voice.

"What's that, lass?"

"Are you holdin' anythin' back from Sinclair?"

"No. I don't think so. At least, I keep getting flashes, but not whole images. As I already told Sinclair, I've seen trees, rocks, and a sparkle of gold, but just quick flashes, nothin' that would make me remember more."

Kitty returned Caleb's hug, saying, "I think it'll come. But I have to tell ya, I think I've about had it for this place."

"What do you mean?"

"Now that that man has me spyin' on you, I just don't know who to trust anymore. And it makes me wonder who else he's got compromisin' information on, that he's also got spyin' for him."

"What is it you want to do?"

"I think I want to pull up stakes and try startin' over someplace else. I feel like I've gone over that waterfall with you. Things just keep going down and down and down for me around here." Kitty rested her head on Caleb's shoulder and gave a deep sigh.

The mention of things going down and down in the waterfall made something click in Caleb's head, and with sudden clarity, he recalled more falling water. Not from inside the cavern that had almost killed him, but another waterfall, quite a bit smaller. And with it came another flash of insight, this one golden. "I know what you mean, but I don't think we should quite give up on things here yet."

Kitty dabbed her kerchief at her nose and looked up to Caleb, saying, "Why, did you just recall somethin'?"

"I may have. At least somethin' that might help me recall more. And besides, I kind of like it here in this valley. I thought you did too?"

"I do, but I don't know if I can stay in my current situation. With all this conspiracy and everythin' else happenin', I think I might just take what little money I've saved and try my luck in the next gold town I find."

Shaking his head, Caleb said, "Well, thanks to your recent comment, if my memory is working again like I think it is, you might not have to go anywhere."

"That's wonderful!" Kitty hugged Caleb once more.

Caleb nodded and hugged her back, saying, "Aye, that it is." But it wasn't just what Kitty had said, of course. It was also how he felt about her, his thoughts about this valley, and his desire to settle down and stop running from his life. He would be damned if he was going to let Sinclair threaten this woman with jail. No, there was something he could do about it; he was sure of it now. He gave her a bigger smile than he felt and said, "It was good that you told me all this. And besides, there's actually more keepin' you here than you realise."

"Really? What?"

This was the moment Caleb had been both dreading and looking forward to all at the same time. He looked deeply into Kitty's pale blue eyes, feeling as if the butterflies in his stomach would fly from his mouth when he spoke. He brushed aside a lock of Kitty's chestnut-coloured hair from her eyes and said with a deep breath, "Me."

Taking her hand in his, Caleb continued, "I want to be here

with you, Kitty. Since the first day I met you, I've felt that there was somethin' special about you, and I don't just mean because you saved my life on the shore of that river."

Kitty laughed slightly and wiped at her eyes again, saying, "And what is it that's so special about me?"

"Well, despite what you do for a livin', I can see you are a bright, kind, carin' and compassionate woman, not to mention beautiful to boot."

Blushing slightly, Kitty said, "Go on."

Caleb smiled, adding, "I've seen how people react to you and how you treat others, and I can see you are an honest and genuine soul, which I need in my life now more than ever."

"What are you saying?"

Swallowing hard, Caleb said, "I'm sayin'... I think I... That is to say... I believe that I..."

"Yes?" Kitty leaned slightly closer, a hint of her perfume drifting Caleb's way.

"I think I love you, Kitty Welch."

Kitty's eyes grew large at this news, and Caleb thought he'd gone too far, letting her know too much of his heart too soon.

Her eyes glistened as she gazed into his. After a long moment, she replied in a small voice, "When I first met you, Caleb Cantrill, I thought you were a piece of debris washed up on shore. But when I got closer and saw you lyin' there, lookin' so sad, wet and pathetic, like you were on the edge of death, I knew I couldn't leave you there. And now, I'm glad I didn't."

Caleb looked expectantly at Kitty, hoping she would continue. After another moment, she did.

"I've spent most of my life like you, runnin' from my past. After I met you on the beach, I started to think of you more and more and that maybe I was done runnin', and you were the reason why. But now, with everythin' happenin', I just don't know what I should do anymore."

Looking into Kitty's troubled eyes, Caleb almost felt he could see her beautiful, sweet soul inside, and said quietly, "I do," and then kissed her.

Kitty kissed him back, hard.

Thoughts of monsters, gold and greed fled Caleb's mind, and he realised he'd found the one thing he'd been searching for ever since he'd been discharged from Her Majesty's Fifth, the one true treasure of his life, Miss Kitty Welch. And he was not going to lose her, ever. From this moment on, he knew that he would fight for her, keep her safe and provide for her, or die trying.

Kitty and Caleb lay back on the bed, their eyes locked on each other, and for the next little while, Caleb showed Kitty just how much he wanted her in his life.

CHAPTER ELEVEN

The soft morning breeze ruffled Sandy's fine blonde hair as he walked rapidly down the wooden sidewalk. His early shift with Angus at the smithy had just ended, and he was a man on a mission right now. With only a half hour before he began work at the Nugget for the day, he was heading for a quick visit to Vicker's Five and Ten.

Sandy mulled the reason behind his mission as he moved down the sidewalk—books. He was running low and needed to fill up his word bin, as he liked to think of it. Thanks to the cost of stories, he sometimes reread a book two or three times if it was a good one. Right now was one of those times, and he wanted to reread one of those books, except that he'd lent the book in question, along with several others, to Caleb Cantrill. And it wasn't as if he was about to ask for any of them back quite yet, not just after lending them out.

So now he was on his way to Vicker's Five and Ten. Almost finished his latest novel, The Mysterious Island, he had finally saved enough money to buy another new book. It was sort of a Dominion Day treat for himself, and he hoped the book he wanted hadn't been sold yet. He realised he should have asked Mrs. Vicker to put it away for him until he got paid. Fortunately, that day had been today, thanks to his smithy job with Angus Cochrane. Moving through the front door at the Five and Ten, Sandy wore a broad smile on his face.

Though the store carried a surprising assortment of goods, the sweet smell of candy was the first aroma that assailed you as you entered Vicker's Five and Ten. Located right next to the full-service soda fountain, the 'Candy Corner' (as the sign proclaimed) had treats of all descriptions proudly on display in assorted glass jars, bottles and bins. Gumdrops, liquorice whips, saltwater taffy, candy corn, jelly beans, you name it; if it was sugary and sweet, it was probably somewhere in the extensive candy section at Vicker's. Despite all that temptation, it was still early in the day, and no customers were currently shopping for a sugary fix. Normally, it was a section that Sandy could spend substantial amounts of money on, but today was not the day for treats; no, today was the day of the written word.

"Morning, Mrs. Vicker!" Sandy called.

The kindly grey-haired proprietress, Melinda Vicker, gave him a wave and a smile as she watched the mountainous boy make a bee-line for the book section. "Good morning, Sandy! Do you know what you're looking for today?"

"Yes, ma'am!" Sandy called over his shoulder. He was in luck. Up ahead lay the object of his quest. With its vibrant blue cover and embossed silver lettering, The Adventures of Sherlock Holmes was quite eye-catching. Whenever he had a chance, he checked the book section at Vicker's (after checking the candy section first, of course). When he'd done so last week, he'd been more than a little excited to discover this book on the shelves, jam-packed with twelve short stories he could read over and over whenever he wanted.

Thanks to Kitty's introduction to the master detective, Sandy had read a Study in Scarlet last fall, quickly devouring it. Since then, he'd been hungry for more and kept his eye out for further works by Arthur Conan Doyle. And so, when he'd seen this amazing collection of Sherlock Holmes stories for sale, he'd known then and there that someday he would make it his own. And today was that day. Though it was just as expensive as the other novels in his growing collection, he considered it a real find, considering it was even for sale in the first place in this expensive, remote mining town.

Scooping the book up, Sandy rushed back to the till to pay, a wide grin on his face. "Here you go, Mrs. Vicker, three dollars!"

"Thank you, Sandy." Melinda rang up the sale on the tall nickel-plated cash register before her, adding, "I sure hope you enjoy it."

Giving a large nod, Sandy said, "I should think so. I really liked the last one by this fella." He held the book up, marvelling at its beauty and still in disbelief that it was now actually his.

"It's imported all the way from jolly old England, you know."

Sandy nodded and replied, "Yes, ma'am, I know. I tell you, I can't wait to read it! That Mr. Holmes is a really smart guy. Miss Kitty says if I keep reading books, I might get to be smart like him someday, too! What d'ya think of that?"

"I think that sounds wonderful."

A look of concern crossed Sandy's face. "Speakin' of wonder, I was wonderin' somethin'."

"What's that?"

"Well, have you heard what happened to Farley Jones?"

"I heard he died of a spider bite."

Sandy nodded and added, "Yes, ma'am. More than one, from what Mr. Caleb told me."

"Is that your Irish friend?"

"Yes, ma'am."

"He was in doing a little shopping the other day. Seems like a nice fella."

"Sure enough. He's a heck of a nice guy, but he sure has got his fair share of troubles right now. And one of them involves spiders. Which is why I was wantin' to ask you about it."

"What is it you'd like to ask, Sandy?"

"Well, Mr. Sinclair wanted me to help Mr. Caleb look for spiders around town. There's an infars... infaster... interfest...

"Infestation?"

"That's it! Thanks, Mrs. Vicker. Some nasty spiders are runnin' around this town that are pretty dangerous. Mr. Caleb and the Doc went to the ice house yesterday to check and found one of them-there infestations." Sandy spoke the end of his sentence slowly, seeming to enjoy the syllables in the new word he'd recently added to his vocabulary.

"The ice house? Isn't that a little cold for spiders?"

"No, ma'am. Doc says it's a great place since it's dark and cool. He figured that was where Farley picked up the spider that bit him. Did you know they can live in temperatures down to almost freezin'?"

"No, I didn't, Sandy."

"Yeah, I learnt that from the Doc. He's a real smart man, too—a regular Sherlock Brown."

"Yes, the doctor is very nice, when he's sober."

"Yes, ma'am," Sandy nodded in agreement, "He does like his drink, doesn't he?"

"A little too much, I'd say," Melinda said, shaking her head sadly.

"So gettin' back to my question. Like I mentioned, I'd promised Mr. Caleb and Doc I would help them go around town looking for signs of those consarned spiders. So, I was just thinkin', the basement of your store here might be a possible place since it's so dark and cool there. Would you mind if I checked your cellar, Mrs. Vicker?"

"Of course, Sandy, if you wish. Do you know where the lantern is?"

"Sure enough," Sandy replied. "I remember from the time I helped bring in your shipment off the stagecoach a few weeks back." He'd been stopping by to check the shelves for new books when he'd seen Melinda struggling near her delivery door with a stack of cardboard cartons that had just arrived from the coast, containing more books, some hats and stationery and, of course, candy.

"That's right, you certainly would know. Okay, then feel free to inspect away."

Sandy nodded, tucked his new book into the oversized front pocket of his overalls and moved toward the cellar stairs.

Not all the buildings in town had basements. Some were only basic wooden structures, slapped up in a hurry to take advantage of the rush. But others, like the Five and Ten, were built to last, with foundations, cellars and indoor plumbing. Next door to the Five and Ten was the Bank of Montreal, which also had a cellar and shared its foundation with the Five and Ten. Together, they leased their building space from none other than Sandy's employer, Mr. Thomas Sinclair.

A lamp hung on a peg near the top of the cellar stairs. Sandy lit the wick and moved down the steep stairs, his eyes scanning for any sign of webbing. The basement was sizeable and dark, and it carried a slight smell of mustiness, despite the relative newness of the building. A series of storage shelves lined the walls with a set of central shelves dividing the room in two, and in the far corner squatted a large coal-fired furnace. There wasn't an overabundance of backstock on the shelves, but what there was, was divided into categories. Stationery and books were at one end, clothing, hats, and other mercantile items were in the middle, and the far end contained assorted candy and novelties ready to refill the displays upstairs, should they get low.

The lantern's flame danced across the cellar walls, and capering shadows appeared to scuttle away on tiny, wavering legs as he moved into the darkness. Not normally a person squeamish about bugs, that had all changed recently. Sandy now had a powerful dislike for spiders, especially after what had happened to Farley Jones. He'd been the unfortunate soul who'd moved the man's mortal remains from the Doc's examination table to the home and office of the town undertaker, Ezra Randall. At that time, the Doc had shown him the jarful of baby spiders that had come out of Farley, and he'd decided then and there that he didn't ever want to have something like that come out of him, if he could help it.

In the corner where he'd shelved some of the cartons of candy from the stagecoach, he was sure he'd seen something moving just on the edge of the lantern's reach, but when he got closer, there was nothing in sight. He turned and looked toward the small stream of water which ran across a corner of the basement, trickling in from a crack in a huge, immovable boulder, the building's 'pet rock'. It had been too large to move or blast through, and part of the foundation had been built around it. The water gently burbled away into a small outflow pipe in the corner, draining into the porous gravel and rock on which so much of this town was built. But he wondered, had he actually seen something just now, and had it crawled into that pipe as he'd approached? Was something using these drainage pipes as a way in and out of this cellar?

The outflow pipe was about six inches in diameter, and Sandy was pretty sure it was not the kind of place a spider would spin its web. He took the lack of spiderwebs anywhere near the 'pet rock' or the storage shelves as further proof that the basement was not infested. However, as he poked around more with his lantern, he could have sworn he heard something moving about in the dark with him.

He returned to look more closely at the cartons where he'd thought he'd seen movement. Everything seemed normal until he checked at the back of one of the boxes marked 'Candy Corn'. One corner of the carton had been chewed open, and a small pile of tri-colour rectangular candy had spilt out from the paraffin paper in which it had been packaged. Candy was not something Sandy thought spiders liked. Perhaps it was a mouse instead? And maybe he'd scared the creature into the outflow pipe when he'd approached.

Either way, Sandy wondered about the Bank of Montreal next door. It was from the bank's cellar that the trickle of water flowed, its foundation built around the same large rock it shared with the Five and Ten on the other side. And it wasn't likely he could just walk in there and check the bank's basement outflow pipe, either. Thanks to the holiday tomorrow and the bank being closed on weekends, if something were lurking around in their basement, they wouldn't know about it until Tuesday. He made a mental note to mention it to Mr. Worthington, the bank's manager, once it was open again after the holiday.

With a sigh, Sandy decided not to waste any more energy worrying about it since he'd prefer to think about something he was looking forward to, like having the day off tomorrow. He got Sundays off twice a month, but this wasn't one of those weeks; otherwise, he would have had two days off in a row, which was almost unheard of around these parts.

Despite his absence, the saloon would still be open. Mr. Sinclair was having Ernie fill in for him. Ernie wasn't as big as Sandy, but he was still formidably strong for his age. A retired master corporal from the Canadian Militia, Ernie was a no-nonsense man who smiled seldom and frowned often. He also enforced the house rules just as well as Sandy did. After all of Ernie's years in the military, he'd perfected his frown on many thousands of troops, and he used it now with similar success on the patrons of the Golden Nugget Saloon.

Another part of Sandy's excitement for the holiday was due to his helping out at the city park's pools as a volunteer lifeguard during the Dominion Day festivities. The park incorporated three naturally-formed pools, providing a lovely green oasis in one corner of the town. With public swimming occurring during the warmer months, the pools were home to geese and duck the rest of the year, along with the fish that found their way in through the aquifer which ran beneath.

Thinking of his upcoming volunteer position over the holiday, it was with a start Sandy realised his current bug-hunting quest was going to make him late for his last day of work before the holiday had even started. Giving the basement one final sweep with the lantern, he climbed the stairs back to the welcoming brightness of the summer day above. He extinguished the wick and hung the lamp back on the hook near the stairs.

On his way to the door, Sandy stopped to say, "I didn't see any webs or anythin' down there, Mrs. Vicker."

"That's a relief. I do so try to keep the place clean."

"Well, you'd know the webs made by these things if you saw them, trust me."

"I'll make sure to keep my eye out."

"And you might want to keep an ear out as well."

"What do you mean?"

"I thought I heard something crawlin' around down there, though I don't think it's spiders. Looks like it got into one of your boxes of candy corn. It could've been a mouse, maybe. And it might have come through from the drainage pipe in the wall next to the bank. But with that said, since I don't know what was makin' the noise, I'd caution your going down there." Sandy glanced at the clock over the door and saw it was only minutes before ten o'clock and the start of his shift at the Nugget. "I gotta run, Mrs. Vicker. I'm gonna be late for work!"

"Maybe it's burglars tunnelling their way into the bank?" Melinda called out to Sandy's receding bulk.

Heading rapidly for the door, Sandy replied over his shoulder, "For the bank's sake and yours, I hope burglars are all it is."

CHAPTER TWELVE

Caleb reached the top of the basement stairs with a small grunt. He hopped to a table nearest the batwing doors and Sandy's currently empty stool, then plopped down with a puff. He'd just finished a bit more creative writing in the journal that Sinclair had given him.

He'd suspected his new partner, Thomas, was most likely having someone bring the journal to him when he was out and about from his basement room. As a bit of a test the other day, Caleb had left the journal sitting in plain view on the table. He'd plucked a single hair from the top of his head and placed it across the book's catch. When he'd returned later that same day, he'd found it missing, confirming his suspicions that he was being spied on.

And so, for the last few days, he'd been doing some creative writing, and the fun had continued this morning. He threw in the odd bit of truth here and there, mixing it in amongst other, more fanciful recollections. His most recent fiction was set a month in the future, mostly comprised of things he would like to have happened if there hadn't been so many other complications currently playing out in his life, such as monsters from hell and blood-thirsty bandits wanting his hide.

The day was still relatively young, now approaching ten,

according to the pendulum clock over the bar. A warm breeze sighed through the open doorway at Caleb's back, hinting at the heat that would come later in the day. Sandy wasn't at his post yet, since the bar wasn't quite open.

Muddy, the bartender, had just arrived. He threw Caleb a quick wave and began to give the bar a brief polish. With that done, he moved on to some beer glasses, perhaps in anticipation of some early but thirsty regulars.

Caleb was not one of them. If he was going to imbibe, which he rarely did anymore, he usually tried to wait until it was at least noon hour somewhere. One beer with lunch or dinner was a pleasant thing, he found, but that was about the extent of it. The last time he'd had more than a single beer, he'd agreed to burgle gold bullion from the Bank of Montreal in Red Deer and look where that had gotten him. He grimaced and sighed.

At the moment, he wanted neither a beer nor breakfast since he was still too wound up from yesterday afternoon. His quick visit to ask Kitty to the Dominion Day picnic had turned into much more than he'd anticipated. But that wasn't a bad thing. He loved Kitty Welch even more now and would do whatever it took to keep her safe. And if that meant going on another bug hunt with Doc Brown today, then so be it.

After their interlude yesterday afternoon, Kitty had said she needed to go back to work, or else she would hear about it from Angeline. And so, despite his reservations and in light of his new feelings towards Kitty, he'd let her do her thing.

Caleb felt more determined than ever to remember things. His flash of insight yesterday afternoon was a welcome thing, but he needed more of them. He'd been racking his brain since his recollection of the waterfall and the flash of gold but, so far, had managed nothing more.

Still feeling particularly energetic after yesterday, he'd been out for a bit of exercise earlier this morning. And so, he'd hopped a few blocks around town and checked out the site of tomorrow's party, the town's park. In anticipation of some upcoming swimming competitions, wooden bleachers had been constructed near the largest of the three natural pools. Across from the bleachers was what appeared to be a diving tower, at least it would be when it was finished. From the looks of things, the person in charge of that operation still had their work cut out for them.

He'd met an elderly lady who said she came to the pools regularly to feed crusts to the ducks and geese. As they'd chatted, she'd mentioned something strange. The birds that had greeted her daily since the spring thaw had recently disappeared. Perhaps the construction had scared them away, Caleb had suggested, but the little lady hadn't seemed convinced. Apart from that conversation, the walk, or hop, had been peaceful, invigorating and calming to his nerves, and it looked like the day would indeed be a pleasant one. In light of his upcoming appointment with the Hole-in-the-Wall Gang, he sincerely hoped that to be true.

Adjusting his position in the chair, Caleb pulled out the remaining gold nugget from the pocket of his dungarees, then scowled at it as he examined it for the millionth time. The breeze kicked up again as he did, the swinging door's hinges creaking slightly at his back as if an invisible visitor had just entered the saloon. He hoped that gazing intently at the nugget would somehow unlock his memory of its golden origin, which currently lay hidden somewhere between his two ears. But that didn't happen, as much as he wanted otherwise, because he was suddenly distracted.

"Good morning, my boy!" Doc Brown called. He sported his usual white lab coat and his leather satchel slung across his shoulder, but today he had an added accessory underneath one arm.

Placing his nuggets back in his dungarees, Caleb said,

"Mornin', Doc. What have you got there?"

With a grin, Brown said, "I've upgraded to a bigger tank." A brass fire extinguisher rested in a sling under the doctor's arm so he could easily pump it as he sprayed. Dangling from the end of a pole over his other shoulder was a small bird cage containing the spider from hell, his lethal hobo's bindle now decoratively upgraded.

"Well, that's a bit more like it!" Caleb said, then added quickly, "The sprayer, I mean, not the spider."

With a grin, the doctor said, "Yes, I've upgraded the solution inside the tank, too. Mama here doesn't like it at all."

"Mama?"

Nodding to the spider, the doctor said, "With as many offspring as she has, I figured the monicker was a natural fit."

Caleb shook his head. Though afraid to ask, he did anyway, "What did ya go and do to your spider spray, Doc?"

"I've increased the level of acid that I've been using. I have plenty, thanks to my experiments."

"Experiments? What kind?"

"I've been studying a relatively new process of separating gold from ore using acetic acid and sodium cyanide."

"Cyanide, Doc?" Caleb sat up a little straighter at the mention of the poison.

The doctor continued, "I use it in the cyanidation process. Mixing a mild solution with the ore allows gold to be extracted using regular water. But don't worry. The cyanide is neutralised through the application of acetic acid. So it's almost perfectly safe."

"Almost?"

Brown shrugged slightly and admitted, "Well, you wouldn't want to breathe in the fumes if you can help it." He patted the extinguisher and added, "However, this is just the acetic acid solution and should suffice for the spiders. And as I mentioned, I have increased the ratio of the acid to water since I want to better penetrate the exoskeleton of the bigger animals or at least dissuade them as it does with our friend here in the cage. In any event, I want to go back there again today to check on things and spray any remaining spiders."

"What, the ice house?"

Nodding, Brown said, "I want to ensure the building is cleared of any further arachnid presence. And this new solution will help because it should neutralise them more quickly, especially if we encounter any more of the younger ones. As I mentioned, we want to get to them soon before they get loose. They'll be much faster and perhaps breed even more quickly once outside in the warm weather." He patted the side of the brass fire extinguisher and added, "This gives much better spray coverage than the mister did, so I think we should be more than prepared."

"Well, that is good news, I suppose," Caleb said with a nod of resignation. "But until we go, could you do me a favour?"

"Certainly, my boy."

Caleb shivered slightly and looked to the spider's cage, saying, "Do you think you could put him out of sight while we're here, Doc? That thing's givin' me a case of the willies." It was bad enough that he'd agreed to return to the ice house, but before then, he didn't need to look at the horrific thing any longer than required.

As the doctor moved to the cloakroom to secure the spider,

bad news in the form of Lucias entered the saloon from the direction of Sinclair's office. Dressed as usual in his trademark black attire, hat and boots included, he sauntered across the room, fixing Caleb in his steely stare as he approached.

Caleb gave the man a small smile as he arrived, saying, "I hope you're not here to help me see the light, are ya?"

"Always the funny man," Lucias said coldly.

"Whatever I can do to keep that handsome face of yours smilin'," Caleb replied, a broad grin on his own.

"To what do we owe this honour?" Brown inquired, adjusting his extinguisher's sling as he arrived.

"The boss said I should come out here and keep an eye on things."

"Whatever for?" Brown wondered.

"The boss wants me to protect his investment," Lucias replied.

"His investment?" Caleb asked.

Lucias pointed one well-manicured finger at Caleb and said, "Yeah, you. Since your outlaw friends from south of the border will be back looking for their missing gold soon. Let's just say Mr. Sinclair doesn't want to see anything happen to you."

Caleb nodded. "I should've figured that out. I must admit, it'll be handy to have you stoppin' them from fillin' me full of lead if I can't remember where the gold is."

Lucias opened his duster. In addition to his Colt Lightning slung at an angle off one hip, a sawed-off shotgun rested in a leather sling under one arm, just opposite the chopped-down

Winchester under his other. He briefly dropped his eyes to the weapons, then looked back to Caleb, saying, "Don't you worry about them filling you full of holes."

"I appreciate that," Caleb said.

Lucias nodded and replied, "Because I'll be doing it to you myself if you can't remember where that cavern is located pretty soon. But hey, no pressure."

"Now who's the funny man?" Caleb wondered aloud.

"I always keep 'em laughing right to the end," Lucias replied with another small nod.

"Words to live by," said a voice at their backs from just outside the batwing doors. The group turned to see Jesús Oritz entering the saloon, flashing his golden smile for all to see.

Caleb was surprised to see the gang so soon and thought they'd said twenty-four hours. But though they were a few hours early, he didn't know if the full amount of time would have mattered anyway since he still couldn't remember.

Oritz's lean, scar-faced sidekick followed through the doors behind him, an intense frown gracing his unpleasant face. Behind him were two even uglier mugs, quite different from the flunkies of the day before. These rough-looking individuals seemed to have all their fingers on each hand and both ears attached. One sported a bad haircut, and the other seemed neckless. Either way you sliced it, both were bad news. Trailing through the doors at the back of the group was an older man with a bushy white beard and hair to match. He nodded as he muttered to himself, "Gonna get my pots and pans back."

Scarface whipped around and shot a dagger-filled look at the grizzled man. About to say something more, the man's eyes widened when he saw he'd been overheard, and he clapped his mouth quickly shut.

"Saludos, mi amigos," greeted Jesús.

"Well, well. Were your ears burnin'? Cause we were just talkin' about ya," Caleb said.

"Is that so?" Jesús said.

Caleb replied, "Yeah, we were discussin' bothersome pests, and then just like that, you appeared."

"Oh, you are very droll, mister," Jesús replied.

"He's a regular comedian," Lucias agreed flatly. His sharp eyes darted from one man to the next, seeming to assess the threat level of each new arrival as he spoke.

Oritz looked briefly to his scarred sidekick, and the man brought a chair over and placed it next to Caleb. Turning the chair around, Jesús straddled it and sat down. He leaned against the chair's back and looked Caleb intently in the eyes for a long moment but said nothing.

Growing uncomfortable after several seconds of this, Caleb said, "If you keep lookin' at me like that, you're goin' to have to buy me flowers."

Jesús grinned and said, "I am looking for signs of recollection."

"You won't find your gold in my eyes. I haven't recalled where I hid it. Not yet, at least. I've had a couple of flashes, but nothing definite so far." This was true, apart from his brief remembrance of a waterfall with Kitty yesterday. Caleb felt sure he might recall more if he had a bit more time. He was about to mention this when Jesús responded.

"That is unfortunate. You know what I said would happen

if you didn't come up with the gold."

Doctor Brown stepped in, saying, "Killing him is not going to get your gold back; you must know that. And you don't look like a stupid man to me."

"You would be correct, doctor. If I were, I wouldn't have gotten to where I am."

"And where is that?" Caleb asked.

"Let me tell you something, Mister Caleb Cantrill. I have studied many books, travelled many miles and seen many unfortunate acts befall my fellow man. At the same time, thanks to my association with the Hole-in-the-Wall Gang, I have also been responsible for many more acts, most of which have been unfortunate for the person upon which they were perpetrated, but ultimately acts that were necessary. And I have been successful because of my drive to do whatever it takes to get the job done. I have never been denied what I, or the Gang, was due and never will. And, after all this time, there is one thing I know for certain."

"And what might that be?" Caleb wondered.

"When a person's time has finally expired, and they have no other hope, that is when they usually start to talk." He pointed to the pendulum clock next to the house rules sign, adding, "And I would suggest you start talking. In two hours, your time is officially up."

Lucias stepped forward and asked, "How much gold was misappropriated by Mr. Cantrill?"

Jesús looked from Caleb over to the man in black and stated, "Eight sacks of pure, sovereign gold."

Caleb was about to add that some of that gold was also technically his since he'd helped with the bank job, but didn't want to argue the details at this point. If he remembered where the gold was, he figured he would give it all to the gang just to be done with them so they'd have no further claim on him. Besides, the gold up in the cavern far surpassed the paltry eight sacks of gold with which he'd fled.

"All right, Mr. Jesús Oritz," Lucias said.

Jesús raised his eyebrows. "All right, what?"

"You have yourself a deal."

"A deal? I did not realise we were in the middle of negotiating one."

"Be that as it may, Mr. Sinclair has authorised me to negotiate on his behalf. He's willing to assume Mr. Cantrill's debt to you and pay back your missing gold. Then, you can go on your way, and Mr. Cantrill will only be beholden to Mr. Sinclair."

Caleb was stunned by this news. He had not expected his newfound business partner to spring for his indebtedness.

Jesús appeared to mull the offer over for a moment, then said, "As much as I would like to take our payment out of Mr. Cantrill's hide, your offer is a reasonable one."

"And?" Lucias asked.

"I will accept it."

Lucias nodded and said, "I'll inform Mr. Sinclair. We'll have your gold ready for you tomorrow afternoon." At his back, the Large pendulum clock on the wall began to chime the hour.

Jesús stood to leave, saying, "Very well. We will return tomorrow."

"I hoped you were already long gone." Kitty Welch said from the doorway. She had just arrived on the scene from her morning commute from her cabin to work. Behind her stood Lucy from London, Carla and Monique. Kitty entered first, followed by the rest of the Golden Nugget's entertainment staff. With disapproval, Kitty added, "Is there no getting rid of you?"

Jesús flashed his golden grin and said, "Do not worry, senorita, as of tomorrow, we will only be a memory."

The gang members were about to exit when they discovered Sandy had just arrived on the other side of the batwing doors and now blocked their way with his formidable presence.

"This seems like a popular destination today," Jesús observed as he looked up at the unsmiling young man.

Peering down over the doors, Sandy said, "You bunch just keep turnin' up like bad pennies, don't ya?"

The two ugly mugs stepped around Jesús and Antonio, then stood on the other side of the door, glaring at Sandy. The taller of the two with the bad haircut said, "You might want to move aside, boy."

Lucias looked toward Sandy and said, "Let them pass, Sandy."

"Might want to listen to your friend," the shorter mug said on his way by. He would have been as tall as his companion, except he seemed to have no neck, his bald, potato-shaped head flowing to his shoulders like a blob of clay on a potter's wheel.

Sandy nodded at Lucias and stepped aside grudgingly as if he'd been preparing to enforce some of the Nugget's rules on these troublesome men.

The gang members pushed through the doors. Bad Haircut stopped on his way by to say, "Don't get in my way again, boy, or you'll find yourself in a world of hurt."

Saying nothing, Sandy merely glowered at the man. But once the mug saw he wouldn't get a rise out of the boy, he turned and moved down the steps to the street. The grizzled man with the bushy white beard trailed out last, muttering, "I knew I wasn't goin' to see my pots and pans today!"

Caleb watched the gang members depart, then looked to Lucias, who was heading in the direction of Sinclair's office once again. His mind was awhirl about this new position in which he found himself, now doubly indebted to Thomas Sinclair, as opposed to being singularly indebted to the Hole-in-the-Wall Gang. With a sour feeling in his stomach, he realised he couldn't decide which one was worse.

CHAPTER THIRTEEN

After their meet and greet with the gang members, as promised, Caleb joined the doctor on a sequel to their first bug hunt. He had decided to forgo another bumpy ride on Emily and had instead hopped on his crutches back to the ice house. Over the last day or so, the pain in his ankle had noticeably lessened, and he'd decided to get some exercise today.

He shivered slightly and pulled his borrowed winter jacket more tightly about his shoulders. It was not the same one he'd worn the day before; that had stayed where he'd thrown it, and it was still draped across the catwalk's planks over the ice pit. When he'd selected a new jacket to wear, Caleb had been extremely cautious, unsure if any spiderlings might have remained in the entrance to ambush someone by hiding in the jacket's sleeves. Small plumes of vapour rose from Caleb's mouth as he said, "I don't see any live ones anywhere, Doc."

"Yes, it does seem rather lacking in test subjects for my new spray."

There were plenty of dead ones, however. Thanks to the doctor's previous spray spree, they were scattered all over the ground, curled into little balls of death. Not only was it disgusting to accidentally squish one and have its greenish-black innards come gushing out, but Caleb discovered they were as slippery as a banana peel to boot. Crossing the catwalk over the ice pit, he'd been extra cautious since the last thing he needed was to place a crutch on one by accident, then slip and fall to his death onto the frigid ice far below. As to how many of the loathsome little buggers remained scampering about, or where they were now located was anybody's guess.

As Caleb hopped into the cold storage room behind the doctor, he saw it as devoid of live spiders as the rest of the place. The boy's body had disappeared since their last visit, presumably removed by the undertaker, Ezra, as promised by Sinclair. Caleb stood a safe distance from the stack of produce bins, well back from where they'd found the boy's desiccated body, although Doctor Brown apparently had no such reservations.

Cornelius scratched his unkempt mane of white hair as he stared at the bins. "Yes, this is strange. I thought for sure we'd see a few live ones at least." He poked the nozzle of his fire extinguisher around the gaps and crevices in the stack of bins, its top still covered in silken web. "There seems to be no sign of them anywhere." Brown stepped back from the containers and added, "I think we'll have to contact Ezra to see if he saw anything when he was here."

Leaning on one crutch, Caleb said, "I agree. But I have a question."

Brown adjusted his fire extinguisher's sling slightly, peering around the stacks of empty produce bins in the storage room as he did. "Of course, my boy. What is it?"

Caleb glanced about for a moment before he spoke, still not convinced the spiders were actually gone and were, in fact, lying in wait somewhere, ready to strike. "D'ya think they just died off like you figured they might?"

"That is indeed a great question. There is a chance of that, and I hope it will be the case, but sadly, I suspect some are still alive."

"I was afraid you'd say that."

"However, I can't imagine they would have gone too far, being small and vulnerable as they were. Perhaps they escaped when Ezra came by?"

"Maybe," Caleb said, not feeling convinced. "But if that were the case, and Ezra let them out, then that's not good either."

"Quite true." The doctor took the pole from over his shoulder and looked closely at the spider dangling at the end in its cage. "I'm surprised our friend here hasn't brought us any success in finding them either. I was sure the spiderlings would sense their mother and come running as soon as we arrived."

Caleb was quite happy that that hadn't been the case. The thought of having hundreds of spiders advancing menacingly toward them once more was not something he was keen to repeat.

Cornelius shook the cage slightly and added, "We need to find them before they become your size. Isn't that right, Mama?" The bird cage wasn't the largest, affording the creature little room to move; however, it did have room to hiss and did so vehemently while clattering its chitinous legs against the cage's thin metal bars.

"I agree with you one hundred percent, Doc." Brown's pet spider's limited mobility was fine with Caleb since he didn't want to see the monstrous thing moving about any more than he had already. Just being in this building looking for the creature's offspring was almost too much to bear.

Brown moved back into the tool room with Caleb hopping behind on his crutches. Brown turned to address his friend, saying, "And I believe there's only one more spot to check around this neck of the woods, and then our little inspection will be over for now."

"Where's that?" Caleb queried with interest. This was good news since he was more than ready to change locations.

"Well, there's another smaller building behind this one which I'd like to check out. I believe there's a chance they might have migrated there."

Happy to be departing to a place much less spine-chilling, both in temperature and multi-legged inhabitants, Caleb said, "Let's hop to it then."

***

They discovered the smaller structure behind the ice house was a storage shed. It smelled here, but not unpleasantly so. The air carried a slight sweetness from the many apple bins stacked high, hinting at harvests long past. No lantern was required since the building had several windows, making it much warmer here. Sweat dripped down Caleb's brow onto his cheeks, running into the corners of his mouth. He could taste the salt and relished it slightly, knowing he wouldn't trade it for the world to be cooler since that would mean going back inside that frozen hell. With a slow nod, he looked about the building and said, "This looks like the sort of place they might have moved on to."

"I agree there's a good chance that some of them might have relocated out here." Brown adjusted his extinguisher cum bug sprayer slung under one arm, then poked its nozzle into crevices around several of the stacks of bins but found nothing worthy of spraying.

To one side of the building was an oiled tarp, behind which presumably lay more produce bins. With the doctor across the room poking his sprayer here and there, Caleb decided to investigate behind the tarp. He whisked it aside, then exclaimed, "Shite almighty!"

A multitude of spiders dropped onto his head and shoulders, and he flung his crutches to the ground in panic. Hopping about on his good leg, he swatted and brushed at the eight-legged beasts while continuing to curse a blue streak.

Hearing his cry, the doctor appeared at Caleb's side and started to pump the sprayer at the creatures but suddenly stopped.

His voice high and panicked, Caleb said, "What're you doin', Doc?"

The doctor touched one of the spiders with the tip of his boot, saying, "There's no need to waste precious solution on these."

Caleb was shuddering repeatedly and had to force himself to calm down. He took a few deep breaths and said, "What? What d'ya mean?"

The empty bins behind the tarp were a bit smaller, looking to hold grapes when full. Despite that, they were stacked just as high as the others. But on a lower half-stack in front, several spiders still crouched, seemingly frozen in place. Caleb looked down at the others on the ground, saw that none were moving there either, and asked, "Your solution did that?"

"Hardly. Look more closely, my boy. It's something I was afraid of."

Approaching the spiders on the top of the bins with caution, Caleb saw what the doctor was talking about. They were not spiders at all, but merely, "Skins! All of these are only spider skins! Where's the rest of them?"

"It's as I feared."

"I hate it when you say that."

"Sorry, my boy, but their maturation rate is as accelerated as their gestation rate within Farley and that poor unfortunate boy we found—it seems they've already shed their exoskeletons."

"So what you're tryin' to say is these discarded skins are like a pair of shoes that got too small for a growin' lad." He shook his head slowly in wonder and added, "Which means they've gotten bigger."

Brown toed at the moulted skins on the floor and said, "Yes, and it'll probably happen again, several more times, in fact."

His brow furrowing in concern, Caleb asked, "How many more?"

"Some spider species can moult up to a dozen times before reaching maturity, while others continue to do so their entire life. And the rate these creatures have been doing so is astonishing. They haven't been outside the ice house for more than a day, and they've already moulted once."

"So you're sayin' these things could get the same size as that monster on your pole in short order?"

"Yes, some of them, at least. The females are always bigger than the males."

A small spark of hope ignited in Caleb's heart, and he asked, "Are there more males than females?" Smaller spiders were always better in his book.

The doctor shook his head. "No, most spiders are fairly evenly split between the sexes, much like other species."

Caleb's shoulders slumped, and he said, "That's what I was

afraid of."

"And with the warmer temperatures out here and the abundance of prey, it will certainly aid their growth."

"What prey are you talking about?"

The doctor gave a slight shrug and said, "Any mammal could serve as a host to these creatures."

"Well, that's a lovely thought, too. Thanks, Doc."

"You're welcome," Brown said with a nod, apparently missing Caleb's sarcasm. "However, there is one other thing to consider."

"And what might that be?"

"The proximity of these spiders in relation to each other."

"What're ya gettin' at, Doc?"

"They moved from the ice house together, and it seems they've stayed together out in the world and even moulted as a group. Which leads me to an even more concerning possibility."

Caleb shrugged slightly and said, "Okay, Doc, lay it on me."

"These creatures might be social animals."

"Meaning they enjoy each other's company? Like friends?"

"In a way. And this leads me to that concerning possibility."

"Hit me again, Doc."

"I believe these creatures might be pack-hunting animals

once there are enough of them." He shook the pole for emphasis, and the spider let out another low hiss.

"Pack hunters?"

"Yes. I've heard of some spider species capable of taking down prey over seven hundred times their size, such as birds and rodents. Which for small spiders is very impressive."

Caleb envisioned some hapless doe foraging in the woods, encountering a nest of monster spiders the size of Mama, then getting swarmed and injected with their venom and being paralysed almost instantly. After that, the monsters would lay their eggs inside the deer's lungs and... He shuddered, unwilling to finish the thought since the possibility was staggering. "Sweet mother in heaven! That's absolutely terrifyin', if you don't mind my sayin'."

"No, not at all, my boy. You go right ahead. In fact, I concur with your assessment of the situation. And do you remember when I said we should check other likely-looking spots for these creatures?"

"I do. Has that changed?"

"Somewhat. I now believe it's safe to assume that pretty much any spot around this area is potentially a place for these creatures to hide."

Caleb's head slumped forward briefly in resignation, then he looked back up and said, "How many d'ya think there are right now?"

"Hundreds, possibly thousands."

"And if we don't find their nest soon..."

Shaking his head, the doctor replied, "I'd need to calculate things more precisely. But off the top of my head, I'd have to say…" His gaze went heavenward as he tallied things up. After a brief moment, Brown looked earthward again, his eyes wide, and said, "We're in very serious trouble."

CHAPTER FOURTEEN

With a satisfied nod, Jesús looked around the room, finding the atmosphere over here at the Kootenay Saloon much more comfortable than the Golden Nugget across the street. The air was thick with tobacco smoke which hovered over the tables in a foggy haze. Some men played cards, others played dice, but all talked in low, rumbling voices, not wanting to be overheard as they plotted their next misdeed. The ashtrays were full, and the spittoons that dotted the floor even fuller. Yes, it felt like home.

Oritz took another sip of sherry from the small glass before him, feeling melancholy for things he no longer had access to, now living on the North American continent as he was. Good sherry was at the top of a long list of things he missed. Like many important families in Spain, his had grown rich from the exploitation of others, and the people of Mexico in particular.

After the Spanish colonisers had introduced opium poppies for medicinal purposes in Mexico, the drug's recreational use and economic potential had soon been realised. And so, young Jesús had come over from Barcelona to supervise his family's poppy-filled land holdings. That had been just a little over twenty years ago, and he'd never looked back, except in reminiscence of his homeland's excellent food and drink. He took another sip of the sherry and made a sour face. According to the barmaid, it was made right here in Canada, and it tasted like it.

Jesús had come to know the Hole-in-the-Wall Gang through his family's trade in the drug business and had become enamoured with their 'take no prisoners' and 'burn the town to the ground' approach to life. And so he had begun working more and more in the field selling drugs and finding profit in other illegal dealings along the way. Over the years, he had come to love being on the road and its endless parade of criminal activity.

Through his ruthlessness, he had earned his current position, and now, having gang members covering his back and at his beck and call at all hours was something he truly enjoyed. In his posse of criminals, new recruits soon learned who was in charge. And if they didn't, he broke them in pretty quick. Making life miserable for someone else was something Jesús enjoyed almost as much as making money. It was a win-win situation working with the Gang. Some days, as he travelled down the road, he felt like Johnny Appleseed from the American folktales, except instead of sowing apple seeds wherever he went, he sowed death and misery.

However, drugs, apples and misery, although pleasant, were not his concern at the moment; it was gold. Though he'd agreed to Sinclair's offer to repay the Irishman's debt, something about the whole situation made him want to think twice about what he'd agreed to.

Sinclair had seemed exceedingly eager for them to move along, judging by the offer made by the man's representative, Lucias. But why? What reason would the man have to take on the debt of the Irishman unless there was something in it for him?

After talking with his new local henchmen, Jesús had learned more about the wily Scotsman. From what he now knew, Sinclair didn't do anything unless there was profit to be had. That meant there was a reason the man wanted them to be gone and wanted to know what it was.

A change of plans was in order since there was another angle Jesús wanted to play up, one that might get them even more gold. He'd planned on returning to the encampment to grab their gear and ammunition tomorrow, but now figured doing so sooner might be a better choice. That way, they could immediately act upon his new plan after they had collected their gold from Sinclair.

They now had enough hands to finish their business in this out-of-the-way little town. Since there was much opportunity here, he was loathe to take only what was coming to them and leave. No, he wanted more of the gold that flowed through this valley, much, much more. But in the meantime, he would play the game and take the proffered gold from Sinclair. And if the Gang garnered extra riches on top of that, then so much the better.

But first, they would need the ammunition they'd left with the ants back at camp. They had no choice but to go since they couldn't return to the hardware store to buy more ammunition. The last time he'd been there, he'd bought out almost their entire stock. And since the store wasn't receiving another shipment for a week, off to the camp they must go. And while there, they would, of course, retrieve Cookie's pots and pans. He swore if he heard that man talk of his cookware any more, he would dice him up and cook him in his own pots.

However, if all went well, the Gang's coffers would be replenished, and they could head back into the hills and count their gold; Cookie could cook, and they could decide what to plunder next. Yes, the more he thought about it, the more this little valley seemed like a great place to set up a more permanent camp. Once relocated to a safe distance from the troublesome local wildlife, they could have fun robbing the sourdoughs blind and perhaps liberate the odd shipment of gold going to refineries elsewhere in the country. Overall, the Dominion of Canada looked like a great place to start a new branch of the Hole-in-the-Wall Gang.

Looking at the men around the table, Jesús said, "All right, compadres, I have decided we are returning to our encampment to get our belongings tonight rather than tomorrow."

"Bout time," Cookie muttered.

Jesús dismissed his two local hires, telling them to be back shortly after nightfall. The men nodded and shuffled toward the bar, no doubt to obtain a couple more drinks to pass the time.

Antonio queried, "Do you figure those devil ants will be settled down by then?"

"Whether they are or not is of little concern. We need to get our ammunition and sundries, and we need them for tomorrow, so tonight is the time we will go. As with most insects, I believe those ants are likely to be dormant at night, so they shouldn't be much of a problem when we get there."

"Door what?" Cookie asked.

"Dormant," Jesús repeated patiently. "Or sleeping, if you will. And we will be best served if we go there tonight under the cover of darkness." He waved to the barmaid for another round of drinks.

Now, they would just need to wait until nightfall to collect their rides, and he already had a pretty good idea of where to steal them from.

CHAPTER FIFTEEN

"And what have you learned?" Angeline demanded. Her hands rested on her hips as she faced Kitty. They stood in a currently quiet corner of the bar near the billiard tables, away from customers' ears.

"Nothin'." Kitty said with a shake of her head. "He's had some brief remembrance of some gold, a hole and a tree, I think, but that's all I know." She'd been doing her job alongside the other girls keeping the sourdoughs spending freely on food and drink, games of chance and feminine finery when Angeline had appeared out of nowhere and begun questioning her.

"Nothing?" Angeline said, incredulous. "I think there's far more going on than you're telling me." The woman's hazel eyes drilled into Kitty's as if probing into her mind and looking for things she would never dare speak aloud to anyone, least of all this woman.

"That's all I know." It was true; that was all Caleb had shared with her regarding his recollections. There was much more going on between the two of them, quite unrelated to the gold, but she wasn't telling Angeline that and would never share it with anyone else, at least at this point in time.

They had spent an amazing afternoon together, something

special that Kitty would cherish for a lifetime to come. And although she was a woman who currently made her living doing the exact same thing she and Caleb had done, it had been so very different. Wonderful, eye-opening and magical, she'd never experienced anything like it with any man before in all her two dozen years on the planet.

Angeline interrupted Kitty's line of thought, saying, "I know what it is!"

Kitty cast a sidelong glance at Angeline but said nothing.

But, once again, it appeared as if the woman before her could read minds, and Angeline exclaimed, "You're in love!"

Kitty's heart doubled its beat within her chest as Angeline made her pronouncement. How could this woman possibly know that's how she felt inside? Was it showing on the outside somehow? With the amount of rouge on her cheeks, she was surprised anyone could tell if she was flushed with excitement or not. And yet, here was Angeline stating Kitty's most heartfelt, and at the moment, closely-held secret. With a dismissive shake, Kitty said, "I don't know what you mean."

"Hmmph! I highly doubt that. You've fallen in love with that lame leprechaun!"

"Don't call him that!"

"So you don't deny it then?"

Casting her eyes down, Kitty said nothing. She would not admit anything to this woman. Angeline could think what she wanted, but only Kitty would have the pleasure of keeping her time with Caleb solely to herself and no one else ever knowing anything for sure. And she would never share their talk of a possible future together either—his dream of settling down and her dream of having her own little eatery here in this nameless little town. She might call it Kitty's Corner—Good food at fair prices, or something like that. Of course, that name was only temporary since she felt sure she'd think of something else to call it should the wonderous day ever come to paint the sign to hang over its front door.

With wide eyes, Kitty realised Angeline had been talking to her, but her wandering mind had almost completely blocked out what the woman had been saying. With some difficulty, she focused back on Angeline's red lips and saw she hadn't missed much.

"And whatever is going on with you two, I don't want it affecting what you've been hired to do."

"No, ma'am." Kitty scoffed inwardly at Angeline's use of the word 'hired' but shook her head in the negative. She received no extra pay or perks for her new role of spy since it was one she'd been coerced into.

Angeline smirked at Kitty, saying, "Oh, are you feeling yourself ill-used?"

Once again, Angeline seemed spot-on in her assessment, and Kitty admitted, "Of course, wouldn't you if you were in my shoes?"

Angeline chuckled softly and said, "I would never be in your shoes."

Kitty's eyes burned at the woman before her, but she said nothing. Angeline would not break her, and she would not kowtow to her either.

Fortunately, Kitty was spared any further confrontation when the object of their discussion came hopping through the batwing doors. Doctor Brown was at his back, fire extinguisher slung under one arm, the other holding a pole, his pet spider-in-a-cage dangling at the end. The doctor stopped briefly to talk with Sandy about something, then smiled and moved toward the cloakroom, no doubt to stow his eight-legged companion and acid-filled extinguisher.

Looking over to the arriving men, Kitty said to Angeline, "It seems like I should go and do my job if you don't mind."

Angeline sneered slightly and said, "You go right ahead. That's all you'll ever be good for anyway."

Kitty spun and moved toward Caleb and the doctor, her eyes filling with tears.

***

Hobbling into the saloon, Caleb scanned around the room for a moment, finally spying Kitty coming toward him from the direction of the billiard tables. His heart began to beat faster as he saw the distressed expression on her face. He nodded toward a nearby table, and together, they crunched through the sawdust-covered peanut shells toward it. Caleb sat with a puff, and Kitty sat beside him with a sigh.

Work gear stowed, the doctor joined them at the table. His normally disarrayed hair looked more distressed than usual, thanks to the warm, early-evening breeze wafting in from outside. He patted it down with his hands as he plopped into his chair.

Concern heavy in his voice, Caleb asked, "What happened, lass? I saw you talkin' with Angeline over there, so I assume it can't be anythin' good."

"Yes, are you all right, dear lady?" Brown gently queried.

Kitty dabbed at her eyes with her handkerchief and said, "Angeline is usin' her position with Mr. Sinclair to make sure I'm doin' what I'm supposed to be doin' and also bein' her usual, cruel self."

"I'm so sorry, Miss Kitty," Brown said.

Caleb placed a hand gently on Kitty's and asked, "And what's she got you doin'?"

Lowering her voice, she said, "As I told you, she's making sure I'm spying on you like Thomas asked me to do."

"Excuse me, young lady," Brown interjected, a look of surprise on his face. "Could you repeat that, please?"

Keeping her voice hushed, Kitty said, "I'm supposed to be tryin' to get the location of the gold mine out of Caleb, make sure he's not hiding anything from Mr. Sinclair, and keep him informed what Caleb is up to."

Brown gave a heavy sigh, shaking his head.

Now it was Caleb's turn to ask the doctor, "What is it, Doc?"

"I haven't been altogether truthful with you, my boy."

"What do you mean?"

"Regarding what Miss Kitty just said, "I am afraid Mr. Sinclair has compromised our relationship as well."

"Meaning?"

"He has me spying on you, just as he does Miss Kitty."

"What?" Caleb was surprised by this news, but not completely shocked. He'd suspected that Sinclair would have used a woman like Kitty to get information on the gold's location out of him with her feminine wiles. And now to learn the Doc was also employed as a spy was a revelation, to be sure, but not particularly earth-shattering. But unfortunately, it made him wonder about Sandy and everyone else he knew around here; were they all burdened with something from their past that Sinclair held over their heads, just as Kitty had surmised? Could anyone, in fact, be trusted? Or was that part of Sinclair's plan all along?

"But it's not how it sounds," the doctor continued.

"Really? Well then, tell me how it sounds," Caleb replied, eyebrows raised.

"I'm being blackmailed."

"Blackmailed?" Caleb shook his head. Two people he knew, who he considered to be friends, both had their relationship with him corrupted by Sinclair's greed, and both through the same method, extortion.

"I'm afraid so, dear boy. There is a dark period in my younger days on which he has some information and is dangling over my head like the Sword of Damocles," but that was all the doctor would say of his past.

With a small shrug, Caleb said, "Well, despite all that, I'm sorry to say there's not much for either of you to spy on. I still haven't recalled much more than I already told you, Kitty." He nodded toward her and continued, "Just that flash of gold, a hole and some trees."

This was not a lie because that is all he remembered of the flash. However, what he wasn't telling either of them anything about, was his latest idea to find the lost cavern. Despite knowing that Kitty was compromised, he knew it was something she'd been forced into, same as with the doctor, and he held no ill will against either of them. But the little idea that he'd been formulating since seeing Sinclair's cavern was one he wanted to keep as close to his chest as he could. That way, if neither of his friends knew about it, they wouldn't feel compelled to betray him to Sinclair.

Caleb looked to his companions and said, "I realise the pair of you were in a situation where you couldn't say no. I appreciate the honesty and forthrightness of you both. And far be it from me to say anythin' considerin' my own history and all. Besides, I already trusted Sinclair about as far as I could throw him before hearin' any of this from either of ya. And you can trust me when I say I won't let him get the best of me." He looked to Kitty and added, "That, I'll save for you."

Kitty blushed slightly and gave Caleb a small, impish smile.

The doctor took in this brief display of affection with raised eyebrows but said nothing.

About a dozen feet from where they sat, Sandy staggered backwards through the batwing doors. More correctly, he seemed pushed. And for that to occur, he must have been caught off guard.

It was the two mugs that had been here earlier with Jesús. The tall one with the bad haircut stepped across the threshold first, followed by his neckless companion with the potato-shaped head.

"We thought we'd come back for another visit," Bad Haircut called out.

Shaking his head, Sandy said, "You gentlemen best be movin' along. We don't need you gang-types around here."

"That's okay; we're on our own time," Bad Haircut replied.

"We got a little while to kill before we go back to work, and wanted ta finish our little conversation with ya from earlier." No Neck drawled.

Bad Haircut gestured to his waist and that of his neckless companion and said, "And you can see, we're not armed."

111

"Yeah. Yer just a li'l too big for your britches, boy. And we're here ta help ya fit back into 'em."

Bad Haircut looked strangely at his companion for a moment, then shook his head and advanced on Sandy.

Shaking his head, Sandy said, "Your makin' a very painful mistake, mister."

The two mugs chuckled, then got even more up close and personal with Sandy, not paying attention to the rest of the group watching off to one side.

Caleb nodded to Brown and said, "Why don't you introduce those boys to your little friend, Doc?"

"That's an excellent idea, my boy! It would be best to avoid fisticuffs if we could." The doctor flew from his chair toward the cloakroom just off to one side of the now brewing brawl.

Kitty cringed slightly as the doctor emerged with his little friend. The spider's long spindly legs hung through the generous spaces in the bird cage's bars, swinging idly back and forth. Despite their relaxed manner, the spider was no doubt ready to latch with lightning speed onto anything breathing that got too close to its wandering appendages.

All conversation in the saloon had ceased, and most heads had swivelled to watch the developing situation.

As Brown approached the unfolding drama, he said to the spider, "All right, Mama, this is a great opportunity for us both." As if in agreement, the creature's chitinous legs clattered together like deadly castanets.

The two men were crowded up to Sandy, Bad Haircut tall enough to look him in the eyes. No Neck stood to one side, both hands resting non-threateningly on the straps of his suspenders.

Bad Haircut said in a low voice, "This is yer moment to learn some manners, boy." As he ratcheted his arm back to take a swing at Sandy's front, No Neck prepared to do something even more deadly at the boy's side.

With a wicked grin, the neckless man pulled a slender, pearl-handled barber's razor from within the straps of his suspenders, flicking it open in one smooth, practiced motion. The blade gleamed murderously in the orange glow of the setting sun angling through the batwing doors outside. The man's fingers tightened on the pearl handle, his knuckles growing white as he prepared to slice Sandy up nice and pretty with the razor's sickle-sharp blade.

Sandy easily dodged out of the path of Bad Haircut's swing, spinning around and trapping his aggressor in a headlock within his bulging biceps.

As Sandy spun out of the way, No Neck missed his target and cursed under his breath. He brandished the gleaming blade, nodded toward his trapped partner, and said, "Let him go, boy, and maybe I'll take it easy on ya and not cut ya up too much."

As No Neck spoke, the doctor gently lowered the cage behind him. Several of the spider's dangling digits briefly latched onto the man's shoulder and quickly contracted, pulling the cage closer to his body. One of Mama's fangs briefly scraped against the sloped skin where the man's neck should have been but was thick with corded muscle instead.

Brown yanked the cage back just as the neckless man whirled around. No Neck sliced the razor through the air where he thought the threat had lain, not realising the doctor was standing safely six feet away from his whistling blade.

Fortunately, the spider's venom had rapidly begun to do its job. No Neck's eyes grew large as he saw what Brown held in the cage. "What the..." He trailed off, wobbled briefly, then dropped the razor and quickly joined it on the hardwood floor.

Brown gave the spider's cage a playful jab toward Sandy's captive, still imprisoned between his muscular bicep and forearm.

"Keep that away from me!" Bad Haircut shrieked. He tried to pull back but couldn't go anywhere, thanks to Sandy's iron grip.

"Are you sure you don't want to make friends with Mama?" Brown inquired, swinging the cage almost hypnotically back and forth before the man's terrified eyes.

Sandy dragged the man's head closer toward the grotesque arachnid and asked, "Why did you come back here?"

In a conciliatory voice, Bad Haircut looked to his comatose comrade on the floor and said, "Hey, now! Don't mind Claude there. We was just messin' with ya."

Caleb hopped over to join the party and said, "And we had a deal."

Struggling for breath, Bad Haircut rasped, "You still do! Like I said, we was just havin' ya on. Can't you people take a joke?"

Kitty picked up the dropped razor next to the outstretched hand of the motionless man in the sawdust and peanut shells. She stood and held it high, its blade gleaming wickedly in the remaining light of the day. "Was this the punchline?"

"Go back and tell your boss we don't have a sense of humour!" Caleb nodded to Sandy, and he released his captive, who collapsed to the floor, gasping for air.

Next to him, No Neck lay immobile. If it hadn't been for

the slight rise of his belly as he breathed, he would've appeared a corpse.

Sandy prodded the paralysed man with his foot, adding, "And you can take your friend, Sneaky Pete there, with ya."

The tall man with the bad haircut rubbed at his neck for a moment and looked about to say something more but held his tongue. He grabbed his partner's arm and pulled it around his shoulders, then stood with a groan. Using the fireman's carry, he shuffled unsteadily out the bar room doors and down the low steps to the street.

Brown pulled back a bit of his grip on the pole, brought the spider closer to his face for a moment, and said, "Well done, Mama!" The arachnid hissed at him, and he responded, "No, you can't lay your eggs in him."

Kitty edged next to the doctor and spider and said with a slight shudder, "That was amazin' how quickly this beastie's bite dropped that man."

"Yeah, how did that little scratch drop him so fast?" Caleb wondered,

"Well, it was near a major artery, so it took effect rather quickly."

Shaking her head, Kitty said, "Still, its poison must be potent as well, judgin' from the small nick that man got."

Brown nodded in agreement. "It's venom, actually, not poison. But you are correct, young lady, getting even a scratch of a mature spider venom seems enough to cause paralysis. However, I am grateful to that man for his volunteering. I've been wanting to have an opportunity to test this animal's toxins."

"Will he be okay?" Kitty asked, concern in her voice despite her obvious reservations.

"Oh, most certainly," Brown replied with a reassuring smile. "It would seem this creature's venom could make a great local anaesthetic." His eyes brightened at the thought, and he glanced at the arachnid and said, "I'll have to look into that. Maybe I can milk your fangs."

The spider hissed at him again.

He ignored Mama's disagreement and nodded toward the batwing doors, adding, "That man will be right as rain at some point in the near future."

"Some point in the near future?" Caleb queried.

The doctor shook his head dismissively. "That was just a quick nip he received. He would've been down for days if Mama had more time to inject him with a substantial amount of venom. With that nip he received, he might be out a half a day or less, depending on his metabolism" With a shake of his head, the doctor concluded, "Well, after all that excitement, I think I need a drink." He gave a slight bow to Kitty and said, "Dear lady." With a nod to Caleb, he turned, slung the spider back over his shoulder and hailed the bartender as he approached, saying, "Oh, Muddy, my boy!"

Sandy gave a small smile and said, "Never a dull moment around this place," then returned to his post near the front doors.

Caleb and Kitty moved out onto the saloon's front porch. Early evening was settling in, the last of the amber sunlight spotlighting the large ridge at the back of the valley. They stood side by side for a moment, and Caleb surreptitiously placed his hand over Kitty's where it rested on the railing. She turned her hand over in his, and they stealthily held hands for a few, all-too-brief seconds.

As of yet, they hadn't announced their newfound relationship to anyone. Though some around them might have guessed already, both felt it best to resolve some of their multiple dilemmas before becoming more serious about their relationship and letting the world know. Though the physical aspect with Kitty had been magical, Caleb wanted to get to know so much more about the woman and hoped to have the time to do so in the near future.

They watched the final few moments of golden light as the sun dipped behind the snow-covered mountain tops. Brilliant shafts of light shot magnificently through some low cloud near the horizon, looking as if the second coming was close at hand, and trumpets would soon sound for all to hear. Caleb gave Kitty's soft hand a gentle and longing squeeze, feeling the beautiful sight a portent. But he had to wonder how many more sunsets he would share with this woman if he ever found that cavern again.

CHAPTER SIXTEEN

The valley around the Natánik glacier had experienced unbounded growth over the last few years. What had been a small trading post had blossomed into a booming metropolis thanks to the discovery of gold in the valley. And Thomas Sinclair had been right there from the start to ensure he got a slice of everything that happened in this town.

When the Scotsman arrived in the valley, little was known about him except that he was exceptionally wealthy. He bought out the original proprietor of the trading post just before the first gold strike was made in the valley. In fact, he'd already been building what would become the Golden Nugget Saloon before that gold strike had even happened. It was like he'd known there was something special about the area before anyone else had.

Sinclair made a fortune and now owned many businesses in the burgeoning town in addition to the Golden Nugget Saloon. And if he didn't own it, he probably held the lease on the building or had interests in the businesses therein. But despite his monopoly, he had done much good and brought many innovations to the area, including the telegraph office, ice house and delivery business. On top of that, he was rumoured to be planning a hydroelectric dam similar to ones recently built in Ottawa, Niagara Falls and New York. And in keeping with his fascination with all things aquatic, Thomas had also built upon and enhanced something which mother nature had formed naturally.

On the far side of town lay a series of three natural pools, now a focal point thanks to the large park Sinclair had paid to landscape around them. These spring pools were of diminishing size; one ran almost two-hundred feet across, the second perhaps half that, and the third not quite fifty feet around. Above ground, they appeared as three separate and distinct pools, but beneath their calm surface, they interconnected via an underground aquifer. Thanks to the aquifer's circulation, the water remained relatively clear and clean in all three pools, its hue emerald green. In the largest of the pools, the water ran quite deep, with the bottom not easily seen, making it ideal for a diving competition.

Tomorrow was the first annual regatta, and the town was abuzz with activity. Horse races down the main street were planned in the morning, along with a couple of boating displays down at the lake in the afternoon. However, the swimming and diving competitions were to be held here in the largest of the pools. The nearby river had been ruled out since it ran too fast and, due to its glacial nature, was far too cold for swimming.

And so, a diving tower was one of the last things to be constructed for the upcoming festivities, and Kirk Erickson's company had been in charge of getting it done. Barely visible in the growing darkness on the pool's opposite shore, the tower appeared straight and true, and he was quite pleased with the project. Consisting of wooden planks and scaffolding, nailed, bound and screwed together, the tower stood almost thirty feet tall and projected out over the deepest part of the large pool.

Kirk stood next to one of his company's other projects, the temporary bleachers, finished just a couple of days before. On this side of the pool, a sandy beach angled gently into the water for a couple of dozen feet before descending into darkness. However, on the tower side, it dropped dramatically after less than a half dozen feet, making it a perfect spot for the tower.

A frown played across Kirk's lips rather than the smile of satisfaction that should have been there as he stared into the gathering darkness. The lack of light around the diving tower was causing him some consternation. He and Sam had been working from dawn till dusk for the last couple of days to complete the tower, and they'd finally finished just as the sun had set. Now ten o'clock, the last of the day's light was a pinkish-purple band above the jagged mountain peaks to the west. He'd just returned from tending to other business and had expected to see Sam's lantern across the way as he finished inspecting the tower's footings. But this seemed not the case. For some reason, the opposite shore of the large pool lay in darkness.

Sam was the only other employee in Kirk's small company. It had been extremely busy recently, and the pair had been working at several sites around this booming town. Sometimes this required Kirk to leave temporarily to check on something at one of the other sites. And that meant leaving Sam working alone, just as he had several hours ago. Unfortunately, this self-supervision sometimes led to a recurring problem Kirk had to deal with, Sam's drinking. On most regular days, the man waited until work was done before starting. Unfortunately, when they had to work later into the evening, like today, it became problematic.

Erickson stood on the shore in front of the bleachers and called out Sam's name. He waited several seconds, but there was no answer, and he shook his head in frustration. Instead of waiting for Kirk to return so he could report the results of his safety check as instructed, Sam had apparently decided to call it a night. Now, without that information, Kirk would have to do the final verification himself.

"Sam Shepherd! I can't believe you buggered off!" Kirk

called, then gave a frustrated sigh. They would most definitely have to have a discussion about this in the morning. He had only run back to the shop to take care of some paperwork and told Sam he'd be back within a couple of hours. He'd been looking forward to being done for the night when he'd arrived back here, but now, having to double-check Sam's work would take another hour or more. He called out to the darkness again, "Which saloon did you get your sorry arse off to tonight?"

A chorus of frogs was the only response to Kirk's question, cheerfully singing their favourite song near a small patch of marsh on the far side of the pool.

Kirk began to trudge along the shore toward the diving tower. It was quite dark now, the moon having just dropped behind the valley's craggy crown of mountain peaks.

The limited light of his lantern caused wandering shadows along the ground as he moved, extending out into the pool as well. On several occasions, Kirk thought he'd seen something moving next to him in the water but swimming deeper down in the darkness. It must have been the lantern playing tricks since the pool's surface was still. If something were swimming in there, he was sure he'd have seen some ripples at the very least. He sincerely doubted any creature alive today could swim without leaving a trace of motion, so it had to be his imagination.

As Kirk drew closer to the tower, he was surprised to see the tools he'd left in Sam's care lying about on the ground. "Ya lazy bastard! Ya couldn't have been bothered to pick up the tools? It's the least ya could've done after buggerin' off early!" He shook his head in disbelief, then began to collect his equipment near the tower's base.

This area was a lovely spot, to be sure, but a hell of a bugger to build anything on, as Erickson had recently discovered. The grassy loam surrounding this side of the pool was quite soft and unstable until you got down to some proper bedrock. As a result, they'd needed to shore things up around the diving tower's footings, and they'd already had to adjust them once already today. That had been what Sam was supposed to have been doing, checking all of the connections to make sure things were solid and secure after the latest adjustment.

Over near the 'kiddie pool', as Kirk thought of the small one, the ground had given way in a couple of spots. Beneath were what looked like marmot tunnels. So apart from the soft ground, it seemed the new park might also have a rodent problem to deal with. But that would be up to the new city works manager. He gave a small smile since he'd applied for the position a couple of weeks ago, and it might be him that would eventually look after the problem if he were lucky enough to get the job. He hoped his company's completion of the diving tower and bleachers would go far in showing how qualified he truly was. In any event, he would know if he got it after the long weekend ended. Of course, if that happened, any further work he would do with Sam through his construction company would be severely curtailed, which might not be a bad thing.

Finally finished collecting his tools, Kirk stood with a grimace, his back deciding to be ornery again. Now, all he needed to do was verify what Sam had presumably checked already.

The base of the tower was attached to several pylons they'd driven into the pool's shore, and they seemed to be holding fine on that end. He walked out over the water, stepping carefully on the widely spaced temporary decking that ran between the square posts. The other end of the footing was braced several feet down against the pool's rocky side.

Kirk squatted and tried to shine the lantern into the water's wavering depths but couldn't see more than a fathom or so. From what he could judge, everything seemed fine. He dabbled his fingers in the water, enjoying the warm temperature. The contestants in the competitions tomorrow wouldn't have to worry about a chill, thanks to the aquifer's warmth helping mollify the river's bitingly cold temperature somewhat.

Erickson stood and gazed out at the expanse of darkness before him. There was no wind tonight, and the water barely lapped against the shore. Millions of stars reflected off the pool's placid surface, making it seem like he was standing in outer space.

Just as he was about to turn away, Kirk thought he saw small ripples as something moved furtively about in the water beneath the surface, a little further out from where he stood. He held the lantern high to cast as much light as possible but was thwarted due to its short throw.

"Sam? Is that you?" Kirk stood on his tiptoes to shine the light as far out as possible. There was a sudden slosh of water, and small ripples crawled toward him across the calm surface. Whatever it was, it stayed just beyond the light's reach. "Sam Shepherd, is that you tryin' to scare me or somethin'? Cause it ain't workin'!"

Another slosh and more ripples, but there was nothing more in response.

Kirk grabbed one of the tower's supports, then leaned out over the water as far as he could, trying to get a better view. There was something down there for sure; he'd just seen brief movement near the trailing edge of the lantern's light. However, it couldn't be Shepherd swimming that deep since he knew for a fact the man couldn't hold his breath for more than a couple of heartbeats thanks to the number of coffin nails he smoked each day.

Kirk shook his head and turned away from the water. If it wasn't Sam, then what had he just seen? From what he knew, there was nothing big enough in this pool to make too much of a ripple, just a few fish. And if that were the case, what was sloshing around out there?

A short distance down the shore of the large pool was a narrow, floating boardwalk that led out onto a floating platform. Both had barrels beneath and were secured in place with cables and weights. Despite that, the narrow walkway still bobbed and wobbled as a person walked out onto it, and if it were windy, it could be especially exciting.

For the Dominion Day festivities tomorrow, Thomas Sinclair had purchased fireworks which were to be launched from the floating platform once it got dark enough. With minimal rain, the forest surrounding the town was getting rather parched since June had been hotter than usual this year, at least according to the area's aboriginal history. Kirk had heard that bit of news from Maggie at the Golden Nugget during one of his frequent visits for a roast turkey dinner last week. And so the fireworks had been considered safe to use, but only if they could be launched from over the middle of the largest pool. The floating boardwalk and platform, recently installed during the park's landscaping, were deemed the perfect spot.

Wanting one more look at what might be swimming around out there, Kirk figured a better vantage point was in order, and the platform seemed like a great idea. The night was silent; the only noise, apart from the frogs, was the slight slop of the water as he wobbled along the boardwalk toward the platform in the pool's centre.

About halfway, he stopped and shone his light closer to the water's surface, almost certain something was moving next to him as he teetered along. Soon he was standing on the floating platform in the pool's centre. He cast the lantern about, sure he would see a muskrat, beaver, or some other nocturnal creature paddling about. He'd long since given up on the thought that Sam was doing the backstroke out there.

"What in blazes is it?" Kirk wondered aloud as he strained to see through the darkness. There was no further sound of movement, and the water continued to lap gently against the sides of the platform. Perhaps the creature had swum away, getting bored of its game. He was about to move back to shore when he spotted something small and tan bobbing in the dark water only a few feet from the platform's edge, something quite familiar.

Erickson knelt, then leaned out over the water as he tried to grasp the object but couldn't quite make it. So, he lay on his stomach and stretched his arm out, straining to reach. After grunting and groaning for several long seconds, he finally snagged the item with the tip of his middle finger. He fished it out and discovered it was what he thought, Sam Shepherd's match safe.

Sam had always bragged how he could smoke as he stood fishing in the river and not lose his matches. Quite proud of it, the man had carved the safe from a fallen maple's limb he'd found in the forest. But the question remained, why was it here? Perhaps it fell out of Sam's pocket while he was checking the diving tower, and it had floated here? Either way, it was strange Sam wouldn't have noticed its loss.

Creaking and slopping along, Kirk checked both sides of the boardwalk as he made his way back to shore. Fortunately, there was no sign of a floating body to go with the match safe. He shook his head, stuffed the safe into his trouser pocket, and returned to the tools he'd collected near the diving tower.

There was no point in alarming anyone or contacting the constabulary since nothing else could be done in the darkness anyway. And besides, Kirk had no proof Sam Shepherd had drowned, only that he'd been careless with the company tools and had lost his match safe while working. No, Sam was most likely tipping back his elbow at one of the town's numerous saloons, and Kirk felt fairly certain when the sun rose and the party started, Sam would soon pop up.

CHAPTER SEVENTEEN

Cricket song filled the warm, still summer's eve as Sandy returned from walking Miss Kitty and the rest of the girls to their cabin. Tonight, there'd been no peeping Toms outside their window, unlike last week when he'd discovered the Flannel Man. With the girls now safe, it was time to assist Doctor Brown back to his office and residence.

When he'd entered the saloon, Muddy was just giving the last call for alcohol. The Doc was sitting at his usual table, already more than three sheets to the wind, having recently finished several shots of whisky back-to-back. With the amount the doctor had drunk, there was no way his friend would be able to walk back home under his own power, even though it was only a block. And as on so many other nights, he had known then and there he'd be going for another short walk.

Leaning heavily against Sandy as they moved to the batwing doors, the doctor said, "Shay there, young fella! I recoginate... remunerise... renumerate... Don't I know you? Cause you seem awfully familiar."

"Yes, Doc. You know me. It's Sandy." One arm gently around the doctor's shoulders, Sandy gave Muddy a wave with his free hand and led his physician friend down the front steps to the rough-hewn sidewalk below.

"Shandy, my boy! Great to shee you again!"

With each slurred word, Sandy found himself awash in the fumes of the doctor's breath.

Brown squinted, craning his neck to peer closely at Sandy's face, then said, "But wh-which whone are you?"

His eyes watering slightly, Sandy replied, "I'm the one in the middle, Doc. The other two guys aren't really there. You just can't see straight again."

As it was on so many nights, helping Doctor Brown down the block to his practice was Sandy's last duty of the day. It was unpaid, but he didn't mind. He liked Brown and was glad his friend would be safe and dry in his own little cot in his office rather than the alternative.

About a month ago, the good doctor had shuffled out the saloon's doors and into the night while Sandy had been walking the girls home. He hadn't seen the man again until later the next morning. The doctor had wandered back through the batwing doors, saying he'd found himself sleeping on the rocky shore of the Kokanee River using a piece of driftwood as a pillow. Fortunately, thanks to Sandy's friendly assistance, the man would have something a bit softer to lay his head upon tonight.

After a few minutes, with Brown chatting animatedly at his side, they'd arrived at the doctor's office. "All right. Here we are, Doc." Sandy released his arm from the doctor to allow the man to stand on his own.

That was a mistake.

Brown began to slump to the ground, and Sandy's strong arms snapped out to grab him before gravity could do its job. As he pulled the doctor upright once again, the man asked,

"Wherezat, my boy?"

"At your home, Doc." Sandy gestured to the whitewashed storefront. A red cross on the window had a sign just below it with neat, black lettering which stated, 'Doctor Cornelius Brown - Medical, Dental and Barbering Services Provided Within'.

Brown leaned forward and peered at the sign, blinking his bleary eyes. After a moment, he exclaimed, "This is a doctor's officeses!"

"That's you. You're a doctor."

"Why, thash right! So I am! Well done!" He tried to reach around Sandy to give him a hug of thanks, but his thin arms couldn't reach.

A sad smile playing across his lips, Sandy replied, "Not a problem, Doc."

Brown nodded and began sorting through his keys with some difficulty, dropping them several times as he did.

Sandy gently removed them from the doctor's fumbling fingers after the fourth drop and unlocked the door for him. Brown stumbled through the door into his darkened office, muttering something about a T-bone steak hitting the spot right about now.

Pulling the keys from the lock, Sandy returned them to the doctor, who accepted them with a bleary-eyed nod. He gave Brown a small pat on the shoulder and said, "Have a good night, Doc."

With growing anticipation, Sandy carried on down the street to the corner and his final destination for the night, the smithy. While he was there, he would check on the livestock Angus kept, which wasn't much. Besides the pump wagon mules, Ester and Camille, there was sometimes a horse or two left in Angus's care overnight for reshoeing early the next morning.

Though Sandy liked to see the horses and mules, that wasn't why he was here tonight; no, he was here to see his new friend. He smiled as he opened the smithy's gate, finding it funny that he had collected two new Irish friends in the space of only a week, one human and one not so much.

After Farley's passing, Sandy had adopted the man's Irish Wolfhound. And as much as he would have liked to have the animal nearby at all times, he didn't want the enthusiastic canine attacking anyone by accident. It had almost happened on a couple of occasions when he'd first attempted keeping Rufus with him at work. Two different drunken sourdoughs had gotten into his face over the course of the evening, and the dog had jumped into the fray without hesitation both times. The already tall animal would put his paws up on the chest of the man he perceived threatening Sandy and give a low growl. With saliva dripping from his parted jaws and a wild look in his eyes, Rufus had been surprisingly effective in defusing those situations.

However, since the dog couldn't differentiate between what was an actual threat and what was not, for now, Sandy had decided to keep Rufus elsewhere when he was working. He hoped he'd be able to train the dog to better follow his lead and, if successful, might try the canine at work again in the future.

And so, Angus Cochrane had said he would look after the orphaned dog for Sandy when he was working his shifts at the saloon, and that is what they'd been doing for the last few days. Rufus's quarters at the stable consisted of a pile of straw with an old blanket overtop, situated next to one of the horse stalls. Angus closed the dog in with the livestock to wait until Sandy came to collect him for the evening. Sometimes, Sandy came over on his afternoon break with a treat for the dog.

When he did, he received a refreshing face wash, the dog acting as if he hadn't seen him in days when in reality, it had only been a few hours. But that was fine with Sandy; he loved the attention as much as the dog loved giving it.

As Sandy opened the stable door, the dog greeted him as he'd expected and stood, placing both paws upon his chest and began enthusiastically licking his face. The dog was so large it almost looked him in the eyes as it did.

"Whoa! I'm happy to see you too, boy!" He scratched the dog's scruff, and it grunted and chuffed in delight, then licked him some more before dropping back to the ground.

After checking on Ester and Camille and a pair of horses to be reshoed the next morning, Sandy took the wolfhound down to the town's new park for a walk. As the long-legged animal did a few laps around the well-manicured grounds, Sandy enjoyed the peaceful evening. It was cooling down nicely, the air carrying a hint of perfume from the wild rose bushes that grew in the park's centre.

When Sandy finally arrived back at his shack, it was approaching midnight. The place wasn't much, but it was his own space, and he appreciated its solitude after a long day of drunks arguing in his face, and today had been an especially long day indeed. He looked forward to stretching out on his cot, which waited invitingly, just inside.

But he didn't want to sleep quite yet. No, he wanted to stretch out and read for a while and lose himself in a different world from this, one filled with less noise and bother. It was something he looked forward to each and every night and rarely missed. Even though he knew he should be getting right to sleep, he couldn't resist. And besides, tomorrow was the holiday. He could stay up a little later if he wished since his volunteer time at the pool didn't start until nine in the morning.

In his eagerness to get inside, Sandy dropped the key to the padlock he'd installed on the door. Since he'd started collecting books, he had become rather paranoid that someone might wander by his shack when he wasn't home, think he was running a lending library, and help themselves to his books. And so, he'd installed a lock.

As Sandy stooped to retrieve the key from the dirt, Rufus chuffed in his ear. He scratched the dog's head and said, "What is it, boy?"

The wolfhound chuffed softly again and turned to face in the direction of the smithy down at the far end of the darkened alley.

Sandy didn't have night vision as good as the dog's and could see next to nothing. But whatever it was, it was making Rufus cautious and attentive. Was it a spider, he wondered. Perhaps one from the ice house was now on the loose? The doctor had mentioned more of his latest adventure there in passing as Sandy had helped him stagger back to his home. According to Brown, there might be hundreds or thousands of spiders out there by now, all growing bigger by the minute.

And so, wanting to ensure that no one else suffered a fate like Farley Jones, Sandy ruffled Rufus's furry head and said quietly, "Okay, boy. Let's go take a look-see if somethin's goin' on that we need to be concerned about."

CHAPTER EIGHTEEN

When Jesús and the remnants of his motley crew had sauntered by the smithy after the ant attack, he had made note of the fine animals that the blacksmith kept. In addition to a pair of mules in the yard, he'd spotted a couple of sturdy-looking horses just inside the stable. And so, when he'd tried to think of a place to steal some locomotion for their nighttime excursion to the camp, this was naturally the first place that popped to mind. And since it was only a block from the Kootenay Saloon, the smithy was also conveniently located, and he would not have to walk too far, which was always a bonus.

Knowing he and Antonio each had a horse was good enough for Jesús. If his new lackeys had to suffer the ignominy of riding the mules, then so be it. And the fact that the town would be defenceless against fire due to their 'borrowing' of the mule team needed to pull the pumper wagon was of little consequence.

It was just a few minutes before midnight, the evening dark and still, and up ahead through the gloom lay the object of their stealthy approach, the small stable where the smithy kept its horses.

In a voice far too loud for their surreptitious situation, Cookie said, "Yep, there it is! Just like you said."

"Keep your voice down, you imbecile!" Jesús hissed. "I can see it."

After his constant and prolonged exposure to Cookie over the last few days, it had become apparent to Jesús why the man had never amounted to more than, well, the cook. After all, Cookie had been with the gang almost since its inception, so the reason for his lack of progress now seemed painfully obvious—the man was a moron.

The owner's home was separated from the stable and smithy by a small footbridge that arched over a babbling brook. Thanks to the gentle burbling the stream made, Jesús hoped it would mask any noise they happened to make. But still, some attempt at stealth was needed.

They had been slightly delayed in their departure this evening thanks to his new henchmen returning from their adventure across the street a little worse for wear. He had not been pleased. Their visit to the Golden Nugget was not something he had requested either of the simpletons to do, and it could have jeopardised their entire operation.

Fortunately, after a couple of cups of what passed for black coffee out of the Kootenay Saloon's kitchen, along with a couple of shots of grain alcohol, No Neck could stand once more but had done so on wobbly legs. At least riding the horses and mules, they wouldn't need to worry about the man stumbling along loudly behind them any longer, as he had on the way to the smithy. Of course, there was always the chance No Neck might fall off his mount and break his head wide open, but that was a risk Jesús was willing to take.

Several mules and a couple of horses were housed inside the small stable, and as Jesús suspected, there were only enough horses for him and Antonio. The other men would need to ride the mules. But that was okay, seeing how much of an ass they all were. And so, while the local hooligans retrieved some saddles, he and Antonio led the horses from the stable. Cookie remained inside, trying to choose the best-looking mule of the three for himself.

By the time they had the horses in the yard, No Neck was returning, somewhat unsteadily, saddle in hand. Jesús took the saddle and watched as the man lurched back into the darkness to retrieve a saddle for himself. He seemed far from fine, but his current situation was his own doing, and Jesús felt no sympathy for the man.

***

Bad Haircut had delivered a saddle to Antonio and now moved back through the darkness to the tack shed for his own. With a small shake of his head, he noted that his partner had not yet returned with another saddle, and he whispered into the dark, "Where did you get to, ya lazy turd?"

Upon entering the small tack shed, Bad Haircut's question was answered when he stumbled across the man in question, currently sprawled across the dusty wooden floor. Repeated shaking didn't rouse his neckless friend, and he seemed down for the count. "What're ya doin', Claude? Takin' a nap cause of that spider bite?"

From off to one side in the darkness, a mysterious voice suddenly whispered, "And you're going to be joinin' him right quick." The speaker's words were underscored by a low, ominous growl as if a hound of hell had been loosed inside the shed and now stood in deep shadows nearby, ready to pounce.

But instead of ravenous jaws clamping around his throat, there was an explosion of stars as Bad Haircut was introduced to the boulderlike fists behind the mysterious voice.

***

With his saddle secure, Jesús climbed aboard his mount.

He nodded and smiled. The palomino-coloured horse seemed quite sturdy and would do for the moment, at least long enough to reacquire their ammunition and other sundry equipment, including, of course, Cookie's pots and pans.

Antonio was in the process of securing the saddle onto his horse, and he asked, "What happened to those two lugs?"

Cookie was emerging from the stable with his mule, and Jesús said, "Cookie, go look for your friends."

"Ain't no friends of mine," Cookie groused but reluctantly did as requested. He tied his mule to a nearby post and was about halfway to the storage shed when what looked like a black demon stepped from the darkness and into his path. It uttered a visceral growl, its long white teeth dimly visible, then lowered itself to the ground as if ready to spring toward him.

From the darkness, a voice told him, "Lessen you want Rufus to remove one of your favourite body parts, I'd suggest you stay right where you are, mister." Cookie listened to this advice and froze in place.

Preparing to step into his saddle's stirrup, Antonio said, "That sounds like the kid from the saloon."

From his mount, Jesús called out, "What, have you decided to play policeman now, boy?"

"No, the police would be a lot gentler with ya," the blond giant replied as he moved toward them. As he passed Cookie, he gave the old man a pop with one of his solid fists, and the cook crumpled to the ground like a sack of russet potatoes.

The large black dog, barely visible in the darkness at the boy's side, charged toward the horses.

Antonio had just flung his leg over his mount's saddle, but his horse reared up in fear of the snarling dog before he could settle in. He fell backwards, striking his head on the packed dirt, and lay unmoving.

Successful in dismounting one rider, the dog now directed its attack at the other horse.

Flicking his ride's reins, Oritz spurred the frightened creature away from the smithy at lightning speed. For now, he would leave his men to their fate with the large dog and the mountainous boy. Riding hard and fast into the night, he called over his shoulder, "We will meet again, amigos."

Jesús fled to the outskirts of town and reined in his horse. With his current plan derailed, he needed time to think. He had no gang left to back him up, and he was never a man not to have backup. This was especially true when the upcoming enemy at their encampment numbered in the hundreds and possibly thousands.

There was no way he could confront those diablos rojo near the river all by himself. Not only was he alone and with limited ammo, but the moonless night was quite dark, and he was concerned he wouldn't be able to see any of the diabolical creatures sneaking up on him.

But as that thought passed, a new one crept into Jesús's head, carrying with it a plan that would require him to wait a little longer. In the meantime, he would need to find a place in this backward little town that could provide what he required to get his little locomotive of greed and retribution back on track.

CHAPTER NINETEEN

Chief of Police Hildey Dugrodt leaned on the railing of the low porch of the modest police station, gazing in wonder at the sight before him. He stood upright, took his hat off momentarily and ran his hand through his greying hair, scratching his head. Just as he'd been preparing to leave after a very long day, Sandy from the Nugget had wandered up to the front of the station, pushing a large flat-top cart, Rufus trailing close at his heels. The chief placed his hat back on his head and said, "And what have you two been up to this evening, Sandy."

"Howdy, Chief! Got a delivery for ya." Sandy grinned and gestured at the two-wheeled pushcart, adding, "I just finished droppin' off the Doc, seein' as he'd had too much to drink again. Course, that was just after I walked the girls down to their cabin near the river and after I took the dog—"

Dugrodt held up a hand and said, "Take a breath and start a little closer to the moment; if you could, son." As the boy gathered his thoughts, Hildey marvelled at what lay stacked on Sandy's cart. Whatever the story was going to be, it would be entertaining, at the very least.

Two burly men, currently unconscious, were on the bottom of the pile, bound at the hands and feet, and gagged as well. They were straddled by another man lying crosswise and similarly trussed; wiry-looking, he had a white scar running down one side of his face. However, this man was awake, and his eyes burned with hatred at the tall blonde boy he had to thank for his current hog-tied predicament.

To one side of the cart stood an old man with bushy white hair and beard to match. His hands were tied together behind his back. Though not gagged like the other men, his bound hands were tethered to the cart with a short rope so that wherever the cart went, so did he. The grizzled man shook his head back and forth as he muttered softly to himself, "Never gonna get my damned pots and pans."

Sandy took a few breaths, then began again, saying slowly, "I was just about to go inside my shack when Rufus started to let out such a stink. We ended up down at the smithy and found these guys, and well, one thing led to another." He gestured toward the cart and gave a small 'what're you gonna do' expression.

Rufus had settled in next to Dugrodt and was enjoying a nice ear scratch, one leg thumping contentedly as the chief scruffed him in just the right spot. It was something Hildey had done to the dog many times before when he'd visited Jones's house. Farley had been a friend of his, and he'd been saddened to hear the grisly manner of his demise. There was no coroner in this town, so Hildey was taking Doctor Brown at his professional opinion as to the cause of Farley's death. To help convince the chief, the doctor had provided him a glimpse of the reason, the baby spiders he'd captured in the jar.

Seeming quite pleased with his catch, Sandy continued, "And Rufus is a hero, too! He helped me get hold of all these fellas, save one." Once the wolfhound had seen no more scratches were forthcoming from the chief, he joined Sandy back at street level, and it was now the boy's turn to scratch the dog's ear.

"That's all well and good, son." Hildey said understandingly, then nodded toward the cartful of criminals and asked, "Now, maybe you could tell me some particulars about your little collection."

"Sure enough!" I just got back to my shack after walkin' Rufus, and he began whinin' and lookin' back down the alley toward the smithy, actin' right worked up about somethin'. So we went for a look-see and discovered these here fellas sneakin' about in the dark, tryin' to steal Angus's horses and mules from the stable. One of 'em got away, but he's real easy to spot—lots of gold teeth and wears a funny round hat."

"You mean a sombrero?"

"Yessir, I think that's what it's called." Sandy poked the shoulder of the old man next to him, adding, "This one's not much trouble, but them other three are the ones you gotta watch out for. We've been having some trouble with these guys around the saloon. They figure my friend, Mr. Caleb, owes them some money, so they've been making it kind of hard on him."

"Oh, they have, have they?"

"Yessir. And then just now, like I said, I found them tryin' to steal Angus's stock and me' n' Rufus stopped them."

At the mention of his name, the dog proceeded to give Sandy's free hand a good licking. He ruffed the dog's fur again, and it grunted in delight.

"Well, you've done a fine job, son. If you ever think you might want a spot on the force, you come to see me. We could always use a crime-buster like yourself on the beat around this town."

"I'll keep that in mind, Chief, but I'm happy workin' at the Nugget and volunteerin' at the fire department for now."

Hildey nodded and looked to the cartful of brigands once again. Though the two men on the bottom were still unconscious, he knew that wouldn't last, and he would need to do something with these men sooner rather than later. With that in mind, he said, "Can you hang on and keep an eye on them for a moment, Sandy? I just have to straighten things out inside."

Sandy gave a small salute and said, "Yessir."

Straightening things out inside meant emptying the cells; they only had two, and both were currently occupied. As Hildey ambled toward the back of the building, he passed Albert VanDusen, his newly hired constable.

Albert placed his fountain pen down and looked up from the logbook he'd been filling in. "What's up, Chief?"

VanDusen had been almost an hour late relieving Hildey for the eleven o'clock shift change due to his breaking up a donnybrook on his way to work. Two of the most drunken brawlers that wouldn't listen to reason had accompanied him back to the office and were now residing in the new cells in the back of the building. Though the cells had been there since the log police building had been built, they'd had no bars on the windows or the along the front of either cell. The bars had, in fact, just arrived the other day.

Until now, any prisoner spending time in their accommodations was told not to step across the white line Hildey had painted on the floor where the bars should be. None of the prisoners had been willing to do so, and this system had worked very well for the last few weeks while they'd waited for the hardware to arrive from the coast.

There was one little detail Hildey had added to the white line which had sealed the deal in his little jail bar honour system. Across the end of the clean white line in front of the

141

first cell, Hildey had poured some red paint. Several prisoners invariably asked what was to stop them from just walking out of their barless cell or climbing out the window. All the chief would do was rest one hand on the holstered revolver at his hip, point to the splash of red paint and say, "That's what the last guy wondered."

The men currently occupying the cells had been found having a game of fisticuffs along with a couple of other men in front of the Motherload Saloon. Albert had tried to intervene and break things up but had soon found himself being assaulted by both men instead. Fortunately, the constable was a retired boxing instructor who'd taught in the Royal Navy. After he'd taken a round out of each of the men, he'd been able to get the cuffs on them. At that point, he'd had to hail one of Carter's Cabs to transport him and his prisoners to the police station. Carter's was a service Hildey had used himself on more than one occasion. With the police department being so new, along with the rest of the town, they hadn't even gotten their paddy wagon delivered yet, but one was on order from down on the coast. At least they had a horse for more distant policing matters, but it was currently down at the smithy getting reshoed.

His hand on the door to the cells, Dugrodt replied, "Gonna make us an upgrade."

"Sorry?" VanDusen queried.

Dugrodt turned and said, "We're trading in your drunks for something a little more substantial."

"Like what?"

"Horse thieves. Now go outside and give Sandy a hand with them." With that, he turned and entered the jail cells.

It was almost a quarter past the witching hour, and both of VanDusen's sparring partners were sound asleep in their respective cells. The chief picked up a tin cup and ran it back and forth across the bars as he called out, "Fire! Fire! Fire!"

The two drunks woke with a start, eyes wide and stumbled to their feet. Swaying back and forth, the shorter of the two rubbed his eyes for a moment, then said, "Hey, I don't see no smoke or fire!"

With a burp, the other man added, "Yeah, I thought you said you was gonna let us sleep it off here for the night."

Hildey nodded and said, "Uh-huh. Well, things change pretty quick around this town, so you'd better get used to it." He unlocked each of the cells and added, "You can consider yourself on parole for good behaviour."

"But why, Chief?" the taller drunk wondered. "I was just havin' a good sleep."

"We got some actual criminals coming in here, and I don't want to cram you men in like sardines." Theoretically, each cell would hold three if one man slept on the floor, thanks to the fact both had bunk beds. However, he wouldn't make a drunken civilian share the cell with these other malefactors if he could avoid it, so out they needed to go.

"Actual criminals?" the shorter one asked as he staggered out of his cell.

"Yeah, horse thieves." Hildey pointed to the door to the office.

The tall drunk wobbled into the office, saying to his companion, "They hang horse thieves, don't they?"

Shaking his head, the short drunk said, "I don't know. Let's go have another drink and figure it out."

Hildey called, "Don't make me rearrest you both and throw

you back in there with the bad guys."

"No sir, Chief," the tall one said. The short one nodded in agreement, and together, they staggered out the front door.

The chief followed them down to the street to help bring in the new tenants but saw he was late to the party. Albert guided the scar-faced man up the station stairs, his hands still tied behind his back. The other two men were still unconscious. Sandy had the one with the atrocious bowl cut lying over one broad shoulder and was loading the second man across his other.

Hildey recognised both men, a couple of local ne'er-do-wells. The man with the bad haircut was Vern Ogilvy, and his potato-shaped companion was Claude Habner, a man with a grudge against humanity. Neither were in the mining trade but rather the robbing trade, or so he'd heard. There were rumours that the pair were responsible for, at the very least, several late-night robberies of drunken sourdoughs around town, but nothing could be proven. Well, he now had proof of both men's criminality, to be sure.

Sandy grinned at Dugrodt and said, "We left you with the old duffer, Chief."

"Much obliged, son." Hildey untied the rope from the cart and gestured for the old man to follow his friends inside.

Once the prisoner's bonds were removed in their cells, the scar-faced man sat upright on the edge of his cot, rubbing at the back of his head. He spied Sandy in the doorway to the office, then stood and moved toward the bars, saying, "You're going to pay for this, boy!"

Sandy shook his head and said, "Not today, I ain't", and moved into the office.

Hildey clanged the cell door shut, causing Scarface to jump

back in surprise, a startled look on his face, temporarily at least. But the mean expression returned all too quickly, and he began squawking once again.

Fortunately, the door to the cells was a nice thick piece of solid fir, and Hildey made sure to slam it firmly shut as well.

Sandy and the chief bid Constable VanDusen a good night and moved out to the station's porch.

Dugrodt leaned on the railing and looked up to the swath of sparkling stars painted across the velveteen sky. He lit a briar pipe pulled from his vest pocket, puffed on it for a moment, then said, "Gonna be a big day tomorrow, Sandy."

"Yessir, chief. I'm gonna be real busy lifeguardin' down at the pools, and so's Angus."

The dog had followed Sandy down to street level and now stood beside him. As the boy reached down to scruff the animal's head, a curl of sweet cherry pipe smoke wafted toward them, and the wolfhound suddenly sneezed and snorted both at once.

With a laugh, Hildey said, "Gesundheit!" After a brief pause, he said to Sandy, "Since you and Chief Angus have been looking after the dog and are both busy at the same time tomorrow, I was wondering something."

"What's that, Chief?"

"Do you think Rufus would like to be a police dog for the day?"

CHAPTER TWENTY

It looked to be another hot one, and Maggie George was starting this first day of July a little early. A few minutes before four in the morning, the edges of the mountain peaks on the valley's east side were just now beginning to glow a pale purple as the sun's first rays began their ascent behind the hidden horizon. If she could get her cakes, pies and other baked treats into the oven by noon hour, Maggie knew she'd be ahead of the worst of the heat.

Opening the screen delivery door with a creek, Maggie entered the Golden Nugget's kitchen to discover a bored Efrem, who'd been working the night shift. Arms folded, he'd been leaning against one of the counters, a bored expression on his face. With a sigh, he'd said there'd been very few customers and that he'd finished all his prep work for the day shift over an hour before. And so, figuring she could handle cooking the odd sourdough's meal in addition to doing her baking for a little while, Maggie had allowed him to go home and get an early start on the holiday. She'd scheduled Mike and Ed to come in for half shifts around eight o'clock, so she knew she would have the assistance by then if it got busy.

Maggie flipped open her latest edition of the Canadian Home Journal. It was a new magazine that had just started publishing at the beginning of the year. Being kitchen manager at the Nugget, she'd received a free trial subscription and was now making the most of it. The latest issue included recipes for several dishes featuring peanut paste. It was a fairly new ingredient and not widely used, but she'd managed to secure a couple of tins from a restaurant supplier down on the coast.

The peanutty butter had recently celebrated its tenth birthday the year before. In honour of this fact and the upcoming Dominion Day holiday, the magazine featured several peanut paste recipes, including a short biography on its inventor, Marcellus Gilmour Edson. Born and raised in Quebec, he'd been working as a chemist in Montreal when he'd patented his process back in 1884. According to the magazine, he was in talks with several manufacturers vying to take the process nationally and beyond. Maggie hoped this would be the case because the paste, though quite tasty, was more of a niche item at the moment and rather expensive. The only reason she was trying it in the first place was that Mr. Sinclair always wanted her to experiment with new and different things in the kitchen and keep the customers flowing through the doors. When it came to food and drink for his establishment, it seemed price was no object.

Maggie was first introduced to the paste through one of her friends from the second floor, Monique. The girl had described trying various peanut-flavoured treats in Montreal a couple of years back, before she'd headed west, and couldn't say enough good things about them. Well, that had been good enough for Maggie, and she'd ordered a couple of tins to try from a mail-order supply company, and they had only recently arrived. And so, throughout the day yesterday, she'd been busy making various peanut candies and other treats featured in the magazine and had used up the entirety of the first tin.

This morning, the recipe that interested Maggie was a lovely peanut-flavoured cake with peanut butter frosting. But to make it, she needed the second can of paste and bustled across the kitchen to the small pantry in one corner where it was stored. With enough paste for her recipe, she transferred the remaining spread to a latch-top storage jar to keep it fresh. She figured that keeping it cool would also be a good thing and placed it on the top shelf of the icebox.

But before she got into baking, Maggie wanted to dispose of the tin in the trash bin behind the kitchen. The hinges on the screen door to the alley gave another squeak and a creak as she elbowed it open. Despite its protests every time it was used, she felt quite thankful to have it. The screen provided some much-needed ventilation during the heat of the summer while dissuading any wildlife and insects from wandering in.

The small trash bin behind the kitchen was normally kept emptied by Sandy—just another part of his numerous jobs around the saloon. But for whatever reason, the bin hadn't been emptied since the previous day and was now serving to feed the local wildlife instead. The lid of the container had not been fastened correctly and was lying half off, making it easy for a raccoon, woodrat or other forest creatures to get into it. A couple of pieces of trash lay on the ground in front of it, and poking out of the corner was the jagged lid of yesterday's peanut paste tin, the rest of the container out of sight just inside the bin.

With a sigh, Maggie said, "Well, I'd best fix this before we get more of a mess and something else gets in there." She lifted the lid to fit it back onto the top of the bin correctly. Though the sky was growing gradually brighter, it was still relatively dark outside. Thankfully, a small amount of light came through the screen door at her back.

As Maggie lifted the lid to reseat it, a slight movement caught her attention, and she realised something was still inside the bin. She lifted the lid slightly higher to see what it was.

With a shriek, Maggie slammed the top down on the bin. She backed away, her heart pounding in her chest as she realised she'd just been introduced to one of the creatures

Kitty's friend Caleb had unleashed onto this valley.

Sandy's shack was not far from the kitchen, and so it was the first place Maggie went for help. And within a few minutes, still rubbing sleep from his eyes, Sandy had gone to the first place he could think of.

***

Caleb had been having a most pleasant little dream. He and Kitty had been celebrating Christmas together. It had been some time in the future, presumably, because a towheaded boy and an auburn-haired little girl were scampering about. Both were playing with a puppy on the floor of what appeared to be their house. A beautifully decorated Christmas tree sat in one corner, candles lighting it brightly. Kitty had been right by his side, and he'd felt a sense of peace and contentment as he'd watched the children play with the dog. But then, out of the blue, Kitty had turned to him and begun to say, "Mr. Caleb! Mr. Caleb!"

Now, several minutes later, Caleb stood with Sandy in the alley behind the kitchen, his dream over and living his current nightmare once more. Both men stared at the bin, saying nothing. The first grey light of day bathed everything in monotone grey. Maggie had gone back inside the kitchen, saying she didn't want to have anything more to do with the horrible little creature she'd found in the trash.

Sandy reached his hand toward the handle, saying, "You want I should open it, Mr. Caleb?"

Caleb shook his head and said, "Let me get something to put it in first." He hopped to the side of the kitchen door and grabbed a small wooden crate with a picture of a green pepper printed on its side and a matching lid on top. He'd graduated to using only one crutch and could now carry light things back and forth as he hobbled about the place. Once back at Sandy's side, he handed the crate to the boy, saying, "You'll probably have an easier time than me catchin' hold of it if ya don't mind."

"Not a problem, Mr. Caleb."

Placing his free hand on the lid, Caleb nodded and said, "All right, are ya set, lad?"

"As I'll ever be." Sandy readied himself, one large hand holding the crate on one side of the bin, with the lid on the other.

Caleb yanked the top off the container but saw nothing inside, nothing except garbage that was. He peered further into the bin. "Do you suppose it's gone down inside the..." As he spoke, his eyes flicked to the lid in his hand, and he cut his question short to express his surprise instead, exclaiming, "Shite!"

The animal was not down inside the garbage because it clung to the inside of the bin's lid instead. The fierce-looking red ant peered at Caleb and clicked its mandibles rapidly together in a deadly staccato. That was enough for him, and he slammed the lid over the crate that Sandy still held, trapping the creature inside.

Sandy took over the lid from Caleb and held the crate up to look through the slits in its side, saying, "You're an ugly little spud, ain't ya?" He shook the crate, and the ant made a high-pitch keening sound.

"Careful, Sandy! We don't want to hurt this fella if we can avoid it."

"Sure enough, Mr. Caleb, but why?"

"Scientific experimentation. I'm sure that once the doctor is sober or close to it, he'd love to see a live ant and then try and figure out what makes these fellas tick. Hopefully, he can come up with something to help rid us of these things as he has with the spiders."

Sandy peered through the sides of the crate again. The ant continued its shrill squeal. It snipped and snapped its mandibles, trying to get at the boy's fingers, but couldn't quite reach and instead attacked the wood. "Why do you suppose we only found one of them here, Mr. Caleb?"

A flashback to his military days came, and Caleb replied, "Why, I'd say it's a scout."

"Like the native folk use to check out the territory around them as they hunt and travel?"

"Exactly. And that's just what the army does as well. It's a very dangerous and lonely job, as you can imagine." Caleb had been volunteered as a scout on several missions while in South Africa. However, he'd been fortunate to survive his forays since most scouts were not, from his experience. Some were killed, while others were captured by the enemy, just like he had with this red beast before him. He finished his thought, saying, "If this fella were to have reported back to his colony, he'd have said that he'd found more good stuff to eat, and the rest of them would be hightailin' it over here right now."

Sandy peered into the forest on the other side of the alley with wide, suspicious eyes. "Let's hope it's the only scout then."

With a nod, Caleb said, "Let's do that, because sometimes an army sends out more than one."

CHAPTER TWENTY-ONE

"Here you go. Give this a try, my boy."

With a nod, Caleb accepted the proffered tongue depressor, wincing slightly as Cornelius Brown's alcohol-soaked breath washed over him.

Just a little past nine in the morning, it seemed the good doctor had decided to start drinking a little earlier than usual today, perhaps because it was a holiday and all. But Caleb wasn't one to judge since he knew his friend tried to limit his drinking to after the noon hour most days, though he'd been in as early as ten o'clock one morning, just after Muddy had opened. But whatever time he arrived, Brown invariably had his daily bacon, eggs and two shots of whisky.

Focusing back on the task at hand, Caleb poked the tongue depressor into the crate.

The ant had been making a high-frequency keening for the last little while, but as soon as the depressor got near its pincers, it stopped and attacked the thin wood, slicing through it as if paper. With the threat neutralised, the animal resumed its keening.

"Bugger me, that's got a good nip to it," Caleb said quietly, imagining what would have happened to him if he'd not been successful with his explosive solution to his ant problem up in the cavern. These creatures looked capable of rending a man to pieces in a matter of minutes.

Standing at Caleb's side, Kitty said, "And he's an ugly little blighter to boot. Even more so up close than when I spotted him and his friends on the beach, just before I realised you weren't a piece of driftwood."

Kitty nudged Caleb in the ribs with her elbow, and he laughed. It was something he found himself doing a lot more recently. Especially now that the Hole-in-the-Wall Gang had been taken care of, or most of them at least.

After they'd trapped the ant in the crate this morning, Sandy had relayed his tale of capturing the bandits down at the smithy—along with Rufus's help, of course, he was quick to add. With gold-toothed Jesús being the only gang member not yet in jail, Caleb wondered if he would show up for his payment from Thomas Sinclair today.

Despite his having doubts about Sinclair, not to mention being beholden to the man twice over, Caleb was beginning to feel a little easier about life and a little more hopeful about things in general. Sinclair didn't want to kill him outright as the gang had, at least not yet. With some movement on that front, he had begun to feel a bit more hopeful about getting his creepy-crawly problems cleared up as he tried to recall the location of both his fortunes.

When all that was finally out of the way, Caleb hoped to have more time to explore his burgeoning relationship with Kitty. The small feeling of hope he'd felt just now swelled further when he thought of the woman beside him. Though they'd yet to repeat their afternoon dalliance, it seemed they were growing closer by the day, and he was looking forward to being around her more and more. She was quickly becoming his reason to get up in the morning, and quite possibly his reason for being as well, after all these long, lonely years. With each passing day, he was beginning to believe more and more that he'd truly be lost if he didn't have her in his life.

So, today was a special day. He and Kitty had committed to spending all of it together, and he was looking forward to each and every minute. Horse races were happening shortly just outside the front door of the Nugget. After that, they would head down to the town pools and take in some of the diving and swimming competitions. After those events were over, the pools would be open for public swimming. And though Caleb couldn't swim with his cast on, he hoped that he could encourage Kitty to take a dip. But first, he wanted to learn more about these ants with the doctor, and he watched as Brown returned with something more substantial to try.

Doctor Brown held a small stack of depressors, perhaps ten thick, secured with baling wire. "Here, let's give him a bit of a challenge." He poked the stack into the crate, and the ant attacked it immediately, slicing through the thick wood with ease. His eyes wide, Brown pulled the depressors from the crate and held them up for all to see.

The trio stared at the ant's handiwork wonderingly. It had bitten through the entire stack of wood, including the baling wire, in just a single bite. Caleb grimaced as he imagined what the little beast would do to a person's fingers and toes as it stripped the flesh from their body.

"Bugger us," Kitty said in a low voice.

"Indeed, young lady," Brown agreed.

"What about where we found the ant, Doc?" Caleb asked. "Remember, Maggie said it was makin' moves on that paste container in the garbage bin."

Brown nodded. "That's right. It would seem they enjoy the stuff." The doctor looked lost in thought for a moment as he stared at the ant and added, "And knowing what they like might be something we can use to our advantage when dealing with these creatures."

Kitty looked to Caleb and asked, "How many of them do you think there are?"

Caleb scratched his head momentarily, then said, "It's hard to say. Thousands of them came at me in the cavern. But I wouldn't be surprised if a number of them survived, along with those blasted spiders."

"There have to be hundreds of them, perhaps thousands by now," Brown said with a sour expression. He peered closely at the ant, then added, "However, I've been running some other tests on this creature since its arrival this morning..." He trailed off, lost in thought, one hand under his chin, his elbow propped on the other.

"And?" Caleb prompted.

Before speaking, Brown glanced over to the spider sitting in its undersized cage on a side counter near his barber-dentist chair. "I have discovered the ants share something in common with our arachnid friend here."

"What could these two have in common, apart from wanting to eat me?" Caleb said wonderingly.

"Something that can prove useful to us."

"What's that, Doctor?" Kitty asked. Her face scrunched up in revulsion as she gazed at the keening ant. It moved agitatedly back and forth in the small crate, constantly snipping and snapping its mandibles in a quest to bite anything or anyone nearby.

"They have a shared weakness," Brown said. He moved to the counter, picked up a large jar of clear liquid, and held it out for them to see.

"Making your own booze now, Doc?" Caleb queried.

"Hardly. It's acetic acid."

"Isn't that what you have in the mister and the fire extinguisher?"

The doctor nodded, "Indeed! As part of my experimenting with that gold ore separation process, I'm fermenting, distilling, and extracting the acid myself these days. This solution is much more concentrated than the other one I was using. That was ten percent; this is twenty-five."

"That sounds like it'll make you pucker up," Caleb said with a slow nod.

"It'll do more than that and most likely burn the lining out of your throat and stomach, along with your colon."

Kitty grimaced again and said, "External use only."

"Indeed." The doctor said with a small smile.

Placing an arm around Kitty's shoulders, Caleb asked, "And you're sure it'll work as well on the ants?"

The doctor lifted the lid on the container and held it near the ant's crate, and the creature's high-frequency wailing ratcheted to new heights. Brown nodded and said, "I believe so. From my brief tests with just our friend here, you can trust me when I say he doesn't like this stuff in the least.' He placed the lid back on the container and added, "So, I hope it should dissuade them from further antagonising us when we encounter more of their kind."

"Don't you mean 'if' we encounter more, Doc?" Kitty inquired.

"Sadly, no. I'm convinced it's an eventuality that we will encounter more of these creatures, and sooner rather than later. Fortunately, that thought has got me working on another ant control method which I should have ready soon. But for now, we should be able to use the spray against both species of our multi-legged threats."

It was almost eleven o'clock and time for the horse races. Caleb ushered Kitty to the street, saying over his shoulder, "I hope you're right, Doc."

Brown turned to regard his captive creatures as the bell jangled and the door closed. In a low voice, he replied, "As am I, my friend. As am I."

CHAPTER TWENTY-TWO

The Dominion Day festivities had begun with several horse races down the main street, the winner receiving one hundred dollars, courtesy of the Golden Nugget Saloon. The final tiebreaker had been a close race, only won by Arlo Platt at the last minute when Jeb Petersen was thrown from his horse less than a half block from the finish line. As a consolation prize, Jeb received a voucher for two pitchers of cold beer from the Nugget in which to drown his sorrows.

Many of the businesses in town had closed for the day. There were exceptions, of course, such as most saloons, restaurants and Vicker's Five and Ten, which wanted to be open, at least for a little while, to take advantage of people's celebratory mood and easy spending on the holiday.

One place, while not closed, was nonetheless locked, with no public access at the moment—the police station. A short while ago, the sole officer on duty had locked the front door, placed a sign on it and moved down the street to supervise the crowd at the horse races. This lack of manpower had been precisely what Jesús had been hoping for. He'd grinned happily when he'd watched it unfold since it meant the prisoners were now unguarded. After all, they would not lock the front door if someone were still on duty inside.

Since his escape from the stable last night, Jesús had

decided a lower profile would be a good idea. In his experience, while scouting a planned crime's location or hiding from the results of one, it was best not to stand out. He was quite sure the bulging blonde boy had informed the local police of his description, including that of his uncommon-looking hat. So, he'd swapped his sombrero for a bowler at Vicker's Five and Ten this morning while the proprietress had been otherwise occupied. He'd wandered right out the front door with it tipped jauntily back on his head.

Currently across the street from the jail, he leaned against the wall of a small bakery, enjoying a meat pie purchased inside. He had done his best to blend in with the Dominion Day crowd. The bowler hat helped quite a lot, not that he looked English, however. For whatever reason, that style seemed a popular fashion with the locals in these parts, unlike the American West and their broad cowboy hats. There were some of those, to be sure, but a majority of the men had bowlers or riding caps on rather than cowboy hats. And so now, he seemed to blend right in. In fact, during the recent horse race, he had been just across the street from the Irishman and his Scottish squeeze. Though the man had glanced in his direction several times as he and his lady had enjoyed their day, there had been no flicker of recognition.

There was a chance that his newfound cleanliness was also aiding his incognito look. At daybreak this morning, he'd spent a few moments scrubbing some of the grime from his face and hands at the town's pools. Once he'd removed several layers of grime and road dust, he had been several shades lighter.

But it was strange what had happened when he'd been there.

Just as he'd finished his impromptu grooming session, he'd thought he heard a splash on the opposite shore of the pool. He'd stood, stepped back from the water, and glanced about but saw no sign of anything or anyone. It had sounded rather large, whatever it had been. But the limited light had made it difficult to say for sure, so he'd thought nothing more of it since he'd had other things to occupy his time.

Jesús stifled a yawn. He'd had minimal sleep last night since he'd been busy implementing other aspects of his little idea. So far, things seemed to be working out quite well, and it was time to move on to phase three of his plan.

The horse races had ended several minutes ago, and the crowds had dispersed. Many had headed for saloons further down the street, and the rest had moved toward the pools in the town's park for the upcoming diving and swimming competitions. And now, the general area around him was pleasantly devoid of people.

Ambling up onto the low porch in front of the police station Jesús wanted to check the sign the officer had left. The large, black capital letters read, 'Temporarily Closed to the Public'. Despite the police doing precisely what he'd hoped, he found it somewhat surprising they would lock the place up with prisoners inside. With a shake of his head, he said quietly, "I wonder what the fire marshal would say about that." He tried to peer inside, but there were some muslin half-drapes across both front windows, and due to his height-challenged nature, he couldn't see over the curtain rods.

Located at the edge of town, the unassuming police station appeared, at first sight, a regular pine cabin constructed of sturdy logs. It sat on a small lot, unattached to any buildings nearby, unlike the downtown, where they were sometimes only inches apart. Jesús moved around to its side and peered through one of the narrow windows halfway down. Inside, he saw why the station had been left unguarded—because it wasn't. There was indeed someone on guard duty inside.

Hunkered down on the hardwood floor in front of the office's two desks was a large black dog, its head resting on its paws. As Jesús pressed his face to the glass, the animal's eyes popped open, and it gave a low snarl. It was the same dog from last night, the one with the long pointy teeth.

Jesús grinned at the dog and sauntered around to the rear of the building. Both jail cells had narrow windows near the top of this relatively unseen rear wall, and neighbours were almost nonexistent since the backside of the single-story police station backed onto the forest.

If everything worked out how he hoped, he need not worry about the black beast because it would stay right where it was. He was not going through the front door after all; he was using the back. And since the jail didn't have one, it would make things interesting.

Strolling casually by the windows, Jesús stopped between them and admired the shiny plate glass behind the gleaming steel bars inset in the log wall. It seemed the Canadians were quite progressive in outfitting their jails. Thanks to modern production methods, he'd encountered more and more jail cells in the west using steel for their bars, which was unfortunate since it was much harder to cut through than iron. But that was irrelevant at the moment since he wasn't touching the bars.

He picked up a small handful of gravel and tossed some of it lightly at one of the windows. After a moment, Antonio appeared. His eyes widened when he saw Jesús, and he gave a crooked-toothed grin. Bad Haircut gave him a wave from the other window, and Jesús flashed his golden smile to them both. He held up one finger, then extracted phase three of his plan from his overcoat's large inner pocket.

Upon seeing what Jesús now had in his hands, Antonio's eyes widened even further, and he nodded, then ducked back down inside the cell. In the other window, Bad Haircut gave a small salute, then disappeared from view.

When Jesús had tiptoed back into town in the wee hours of

the morning, he'd initiated the first phase of his revised plan, stealing some horses for his men. With that done, he'd moved onto phase two and broken into a mining supply store where he'd picked up a little something for the final phase of his plan.

Oritz knelt and placed phase three between the two cells. The exterior pine would be a bit weaker here, carved out slightly on the other side to accommodate the interior wall's logs.

Now, he was ready to complete the loudest and most attention-grabbing part of his plan, the part where he put in the new back door.

Jesús lit a cigarillo and puffed it momentarily, enjoying the fresh taste of the newly ignited tobacco and sherry-dipped tips. After a few more puffs, he touched the cigarillo's glowing end to the fuse on the six-stick bundle of dynamite.

With alacrity in his step, he retreated to the safety of the trees at the edge of the forest while the twenty-second fuse burned greedily toward the red tubes of high explosive.

Just as he covered his ears, the sound of multiple people screaming came from another part of town. So much the better, he thought with a smile. Keep screaming, my friends, because I will soon give you more to shout about.

Confusion and mayhem elsewhere would aid his little jailbreak immensely. With fingers now firmly planted in his aural canals, Jesús poked his head around the side of his shielding tree and looked expectantly toward the crackling fuse, waiting for the show to begin.

CHAPTER TWENTY-THREE

Brilliant blue skies stretched from peak to peak with hardly a cloud in sight save for a few grey whisps over the mountaintops in the rear corner of the valley. It seemed a perfect day for a picnic in the park or to eat ice cream in the shade, and plenty of people did both as they enjoyed the warmth of the summer day.

A young boy sat in the sand at the edge of the smallest of the park's three pools. He poked a stick into the water close to the shoreline, entertaining himself while his parents presumably waited for the diving competition to start at the large pool.

While gathering some damp sand from the water's edge to build his sand castle, the boy discovered a new friend hiding in a patch of marsh along the shore. It was a small black creature, quite unlike any fish he'd ever seen. Though not as long as a snake, its body was black and scaly like one, but it was much thicker around, and boy, was it fast!

Construction had been going quite well on the castle, and he hoped to have the drawbridge in place before lunch. Unfortunately, his new friend was taking up valuable construction time, not that he minded since this was much more fun. The boy had corralled the black thing into a small bay he'd created with rocks and sand at the edge of the small marsh. He poked and prodded at the creature with his stick again and again, giggling as he watched it shoot frantically back and forth in the small section of pool in which it was now trapped.

Another smaller boy joined the fun, and the first boy introduced him to the black thing he'd corralled, pointing out how badly the animal wanted to escape. The little boy giggled at the sight and began reaching in to grab at the black creature. But he needn't have worried about trying to catch the animal since it turned out the small beast had wanted to catch him instead.

As soon as the small boy thrust his hand in, the creature shot through the shallow water in a blinding streak and latched fiercely onto the side of his palm. Recoiling with a shriek, the boy snatched his hand from the pool. The black thing dangled down from it, looking like a large, black leech but longer, its numerous sharp teeth firmly implanted in the child's soft flesh. The little boy screamed again and again, no doubt as much from the sight of the creature on his hand as from the pain of the bite. Lashing back and forth as it dangled, the little beast tried to coil its oily black body about the boy's small wrist.

***

Standing on the floating platform in the centre of the large pool, Sandy turned toward the shriek and saw a concerned mother drawing her boy away from another playing near the shore. Something seemed wrong with the boy's hand, but he was too far away to see for sure what it was. However, since the commotion was on the shore and not in the water, he began to direct his gaze back toward the large pool. As he did, he saw Angus Cochrane moving toward the boy and mother and knew things would soon be in good hands. The fire chief was also working as a lifeguard today, but on the two smaller pools, his swimming skills not as advanced as Sandy's.

Today, Sandy's job was to keep anyone from swimming in the largest pool. The diving competition was about to start, and his top priority was to keep it clear of any public swimmers so that those diving from the new tower didn't land on someone's head by accident. He glanced back to Angus and saw the man now hurrying toward him, something in his hands. Sandy moved back to shore along the floating boardwalk to meet him.

Angus wore a look of distaste on his face as he approached. "You'd better see this!" He thrust out what he held for Sandy to see, grasping it tightly with both hands, one just below the creature's toothy maw, the other lower on its writhing body.

Sandy's eyes widened as he took in the creature. About the length of a chair leg, the black beast seemed made of nothing but muscle and sinew as it coiled and tugged in Angus's strong hands. Though not a snake, its head looked similar, except its body was much thicker. On its sides were two small sets of limbs that didn't appear strong enough to support it on dry land but looked like they would help the creature manoeuvre rapidly and dangerously when in the water.

Marvelling at the animal he held, Angus said, "A young fella had this thing captive near the shore, and it latched onto another boy's hand. I had to crack the bugger on the head a couple of times with my knuckles to make it let go of the boy." He shook his head and added, "Its bite left a hell of a welt."

Nodding, Sandy said, "That looks kind of like the thing that killed that man in the river and tried to take a bite out of Mr. Caleb, just smaller."

"Well, it looks like they've found their way from the river into the aquifer down below. If there are ones bigger than this in there, we might have a problem."

"I know." Sandy wondered what they could do and was going to consult Angus further when the subject of their previous conversation hopped into view with Miss Kitty at his side. Sandy smiled broadly and said, "Hey, Mr. Caleb, Miss Kitty, we was just talkin' about you!"

"Good things, I hope," Caleb replied.

Sandy shook his head and nodded toward what Angus held, saying, "Nope, sorry. Not this time."

Caleb and Kitty's eyes grew large at the sight of the thing in the blacksmith's hands, and Caleb said, "Don't be tellin' me you found that in the pools here?"

"I am tellin' you that," Angus replied. He nodded over his shoulder and added, "Bit a little boy down in the small pool."

"Oh no!" Kitty said, her eyes locked on the wriggling black thing. "It's like the ones I saw in the small pools beside the river, but I think it's bigger now."

"Aye," Caleb said. "It looks like they're growin' just as fast as everythin' else that's come out of that cavern." Noting it thrashing in Angus's hands, he added, "I'm surprised it's so lively. And you say it's been out of the water for a while?"

"A few minutes at least now," Angus replied.

"I wonder if it can breathe air as well as water?" Kitty asked.

Looking to Kitty with a smile, Caleb said, "Exactly what I was wonderin', lass."

"Well, I'm going to dispose of this thing," Angus said, squeezing the black creature firmly to stop it from moving.

From over Cochrane's broad shoulder, a voice inquired, "Dispose of what?"

The group turned to see Cornelius Brown looking ready for battle, leather satchel over one shoulder, fire extinguisher slung under his arm.

Angus held up the creature, and Brown's eyes practically bugged from his face. "Heaven's no! Don't dispose of that! I'll take it off your hands!"

The blacksmith held it out to the doctor and said, "All yours, Doc."

Brown took the creature and discovered just how strong it really was, saying, "My, but you're a perky little thing."

Wiping his hands on his trousers, Angus moved back toward the small pool and said over his shoulder, "Yup, it's a real fighter. So you better hang on tight!"

"Yeah, for a fish out of water, it's pretty lively," Sandy observed.

"It's not a fish," Brown said as he looked more closely at the creature, then added, "I think it's an amphibian."

"What, like a salamander?" Caleb wondered.

"Very good, my boy," Brown nodded, seeming pleased at the correct answer.

"What's the difference?" Kitty asked.

Brown replied, "A fish gets oxygen from the water and spends its life there, while salamanders breathe air and live in the water, but they can also go on dry land as well. And though I'm not one hundred percent sure, I think there's a chance this creature can go both ways."

Caleb laughed and said, "What do you mean, Doc?"

Holding the animal up for all to see, Brown said, "Most amphibians can't breathe underwater after they mature. But judging by the gills on the outside of this creature's neck, I think these fellows can do both!" He held it out toward Caleb and asked, "Did you happen to notice if the big one that bit you had them, too?"

With a grimace, Caleb said, "I don't recall, Doc. I was too busy fightin' for my life, but I suppose it might've."

The doctor nodded toward the little black beast and added, "If these creatures have lungs and can crawl around on land, in addition to staying submerged in the water for long periods using their gills, they might be a multi-environmental threat."

"How's that?" Sandy asked. He liked learning words, but sometimes the Doc was far beyond him.

Brown gave Sandy a small smile and clarified, "I think they can live in water as well as on land, making them doubly dangerous." The black thing twisted and curled in his hands, renewing its efforts to escape. If the doctor hadn't been holding it as close to its mouthful of pointy little teeth as he had, he might have suffered a painful bite from its violent lashing.

"Oh," Sandy replied in a small voice. "That's not good."

"No, it's not. But in the meantime, I need to get this fellow someplace moist. Even if they can breathe air, they likely need some water to sustain themselves." Brown looked about the area as he spoke.

Sandy spied a child's green metal pail, ideal for sand castle building, next to the shore, currently untended, and said, "Will this do, Doc?"

"Ah, just the thing!"

Sandy held the bucket out, and the doctor placed the black beast inside with a plop.

Caleb said, "You're getting quite a menagerie there, Doc, what with the spider, then the ant and now this."

"Yes, it would seem I am officially a collector of fauna from your cavern." He shook his head as he said, "I really must see that place with my own eyes."

"Maybe, Doc, once we get these things under control, along with all their friends."

Brown looked at the extinguisher under his arm and said, "I'm hoping my new spray will help in that regard."

Sandy said, "Well, I should get back to my post. I think it's almost time for the diving competition to start." He looked about briefly, then added, "It's supposed to be limited access out on the platform because of the fireworks they've been gettin' ready for tonight. But if you guys wanted to come out there with me to watch the diving, I think that would be okay."

Caleb and Kitty looked at each other. Caleb nodded, and Kitty smiled, saying, "That would be wonderful! Thank you, Sandy."

Brown gave a distracted smile and said, "As much as I'd like to join you all, I will have to defer. He knelt next to the pool's edge with the bucket, scooped several handfuls of water onto the black creature's head and added, "I want to get this little fella back to my office. There's something I want to verify."

With a nod, Caleb said, "All right. We'll catch up with you later then, Doc."

"Indeed you will, my boy!" Brown said as he stood. He gave a slight bow to Kitty, a wave to Sandy, then moved across the park in the direction of his practice.

***

A rope lay across the boardwalk entrance, attached to two posts on temporary footings. Hanging from the rope, a sign read, 'Closed for Fireworks Display This Evening'. Sandy unhooked one side, allowed Kitty and Caleb to enter, and then hooked the rope closed behind them.

The floating boardwalk was a little unsteady, and Caleb was grateful to have Kitty's arm as they moved out to the platform. Though he knew he should probably be with the doctor looking for signs of spiders and the new ant infestation, he hoped that taking the day off to be with the new light of his life would not compromise their little operation too much.

"If ya want, you can sit on one of the fireworks crates." Sandy gestured to a couple of moderately sized wooden crates sitting on their sides, currently empty. "Chief Angus was helpin' the fireworks guy with gettin' things set up when I got here this mornin'."

The fire chief and fireworks company representative had been busy. Several mortar tubes looked ready to launch some of the larger rockets and aerial fireworks. Next to them, sturdy-looking wooden frames and racks held other types of explosive excitement, such as pinwheels and Roman candles, all readied in anticipation of tonight's festivities.

Caleb pulled a fireworks crate toward a corner of the platform that faced the diving tower. He directed Kitty to sit upon it with a wave of his hand, and she did so with a smile. Caleb slid another crate next to her and sighed as he lowered himself, his cast-covered foot projecting slightly over the water at the platform's edge.

Kitty lifted the lid on her basket and pulled out a bag of penny candy from Vicker's, which Caleb had bought for them to share. She took a couple of jelly beans and a piece of waxpaper-wrapped saltwater taffy, then offered the bag to Caleb.

After plucking out a few candy corn, Caleb held the bag out and rattled its contents in Sandy's direction. The boy shook his head. "Can't eat while on duty, but thanks." He turned his attention back to the water, squinting into the brightness as he scanned for anyone swimming where they weren't supposed to.

Kitty placed the bag back in the basket and closed its lid. She patted its top gently with her hand a couple of times, then said, "Thanks again for this unexpected gift. From baskets to jelly beans, Vicker's always seems to have what a girl needs." She gently placed her other hand on Caleb's, which rested on his knee, and added, "Just like you."

With a smile, Caleb turned his hand over and held Kitty's, giving it a gentle squeeze and said, "I recalled you sayin' how you needed a new one with a lid after that adventure you had with your red flannel friend. I didn't want you to risk losin' any more apples." After a moment, he added, "Just as I don't want to risk losin' you."

Giving Caleb's hand a squeeze in return, Kitty smiled. She said nothing more and looked out at the pool. Though the water before them sparkled like a million diamonds in the noonday sun, it paled in comparison to Kitty's dazzling smile.

Seeing that smile on Kitty's lovely face was reward enough for Caleb, worth more than all the gold in his cavern up in the hills. Despite his fancy's romantic protestations, he still needed some gold to live on and recalled he was down to only one of his nuggets left to spend after his most recent shopping spree.

After losing his brown felt companion of many years in the cavern waterfall, Caleb had wanted a new hat for the upcoming holiday festivities. He figured he'd be sitting in the sun a lot, and so he'd stopped by Vicker's Five and Ten the other day to go hat shopping.

Fortunately, the proprietress had been more than happy to allow him to use one of his nuggets as payment, and he'd bought a new felt hat—brown, just like the old one. On top of that, Melinda Vicker had issued Caleb store credit for several hundred dollars as 'change' from his purchase. He really had to give it to the people of this town; apart from Thomas Sinclair, most seemed above board, earnest and, like himself, just trying to survive.

As a result of the credit, he'd gone on a bit of a shopping spree for his friends. For Sandy, he'd picked up a book by a new writer called Wells, all about a time machine, which he knew the boy would enjoy immensely. The Doc had been in need of a new magnifying glass since he'd broken his old one during the panic of collecting and killing the baby spiders pouring out of Farley Jones. And, of course, Kitty's basket had been an easy guess. He valued the friendships he'd forged with these new people in his life, and the gifts he'd given were a way of showing them just that. He found that giving back something to those who had given him so much made him feel good inside.

A light breeze had sprung up, and small wavelets slapped lazily against the floating platform's sides, rocking it gently. The bright blue sky of early morning now had some company. Ominous, dark clouds were creeping over the tops of the snow-covered peaks at the back of the valley, adding an element of doubt over the rest of the day's weather.

Across the rippling water, off to one side of the bleachers, several vendors sold everything from meat pies and french fries to doughnuts and butter tarts, and probably everything else in between. From the other side of the bleachers, a small assembly of bedraggled musicians switched from playing a ragtime ditty and began pumping out a blast of fanfare—the diving competition was about to start.

Standing in the shade of the diving tower, a tall, thin man stepped out into the sun holding a long, brass, speaking trumpet. He began the proceedings by welcoming everyone to the first annual Kootenay Regatta and received a great cheer. He followed it up with some bad news, announcing, to some disappointment in the crowd, that the contest to name the town had been deferred until the fall fair at the beginning of September. He added that Natánik would continue to be the unofficial name of the town until then, and there was still plenty of time for people to get their entries in. With no further explanation, he directed the crowd's attention to the small sandy beach in front of the bleachers, saying a brief bit of entertainment was now in order for the youngsters in the audience, along with those still young at heart.

Two men dressed as clowns in patchwork clothing had been working the crowd before the event. They now bumped into each other on the beach, their collision leading to an argument. One clown clouted the other with what looked like a large salmon, knocking his opponent to his back in the sand. The man quickly recovered, clambering to his feet with a piece of twisted driftwood which he then used to chase the other clown around the beach. And so it went for the next few minutes, and they alternated, each seeming to find something new, strange and funny with which to swat or poke at the other. The children in the audience watching this were beside themselves with laughter, and many adults were cracking a smile as well.

Caleb studied Kitty surreptitiously, pleased to see the entertainment also tickled her inner child. Her bright, clear eyes sparkled with merriment as she watched things unfold on the beach, and he was struck again by the luck he'd had to come across such a beautiful, sweet, gentle and caring woman.

Another short musical interlude came from the band. The clowns suddenly abandoned their attempts to assault each other and moved back into the crowd to watch. The thin man with the brass trumpet was back and announced that the diving competition was about to begin. Sounding like a barker at a carnival, he announced the name of the first diver, Bill Burton from Boston Bar British Columbia, his excitement growing with each B he bleated.

Burton, a handsome young man with dark, wavy hair, climbed the tower with athletic ease. Once on the small platform at the top, he pulled a swimming cap from his waistband and placed it on his head. After adjusting his striped, knee-length, one-piece swimsuit, he moved to the platform's edge. Burton knew he was the focal point of everyone's attention and smiled broadly at the audience, then looked down into the pool. His smile faltered slightly, and he briefly rubbed at his eyes as he continued to stare into the water. After another moment, he gave his head a dismissive shake and prepared to dive once again. A breeze had sprung up, and the water's surface below him now rippled with small wavelets.

Just as Burton began to launch into his dive, he suddenly attempted to abort the whole operation. Something he'd seen from his bird's eye view of the choppy water below had suddenly changed his mind. But it was too late, and he'd committed to gravity's embrace.

But instead of a graceful piercing of the water's skin, Burton gave a slapping belly flop which geysered water into the air, sending small waves echoing out from his point of impact, and then he sank from sight.

As Burton struck the water, the crowd let out a collective "Oh," and a young woman standing near the tower's base let out a small scream of concern. Everyone craned their necks to see if he would appear again.

Sandy removed his shirt and overalls, revealing a one-piece swimsuit beneath. When the diver hadn't surfaced after another moment, the boy leapt into the pool with a mighty splash, giving Caleb and Kitty some refreshing spray. The after-effects of his forceful dive into the water were enough to rock the platform quite substantially, adding to the wake of the incoming wavelets caused by the growing breeze.

The relatively calm water surrounding Kitty and Caleb when they'd first boarded the floating platform now slapped and chopped against its sides instead. The platform had already been rocking slightly due to the growing wind that accompanied the increasingly cloudy day, and Sandy's dive hadn't helped things much.

Beneath Kitty and Caleb, the wood creaked and groaned as the waves slapped against the barrels keeping the platform afloat. It got so rough that Caleb's cast was sloshed with a substantial amount of water, eliciting a "Shite" from him as he pulled his leg back.

The effects of these waves also drew a response from Kitty. But unlike Caleb's profanity, hers was a scream of disgust and horror.

A man's head and part of one shoulder bobbed out of the water from under the edge of the platform. As he floated further into the pool on the rippling waves, it became evident the rest of his body was missing from the shoulder down. The bloated cadaver's glazed white eyes bored directly into Kitty's as if willing her to scream again.

She obliged, loudly and repeatedly, as did other women nearby, along with quite a few men close enough to see what had caught Kitty's attention.

With horror, Caleb realised the entire time they'd been sitting there, the corpse must have been wedged directly beneath them, and the wind, along with the wake from Sandy's dive, seemed to have somehow dislodged it.

Kitty turned away from the gruesome display and buried her face in Caleb's muscular shoulder.

Near the diving tower, Sandy popped to the surface for a gasp of air, then dove back under, still looking for the errant diver.

Caleb prepared to stand and escort Kitty away from the grisly sight when in the distance, on the other side of town, a huge explosion ripped through the hot afternoon, temporarily silencing even the loudest screams.

CHAPTER TWENTY-FOUR

"Here's a bit more moisture for you, my deadly little anachronism," Cornelius said. He poured water from a glass carafe into the bucket, just enough to cover the creature's slimy obsidian body. On the way back to his practice, thanks to its coiling and writhing, the little black beast had splashed much of the pool's water out of the beach pail and had been left floundering in a small puddle in the bottom.

Brown had upgraded the creature's accommodations from the green beach pail to a more spacious wooden bucket as soon as he'd returned. Of course, he'd first had to remove the mop from the bucket and then get rid of some of the sediment in the bottom. But with that done, the little beast now darted back and forth in its new mop bucket terrarium, appearing much happier with the added water and space.

After retrieving the little obsidian beast from the pools, the doctor had been in a hurry to get the creature back to the office as quickly as possible. However, on the way, a series of screams had rung out in the distance, followed by an ear-ringing explosion, not a block from where he'd been walking. He'd hurried to investigate and arrived just in time to see the prisoners from the jail escaping on horseback. Rufus had been barking excitedly in the offices at the front of the building but seemed unharmed. Thankfully, a thick log wall separating the offices from the cells had been between him and the explosion.

One of the gang members that hadn't escaped, an older man with a bushy white beard and hair to match, had been sitting on the floor of one of the demolished cells, holding his hands to his head as he regained consciousness. He was complaining of ringing in his ears, and Cornelius had tried to assess how the man was doing, but the man couldn't understand him due to his new hearing impairment.

Several moments later, Chief Hildey had come jogging up, but the gang had been long gone by then. After informing Dugrodt of the missed opportunity, the chief had responded that he couldn't have followed the desperados if he'd wanted. It seemed his horse had been the one stolen the night before from the smithy, left there in anticipation of being reshoed by Angus the next morning.

Upon learning this news, Brown mentioned the irony that the bandit who had just demolished the chief's jail had also ridden away on his stolen horse.

The lack of response and flat, cold expression on Dugrodt's face told the doctor all he needed to know regarding the chief's thoughts on irony and fate's capers and japes.

As Brown departed the jail for his practice, the chief had given a sad shake of his head and said it was going to be a long day. Apparently, there had also been trouble down at the pools. Dugrodt hadn't given any details, and Cornelius hadn't pressed him since the man seemed to have enough on his plate. But Brown realised whatever had happened, it must have been the cause of the screaming he'd heard just before the jailbreak. And so, he'd left the chief to piece back together his splintered hoosegow with Rufus sniffing excitedly around the site of the jailbreak and the deafened prisoner now handcuffed to the twisted metal frame of one of the bunk beds.

Now finished situating his new 'wet ward' in the bucket, Brown turned and addressed his medical office menagerie, saying, "And how are the rest of you doing?"

Across the room, on a low shelf, sat the ant, still in its crate. On the countertop above was the spider, hanging upside down inside the small bird cage. Both creatures regarded him with keen interest, and for different reasons—the ant wanting to dissect him into bite-sized chunks for easier transport back to the colony's food stores, and the spider just wanting him to bear her children.

The ant had been in the garbage when he'd found it, so he was fairly certain it had been looking for something to eat when captured. Alternately, since the spider's capture, it hadn't eaten anything, though he'd tried to tempt it with some mice he'd live-caught for that purpose. Fortunately for the rodents, the spider had no interest in them. But then, he knew spiders in the wild could go for weeks, if not months, between meals if they had to. There was a chance the arachnid wasn't hungry because it had eaten something just before he'd caught it, or he hadn't yet figured out the right food with which to tempt the creature.

Brown recalled his chats with Caleb, who'd told him of his introduction to the spider in the cavern. What struck him now wasn't something the Irishman said directly but rather something he had inferred from his friend's colourful descriptions—that the spider appeared to have led him to the lake-filled cavern. Had the arachnid in the cage, or one like it, been on its way to hunt the ants? And were these two creatures natural adversaries?

"Well, I suppose there's one way to find out." The doctor retrieved the ant's crate and placed it on his examination table, then sat the spider's cage beside it. Though not touching, the creatures were close enough for each to become the focus of the other. The ant began to chitter and snap its mandibles together, and the spider dropped to the floor of its cage, uttering a long, slow hiss as it regarded the ant.

Brown retreated momentarily to his small office and storage room. In addition to being his bedroom, he used it as a lab to experiment on gold separation. He returned with a steep-sided, galvanised steel washtub. It was oval, about three feet long, two feet wide and a foot and a half deep. The doctor placed it on the floor against the base of the examination table, just beneath his captive creatures.

The bell over the door jangled, and Brown turned, surprised to see Kitty and Caleb again so soon. Kitty was supporting Caleb lightly, but for some reason, it looked more like he was supporting her, emotionally speaking, at least. The doctor saw in her eyes that she was troubled and asked, "What happened, dear lady?"

Kitty responded, saying, "It was horrible! That poor man!" She buried her face against Caleb's shoulder and sobbed quietly.

His eyes wide, the doctor asked, "Care to tell me what happened, my boy?"

Caleb nodded, looking rather pale himself. "A man popped out from under that floatin' platform in the middle of the large pool, or at least some of him did."

"Only some of him?"

"His head and a bit of one shoulder," Caleb replied grimly. "Don't know what happened to the rest. Chief Dugrodt has yet to determine if it was foul play. But judgin' by the bite marks, I'd say it's foul all right, but not played by any man's hand." He shook his head and added, "Once Chief Dugrodt releases the remains, Sandy said he'll bring them over straight away for you to examine."

"The chief's got his hands full, what with that and the explosion at his jail," Kitty added.

Frowning, Brown replied, "I saw what had happened at the lockup on my way back to the office. It seems most of the men Sandy captured have now disappeared."

"Just like that swimmer," Kitty said sadly.

"Aye, that's right. The first diver in the competition."

"What happened?" Brown wondered.

Caleb was about to respond when the bell over the door came alive again.

Sandy pushed through the entrance, a bundle wrapped in an oiled tarp over one muscular shoulder. His hair was still wet, and though his overalls were back on, he was without his usual blue cotton shirt.

Nodding toward the blonde giant, Caleb said, "Perhaps Sandy can tell you himself."

"Are you all right, my boy?"

"Sure enough, Doc, but not this here fella," Sandy nodded toward the tarp. "Chief Hildey wanted you to look at him." He moved to lay the remains on the examination table but saw it occupied by the spider and ant.

"Here, let me move those for you." The doctor temporarily placed the ant's crate and the spider's cage on the floor near the tub and added, "Caleb mentioned something had also happened to one of the divers in the competition."

Sandy lay the tarp-wrapped remains on the table and replied with a nod. "Yessir. Fella never came back up. So, I dived and dived lookin' for him, but couldn't see him nowhere. The chief and Angus are at the pools puttin' barricades and signs up in case someone else tries swimmin' and never comes back up. And they ended up cancellin' the rest of the swimmin' display, too." He shook his head and looked to the remains, adding, "I think the same thing that got that divin' fella also got Sam here.

"Sam?" Brown wondered aloud.

"Yeah, you know him. Sam Shepherd," Sandy replied.

'Know him' was an understatement regarding Brown's relationship with Sam Shepherd. The man had been a barfly just like himself, and they had tipped back their elbows together on more than one occasion, having many a good conversation at one watering hole or another in this town. Seeing his friend come to an end like this was almost too much to bear, especially after another man getting killed with whom he'd also had more than a passing acquaintance, Farley Jones. Feeling nearly a physical thing within his chest, Brown's resolve to rid this town of these menaces from out of time suddenly became much, much stronger.

"What're you doin' with the tub here, Doc?" Caleb asked, tapping the tub with the tip of one crutch and making it ring like a gong.

As he unwrapped the tarp, Brown replied, "An experiment, but that will have to be put on the back burner for a moment while we examine Sam here."

Kitty turned away as the last fold of tarp was pulled back, and she pressed her face into Caleb's shoulder as he held and comforted her.

Brown noted this and said, "I'm so sorry, dear lady. I should have warned you I was going to do that."

Kitty nodded slightly, her face still buried in Caleb's shoulder.

Smiling grimly, Caleb said, "It's okay, Doc. Go ahead with

what you need to do."

A deep frown crept across the doctor's lips when he saw what remained of his deceased friend. Seeing him this way was much more emotionally impactful than he'd thought. He shook his head sadly; how the poor man must have suffered. He'd been bitten more than once by a creature with a bite span that seemed quite substantial.

"Would you do me a favour, my boy?"

"Sure, Doc. What's that?"

Brown pulled a cloth measuring tape from the inner pocket of his white lab coat and said, "Could you pull up your shirt, please."

"Huh? My shirt?"

"I'd like to see where you were bitten."

Caleb nodded and said, "Sure thing."

Cornelius had examined the bite marks on Caleb's side at the same time he'd set his ankle in the cast but hadn't thought to measure them and wanted to do so now. His eyes grew wide as the Irishman pulled his shirt from his trousers. Measurement was still possible, but just barely.

What had been red, inflamed bite marks in an oval pattern around one side of Caleb's flank had now healed and appeared merely scar tissue, which seemed impossible. The wound should have only been scabbing over at the most, yet somehow, the bite marks seemed only a memory, looking for all the world like a wound Caleb might have received during the Boer War a decade and a half before.

"My, but you heal fast," Brown commented.

Sandy replied, "He's a regular Ash... Akil... Ashill..."

"Achilles?" Brown inquired.

"That's him, the guy with the bad heel."

Brown nodded, "Yes, he was a quick healer as well, according to legend."

Kitty suggested, "Maybe it's the air around here. All that mountain freshness or somethin'."

Brown nodded in agreement, saying, "Or something." He measured the distance between the marks on Caleb's flank as best he could, then asked, "How's your ankle feeling?"

"You know, now that you mention it, it's not bad at all. It had been hurtin' pretty bad the first few days, but now, it feels much better." Caleb looked at the cast and added sheepishly, "I should mention that I got it a bit wet down near the pools when I was on that platform."

"I'll take a look in a moment; first, I want to finish with my friend Sam here."

"Sure, Doc. Take your time."

Brown returned to Sam and measured the bite marks on what remained of the man's shoulder. "Interesting indeed."

"What is it, Doctor?" Kitty asked.

Cornelius turned and faced the trio saying, "Assuming it was the same creature that bit you, there's one of two possibilities here."

"What's that?" Caleb queried.

"Either, there are two of these full-sized creatures..."

Brown trailed off as he looked at Sam's remains.

"Or?" Kitty asked.

"There's one, and it's getting bigger," Caleb finished.

"Precisely," Brown said with a nod.

"Both of those possibilities are bad," Kitty said quietly.

"Sure enough," Sandy agreed, then asked, "How big do you think it'll get?"

Shaking his head, Brown replied, "Hard to say. But I'd imagine the creature's growth could continue for a little while, especially with the wealth of food it's recently had. He turned toward the remains of Sam and added, "Apologies to Miss Kitty." He gestured toward the teeth marks that fringed the edges of Sam's shoulder and upper chest, saying, "If it is the same creature, it would appear the bite radius has increased by several inches since you were first introduced to each other. This amount of change in a week is most distressing."

"I agree. Caleb said. "But it's not the sort of encouragin' stuff we want to hear, Doc."

The doctor shrugged, saying, "I wish I could be the bearer of better news." He rewrapped Sam's remains and said, "Sandy, would you mind?"

"Not a problem, Doc." He picked the tarp from the table, slung it over one shoulder and said, "You want I should take him to Ezra like I did, Farley?"

"If you would, son."

Sandy got to the door, then turned and asked, "Do you think he's open today?"

Kitty replied, "Around this town, I think he's open seven days a week."

Sandy nodded, said, "Sure enough," and departed with a jingle.

Brown wiped the examination table with a small towel hanging off one side, then turned to Caleb and patted the top, saying, "Hop on up."

"I've been doing a lot of that recently with this thing." Caleb sat on the table's edge, swivelled his legs up and lay back.

The doctor shook his head as he looked at the slightly sodden cast and said, "You really have to avoid getting water on this thing, my boy. It looks like I might need to replaster you."

Kitty moved around and kissed Caleb on the forehead, saying, "That's for good luck, once again."

"I'm lovin' that luck." Caleb touched his forehead and smiled.

Kitty returned his smile with one of her own, the room seeming to grow brighter with its brilliance. But its radiance faded quickly, and her smile became one of sadness when she added, "I think I'm goin' to go lie down in my room at the Nugget for a little while. All of this excitement has been a wee bit too much for me."

"You do that, lass," Caleb said. "I'll hop on over when I'm done."

"Sounds fine," Kitty said and moved toward the door. She paused with her hand on the doorknob and added, "I wonder if they're still havin' those fireworks tonight in light of what's happened."

"I don't know. It depends on what Angus and Hildey figure, safety-wise. Angus was sayin' with the forest around town gettin' so dry, they might hold off if there's a breeze since they wouldn't want to start a fire." Caleb finished and looked into Kitty's eyes with a grin, saying, "But even if they cancel them, I'm sure we can figure out somethin' to do."

Kitty blushed fiercely and jingled out the door to the street.

The doctor gave a small smile and said, "I see things are proceeding well in your quest to win over the heart of our fair friend?"

Nodding, Caleb said, "That's a good way to put it, Doc. And yes, things are going well."

Brown pushed up his sleeves, then picked up something from the side counter that looked like an oversized pair of scissors with a slightly angled blade and a serrated edge on one side. He snapped them together several times as he moved toward Caleb, saying, "Plaster shears." Once at Caleb's side, he snapped them a couple more times and added, "All right, let's see what we shall see." Just before he started to cut, he advised, "And by the way, try not to move."

"Just a patient-care tip for the future, Doc," Caleb said as he stared at the shears.

"What's that, my boy?"

"Maybe don't snap those things together like that unless you want to give your patient a bad case of nerves."

Brown nodded and said, "Duly noted." The doctor went to work on the cast for several minutes and soon had Caleb's lower leg exposed to the air.

Caleb sat up and leaned forward to scratch the skin that

had been hidden beneath the cast, saying, "Ah, that feels better." He looked up to the doctor as he finished scratching and saw Brown's face filled with concern. "What's wrong?"

The doctor shook his head and said, "It's your ankle."

"I know it is, Doc. What about it?"

Brown probed where the break had been, noting how clean the skin looked. Before he'd set Caleb's ankle last week, the bone had been on the verge of rupturing through his skin, but now, it seemed almost unscathed. He poked and prodded for another moment, then said, "Tell me if that hurts."

"A little late to the party with your warning again, Doc. But no, fortunately, it feels fine." There had been no pain, and this seemed a promising thing. Caleb nodded toward his leg and asked, "How much longer do you figure then?"

"For what?" Brown asked distractedly.

"For my ankle to heal! Another five weeks or so, right?"

Brown shook his head and said, "No, my boy, I'm afraid not."

With alarm, Caleb said, "I sure hope you're not going to tell me it's gangrenous and you need to amputate!"

"Hardly." Brown continued to stare at Caleb's leg.

"Then what?"

Brown looked up at Caleb, his white brows knitting together. "From all outwards appearances, it would seem that your ankle is completely healed."

CHAPTER TWENTY-FIVE

The dynamite had done its job well, perhaps a little too well, Jesús realised. In retrospect, he may have used a bit too much explosive since he'd blown out most of the rear wall of the city lock-up. Maybe three sticks of dynamite would have been preferable over the half-dozen he'd used. Oh well, live and learn had always been his motto.

Bad Haircut had been unlucky enough to catch a piece of shrapnel in the explosion. He'd staggered out of the gaping hole in the jail's wall, clutching his arm in agony and leaving a crimson trail behind. A long wooden splinter had pierced his flesh like an arrow, and blood flowed around the piece of shrapnel in pulsing gushes.

Antonio had tended to the wound, taking Bad Haircut's belt and tightening it around his arm in a makeshift tourniquet a couple of inches above the puncture. With the blood flow stemmed, he'd led the man to the waiting horses. Since time was of the essence, they couldn't extract the wood immediately, so that was where the splinter stayed until they had time to tend to the wound properly.

Unfortunately, Cookie had been left unconscious on the floor of the jail cell. In the confusion and dust, no one had realised the cook was missing until they were out to the horses, and then it was too late to go back for him. The explosion had been enough to wake the dead on this peaceful day. On top of that, the infernal dog in the office had been baying like a hound from hell, likely drawing even more attention to what had happened behind the jail than the dynamite.

As they'd mounted their horses and prepared to gallop away, the drunken doctor had arrived on the scene at the last minute, witnessing the direction in which they were heading. And so, Jesús had changed his trajectory, and they'd gone the opposite way at the last minute.

Oritz had been tempted to shoot the doctor but didn't want to waste any of his remaining precious ammo before they got to the encampment. There was a fairly high chance they might need what remained for something more important, like killing monster ants as they recovered their belongings. And besides, he didn't need the law hunting him down for murder on top of his recent acts of horse thievery and aiding and abetting a jailbreak.

Now that they were a safe enough distance away, they'd stopped to tend to Bad Haircut's wounds. Antonio kept the belt tight on the man's arm, knowing he would need to remove the piece of wood first. If he did so with the tourniquet loosened, the man would most likely gush blood like Old Faithful and bleed to death within minutes.

Antonio steadied his hand on the man's shoulder and yanked the piece of branch out without any warning, saying as he did, "This is probably going to hurt."

Bad Haircut's shriek was not unexpected, given the circumstances. His forehead bathed in sweat and eyes wide, he responded, "You're right. It bloody well did!"

Jesús now wished Cookie were at hand. Over the years, the cook had acquired some serious skills stitching together assorted knife wounds and bullet holes to which the gang seemed so prone to collecting. But there was no turning back now, so he would have to make the best of his decision.

Taking hold of Bad Haircut's shirt sleeve, Antonio tore off a long portion and bound it tightly around the now oozing wound, saying, "This will have to do for now."

Soon, everyone was back in their saddle and ready to ride once again. As they made their circuitous route toward the river, No Neck had difficulty staying upright in his saddle. It seemed the man still felt the effects of the spider bite from the day before, saying he felt drunk but without the buzz.

Just outside of their encampment, Jesús turned to address his crew, saying, "I want us to go in there as quietly as we can since we don't want to attract any attention. And we need to watch where we step at all times. We don't know for sure where those diablos rojo might have burrowed."

His eyes squinting in concentration, Bad Haircut had wobbled slightly in his saddle as he listened to the words of warning, no doubt suffering from some major blood loss. No Neck pulled his horse beside his buddy's and snickered slightly as Jesús finished his speech.

"Is something funny?" Antonio asked.

"No, I'm just tryin' to imagine how large these ants could possibly be. I really need to see these things because you gotta be exaggerating."

"Are you calling me a liar?" Jesús inquired.

No Neck realised what he'd just said, and his eyes widened. "No! No, of course not!"

"Good. Because trust me, if you see them, that means that they see you, and that is not a good thing."

"How big are they, really?" No Neck inquired again.

"Big enough to dig the same-sized hole as a damned gopher," Antonio replied.

"All right," No Neck conceded, "Maybe I don't want to see them after all."

Shaking his head, Jesús said, "Trust me, you don't."

Jesús gave the signal, and they began to move toward their encampment once more, now following along the river's shore. Approaching from upriver seemed the best route rather than their original direction through the forest, which they'd taken upon their arrival in the valley.

At a bend in the river, a deadfall of driftwood had piled up from changes in the water level caused by storm swells over the years. The way past the twisted mound was narrow, and they were almost forced to lead their horses into the river to get around it, but fortunately, there was just enough room to file past one by one.

In the lead, Jesús paused as he passed the drift of dead wood. His brow knitted together in a mixture of horror and anger as he witnessed the after-effects of the ants' insatiable appetite. He shook his head; so many good, bad men had been lost due to the ravenous red devils. He mourned their passing but knew he would avenge them someday soon.

Sticking out of the driftwood were two skeletal legs. Stripped bare of meat, shreds of denim hung from the bones as they now bleached in the sun next to the pale, barkless wood. It must have been the remains of Long, Jesús realised. Cookie had relayed his experience at the encampment during a round of much-needed drinks at the Kootenay Saloon. He'd described in great detail how Lister had come tearing around this very bend as he fled for his life, babbling about Long's demise at the pile of driftwood. That had been just after Webb had been attacked in the river, and about the same time the rest of the men at base camp were being eaten alive. After the tunnels he'd already seen the creatures dig, Jesús wondered exactly how far the ants had expanded their territory since he'd last been to the encampment. Hopefully, they had tunnelled their little red asses out of the neighbourhood by now, but he wasn't holding his breath.

The men followed behind Jesús, each slowing as they passed the pile of wood, eyes growing wide at the sight of the skeletal legs. No Neck came through last, and he shook his head, saying, "No, I definitely don't want to see them ants now."

The group moved further along the shore and soon came upon another grisly discovery. Two more skeletons lay at the bottom of a rather steep embankment, presumably the remains of Stork and Lister if Jesús's memory of Cookie's alcohol-fuelled terror tale served him correctly.

They arrived at a spot about a hundred yards further down the embankment that was less steep and easier to ride the horses up, and soon, they were back at the encampment.

There was no sign of any activity, either mammalian or insectoid. No birds chirped in the trees, and no squirrels chittered from the branches. It was dead silent, the only sound the rushing river in the background. Jesús and Antonio halted their horses off to one side of the encampment, away from the carnage of last time. Bad Haircut and No Neck were across from them on the opposite side of the clearing.

Jesús held his index finger to his lips, signalling silence to the men, and then began to dismount. The other men nodded and carefully did the same. Pausing to light a cigarillo, Jesús took a long drag and felt the nicotine surge through his system, sharpening his senses.

Antonio pointed toward the skeletal remains of the downed

ammunition horse, the object of their quest. Jesús nodded with a grim smile as they approached the remains. The animal had been stripped bare just like the men, and only some tufts of hair from its mane and tail remained.

No Neck and Bad Haircut had been tasked with grabbing some of the pots and pans for Cookie. Jesús realised that if he were successful in springing the man from the arms of Johnny Law in the future and hadn't retrieved some of the man's cookware, he'd never hear the end of it.

At first, Jesús was quite surprised the horse's skeleton was so devoid of flies and maggots but then realised the lack of flesh on any part of the animal, or any of the human remains around it, left nothing for insects to eat or breed upon. The horse lay where it had fallen, the two satchels containing the ammo still slung over the animal's skeletal remains. Together, he and Antonio worked to disentangle the leather of the satchel's straps from the horse's corpse.

Over near the former site of the kitchen, the partially disabled duo worked to collect what they could salvage of the cook's kitchen implements. Bad Haircut looked to his neckless friend and said, "I think I've lost a lot of blood. Feelin' pretty dizzy when I bent down just now." The wound in his arm was still seeping blood, not a large amount, but enough to spot on the ground occasionally as he moved his arm the wrong way and stressed the coagulating wound.

"Tell me about it," No Neck complained. "I still can't feel anything down one side of my body, thanks to that spider bite!" The man seemed to realise he was being too loud just about the same time he looked over to Jesús, who had just snapped his head in the direction of his voice. Anger flaring across his face, Oritz made a gesture drawing his index finger across his throat. About to say something more, No Neck clapped his mouth shut and continued his work. It was hard to say whether the gesture meant to cut the noise or to indicate Jesús would rather just cut his throat. Either way, No Neck didn't seem ready to ask for clarification.

In a hushed whisper, Bad Haircut said, "Let's just get this done and get out of here." He bent with a wobble and collected a couple of pans from a nearby log.

Speaking in a loud whisper, No Neck groused, "Never shoulda joined on. And I still can't hear worth a damn out of my one ear thanks to that 'splosion at the jail."

Jesús and Antonio had finally freed the ammo satchels intertwined in the horse's carcass. They moved to their mounts and secured one bag to Jesús's horse and the other to Antonio's. If something untoward happened to one of the animals, the other would hopefully survive, at least allowing them to retrieve some of their ammunition.

No Neck and Bad Haircut seemed to have gotten everything they could gather of the kitchen implements. After securing them to their horses, they now led their animals quietly toward Jesús's location.

With a clatter, No Neck's cookware-laden horse stumbled and crashed to the ground. Both of its front legs had fallen into a hole hiding beneath a thin crust of dirt which had crumbled away when the weighty animal stepped upon it. The horse's chest now rested almost flush with the ground. It whinnied in fright and quite possibly pain since it may have broken one or both of its legs in the fall. It bucked and jerked but couldn't stand or extract its legs from the hole due to the awkward angle at which it now found itself. No Neck was beside it, yanking on its bridle to pull it free, but the beast seemed well and truly stuck.

Suddenly, the trapped animal's panicked whinnies turned to squeals of agony, and it began to spasm and shake as if having an epileptic attack. No Neck began backing away from the creature in dismay, shaking his head back and forth.

Jesús stood wide-eyed, watching this unfold. It seemed strangely reminiscent of what had happened to One Ear. As he'd suspected, the ground around the encampment seemed riddled with holes like a piece of Swiss cheese, and wherever they tread might be fraught with danger. Some of the ant's holes were apparent and easy to spot, while others were buried in the brush or hidden completely, as was the case with the horse, which had stepped onto the roof of a tunnel excavated too close to the surface. Any person or animal that stepped on one by mistake could suddenly find themselves in a similar predicament to that of the horse.

After a few moments, the animal had thankfully stopped squealing and shaking. In fact, it wasn't doing much of anything anymore. Its head lolled to one side, tongue dangling from its mouth. But after a moment, the horse began to tremble and shake again as if in the midst of another convulsive fit.

However, the men soon realised that was not the case when the first quivering antenna appeared in the horse's mouth, now locked open in a cry of silent agony.

The ants had burrowed their way through the horse's chest and up into its throat, eating it alive from within as they attempted to clear the blockage which had fallen into their underground kingdom. Now, ant after ant poured from the horse's mouth as the first scouts arrived to assess the new threats to their colony.

CHAPTER TWENTY-SIX

"What? How is this possible?" Caleb asked, flummoxed. He leaned forward and poked and prodded at his ankle. It should have felt quite raw and sore still, but instead, he felt no pain whatsoever.

"Your guess is as good as mine, my boy." The doctor briefly scratched the back of his messy white hair and added, "But I have to say, with all of the other improbable things happening around here, it strangely doesn't seem out of place."

"I know what you mean, Doc." Caleb looked down at the floor speculatively and then back up at the doctor, asking, "Should I give it a try?"

"From all outward appearances, your ankle seems healed. So I would say, go ahead, but tread carefully; it may be like a roast cooked in too high an oven."

"How so?"

"Done on the outside, but still a little raw in the middle."

"So, take it easy and don't go runnin' no marathons would be a good plan. Is that what you're sayin'?"

"That about sums it up."

"I gotta say, Doc, it feels good with the cast off, but I'll be as careful as I can." Caleb lowered himself off the examination table. With a deep breath, he slowly stood to see if he could bear weight on his ankle. Fully erect, he realised he could because there was no pain—everything felt normal, as before the fall. With things seeming so promising, Caleb decided to go further.

The bell rang musically as he opened the front door. Standing on the threshold, Caleb enjoyed the slight breeze that wafted through. It carried a scent of wildflowers, perhaps roses. Thinking of the blossoming flowers caused his own sense of hope to bloom anew. If he could heal so quickly and miraculously, perhaps some of his other concerns might just work out as easily.

Without limping in any appreciable way, Caleb returned to the office and sat in one of the chairs in the waiting area.

Brown inquired, "No pain?"

"Nothin' at all. I feel like I did before I dropped into that cavern of horrors." And Caleb wondered at that. He'd never been a remarkably fast healer during his life to date. Though never run through with a Zulu spear or pierced by a Boer bullet, he'd still had his fair share of cuts and scrapes, and they had all taken some time to heal. He'd known a couple of mates in the army whose recuperative abilities seemed almost superhuman sometimes, but he had never been one of them.

"Your recovery is remarkable." The doctor lifted the washtub from the floor and placed it on the examination table.

"I'd be prone to agree with you, Doc," Caleb said, slowly nodding. Apart from the fast healing, he didn't feel particularly different than before, so that was a good thing. Even the bite marks on his side had stopped itching. A thought of his younger years popped into his head, and he asked with wide eyes, "D'ya think it has anythin' to do with that bite I received?"

"What, from the black thing?"

"Yeah. I was just thinkin' of a story a fella told me in the army. Can't remember its name, but in it, a fella gets bitten and ends up turnin' into a wolf!

"Yes, I've heard folklore concerning such topics. And apparently, Alexandre Dumas wrote a tale about one, but I don't believe it's been translated into English yet. But don't tell me you think you might turn into a…" The doctor looked to the mop bucket, seeming unsure how to describe the black, toothy creature it contained.

"Well, no, I guess not. But what d'ya think those things are, Doc? An eel of some kind?" Caleb suggested.

"I've been examining the small one here." Brown poked at the bucket on the floor with his toe, and the black baby beast sloshed around inside. "While it does resemble an eel in some respects, such as its toothy little maw with rows of pointed teeth angling inward, it has other characteristics not found in the eel genus, such as its vestigial limbs, which leads me to believe it has amphibian heritage."

"That's right. You were talkin' about salamanders back at the park."

"Quite correct."

"So, if I lost this now, would I grow another one?" He tapped his now-healed leg for emphasis.

"I don't know if I'd go that far at this point. But you are correct. In addition to regrowing lost tails, some salamanders regrow lost limbs, teeth, hearts, and even parts of their brains. However, with all that said, I would venture whatever was in that animal's bite has affected you in some way, and in this case, it would appear a good way. Rapid healing seems to be the only side effect for the moment."

Brown toed the bucket again, saying, "This creature is like something from out of time." He looked to the ant and spider and added, "In fact, they all are."

"What, like some of those dinosaur things I heard talk of in National Geographic?"

"Precisely! That whole cavern seems like an entire ecology in and of itself."

"Ecology, Doc?"

"A geographic region with distinct flora and fauna, oftentimes found nowhere else."

"That about sums up that cavern from what I've seen so far."

"Well, once again, I would like to volunteer my services should you ever remember its location, my boy. I could provide valuable insights from both a medical and scientific standpoint. As you can imagine, that place needs to be documented and studied."

"I can imagine you're right. Hopefully, whatever has healed my ankle will heal my brain just as quick." Thinking of the bite again, Caleb asked, "D'ya think there'll be other things?"

"I don't know, but you should keep an eye on yourself over the next few days and see if you have any other symptoms apart from this rapid healing. Maybe you should come in for a checkup next week so I can see how you're doing?"

"Sure thing, Doc. If I'm still alive and haven't been gobbled up by one of those beasties behind ya." Caleb gestured to the wash tub and asked, "And what exactly are you doing there anyway?"

"I'm glad you asked, my boy! Something I've noticed with these creatures is their level of animosity toward each other."

"How so?"

"Well, when I've had their containers close by, they've reacted quite violently."

"What're you sayin', Doc? You think they might be natural enemies."

"Yes, and I was just going to test that theory out when you and your lady fair arrived on my doorstep.

"Speaking of people arriving on your doorstep, I was wonderin' how are you affordin' to survive without havin' any patients at your practice over the last few days?"

"Simple, my boy. I told you that Sinclair has asked me to keep an eye on you."

"Yes."

The doctor looked down at his feet for a moment, then glanced back up and met Caleb's eyes. "Well, he's got me on retainer."

Caleb shook his head in astonishment. "He's paying you to babysit me? I thought he was blackmailin' you!"

"Oh, he is, but I told him if I wasn't available for walk-in customers on a regular basis, I couldn't survive in this town. And I've been kept especially busy with this plague of monsters we're now dealing with. So Sinclair offered to cover my expenses while I assist you, which I suppose is fair since I'm working with you to eradicate our problems from the past.

As Lucias so aptly put it yesterday, he's protecting his investment in you."

Caleb shook his head and said, "Ask a silly question..." Though he displayed little emotion externally, inside, he was busy processing this news. Was everyone around here on Sinclair's payroll or being blackmailed by him? Regardless of his suspicions about the Doc, what he felt for Kitty seemed to be genuinely reciprocated by the woman, from what he could tell. And as far as he knew, Sinclair wasn't paying her any extra apart from her normal wages as a second-floor girl. But still, he wondered. Making a person question the loyalty of others was something in which Sinclair probably revelled—pitting friends against friends and causing no one to trust the other. The more Caleb thought about it, the more he became convinced he was correct.

"Speaking of answers to questions," Brown continued, "I think I have a few or at least something to go on. Let me show you."

The doctor retrieved his rose mister from a side table beneath the large barbering mirror. He approached the ant's crate, saying, "Watch this." He gave a small puff of spray in one corner of the ant's small quarters. The creature scuttled away as far as it could to the other side, its mandibles making their impression of a castanet once again. The ant's high-pitched wailing was noticeably louder now as if it were fearing for its life and calling for help.

"Is that the new acid spray like you have in the extinguisher?"

Brown grinned. "It is. And you saw how it pulled away just now?"

"Yeah, just like the spiders."

The doctor nodded slightly and said, "In addition to being

corrosive, I believe the acetic acid also works as a deterrent with the ants because they think it's a marker of another ant species warning them away from its territory. I've read recent studies showing how chemical inhibitors like that are used in nature by all sorts of different creatures."

"How's that?"

"Well, if we were ever to encounter a large number of ants, I should be able to use my fire extinguisher to spray any areas we don't want them to go. And it should also disrupt any scent trails they leave to navigate by."

"And sort of cut them off at the pass, huh?"

"Something like that. But I'll need to see a larger number of them than this one sample in order to verify its efficacy."

"Well, we should probably head down to the river for that."

"I agree. But first, there was something else I'd been thinking about in that lake-filled cavern of yours where you met these ants. And the more I've thought of it, the more I'm convinced I need to try it." Brown began to remove the top from the ant's crate.

"Whoa, Doc! What're you doing?" Caleb backed up a couple of feet in alarm.

"As I mentioned, I was going to test my hypothesis when you arrived. So there's no time like the present."

Brown took the top all the way off the small crate, then turned it upside down over the washtub before the ant could crawl out and scamper up his arm. The red menace dropped into the tub with a clunk. A series of clicks and clacks echoed hollowly in the stainless steel tub as the ant explored its new, larger habitat.

Upon verifying the ant was unable to crawl up the smooth sides of the washtub, the doctor grabbed the arachnid's cage and slowly returned to the tub, the spider growing more agitated the closer he got.

Something he'd heard in school many years before popped to mind as Caleb watched, and he asked, "Are you goin' to have them go up against each other as the gladiators did in Ancient Rome?"

"Quite so, my boy."

"Isn't that kind of cruel?"

Brown shook his head. "In the name of science, and because either of them would just as likely attack you as each other, I would have to say no. However, you're quite accurate in your comparison. Each of these creatures is a warrior for its species in its own right, and this washtub shall be their arena." Saying that, Brown sprung the cage's door and shook it violently until the spider dropped into the opposite end of the oval tub from where the ant was currently exploring.

"Are you sure that spider can't crawl out?"

"Reasonably so," Brown said, focusing his attention on the drama unfolding below like a Roman Emperor at the Colosseum.

The ant turned and froze as it saw the spider, and then without any prelude, it charged the arachnid, its shear-like mandibles snapping a staccato.

The spider limberly dodged out of the path of the ant's frenetic foray and leapt onto its back. It bit down hard, fangs piercing deeply into the soft tissue where the back of the ant's head connected with its thorax. Almost immediately, the ant ceased struggling, and the spider wrapped its long, spiky legs around its adversary in a deadly hug, injecting further venom as it did.

In a manner of moments, the eight-legged predator had deftly spun a silken straight-jacket around the now-paralysed ant, ensuring it could go nowhere if and when the venom wore off. With its victory complete, the spider paused and regarded the two men, not moving from the top of its prey.

"Okay, now we know," Brown said.

"They're mortal enemies!" Caleb said in astonishment.

"More than that, I believe it's as I surmised; the ants are a source of sustenance for the spiders.

"Is this part of that ecology thing again, Doc?"

"Indeed. What I had postulated was, in fact, the truth."

"And I followed that spider through to the source of its food inside the cavern, the ant colony."

"Correct. When hunting inside the lake-filled cavern, these spiders must lie in wait for any ant scouts searching for edible detritus along the shores of that lake you mentioned."

Caleb nodded and said, "I think you're right. But it's strange. You mentioned before how these monsters might be pack hunters. Yet when I was there, I never saw any other spiders, just the one."

The creature in question now crouched atop its prey, busy regurgitating digestive enzymes into the cocoon and dissolving the ant's insides for its next meal.

"And you're thinking the same as me."

"I am?"

"Yes. When this creature has a finite food supply, it naturally limits the animal's desire to lay eggs, which is why Mama didn't impregnate you when you were first introduced."

"You have such a way with words, Doc."

"Thank you, my boy."

Caleb finished the thought, saying, "So, if Mama laid eggs in me up in the cavern, doin' so would have overwhelmed her huntin' ground with predators, in this case, her very own offspring."

"Exactly!"

"And now she's free to lay eggs in a place where there's plenty of prey, from ants all the way up to people."

"Correct! It's making hay while the proverbial sun is shining."

"Remember when I asked you a while back how many offspring there could be if all of Mama's babies survived, and you said you'd have to calculate it?"

Squinting at the spider now sucking up some of the ant's insides, Brown said, "Well, let me see... If these creatures procreate as rapidly as you heal... And if they do so throughout the year... And if the offspring are equally divided..." He looked toward the ceiling, appearing to do the math in his head, then looked down to Caleb and exclaimed, "Great Darwin's ghost!"

Alarm growing within his chest, Caleb asked, "What is it, Doc?"

"We could have well over ten million spiders on our hands by next year!"

"Sweet Mother Mary!"

"And Joseph as well," Brown added.

"What're we goin' to do, Doc?"

"Well, I believe it's imperative to find where those baby spiders went before they reach maturity as soon as possible."

"You hit the nail on the head, Doc. But d'ya think she's only laid one batch of eggs since Farley's?"

"Clutch, it's called a clutch of eggs."

"Okay, thanks. D'ya think she could lay more than one right away?"

"It would be highly unusual. Most spiders that lay throughout the year do so only every few months, not weeks."

"You said 'most', are there any exceptions?"

"Yes, there's the nursery web spider which lays several sacs at once and others that can lay up to a dozen times yearly. If our spider has any of those traits and has already laid a secondary or tertiary egg sac, we could already be in big trouble."

"Okay, spiders are a priority," Caleb said with a nod. "I suppose we should get out there and do some more bug huntin' then."

"Indeed. And don't forget the ants could also be in the millions within the year since they're no longer constricted by their ecology either."

"Crap on a cracker, man! With everythin' crawlin' and slitherin' around out there, I think we'll be lucky to survive until Christmas!"

"Then let's hope our efforts pay off," Brown said encouragingly. He peeked inside the leather satchel across his shoulder as he spoke. His eyebrows furrowed together, and he looked up, saying, "I need to gather a few things before we go. They're just in my back office." With a glance into the tub, he inquired, "Would you mind keeping your eye on our leggy friend there for a moment? I'll be back in just a second."

Caleb's eyes widened, and he asked, "Are you sure it can't get out? Maybe you should put it away first? You saw how it jumped on the ant just now, and remember back at the ice house. I think that tub looks awfully shallow."

Brown moved toward the back office and said, "You'll be fine! Mama's still busy eating, and besides that tub is galvanised steel and the metal quite slick. I sincerely doubt it could jump out; the sides are a good foot and a half high." He turned before entering his back office and added, "But if it'd make you feel any better, grab the net."

Caleb nodded at the suggestion, his eyes locked on the spider. A foot and a half didn't sound like very much of anything. He'd been deathly afraid of spiders for as long as he could recall, or at least since that day in Dublin many years before.

The leggy predator abruptly stopped supping its liquefying ant sorbet and regarded Caleb. Its shiny black eyes burned into his as if reading his mind and sensing how much he feared it. To his dismay, he kept seeing the spider's rather sprightly leap onto the ant's back, repeating in his mind over and over as if time had slowed down as he recalled it. He didn't want to see if the creature was capable of leaping out of the tub, so the doctor's suggestion of the net seemed like a great idea. However, he just had to move around the tub to get to it.

Almost as soon as Caleb had the thought, the spider leapt

from the husk that had been the ant and perched on the edge of the wash tub. It crouched, flexing slightly on its long legs, regarding Caleb.

"Doc! We got serious problems!"

"What is it?" Brown called from the other room.

"Your little friend is loose!"

"Egad! I'll be right there. Don't let it get away. Try to trap it with something!"

Staring hard at the spider, Caleb said, "Trap you? With what?" The arachnid was now between him and the net, currently leaning against the side table near the mirror. Caleb shook his head. Here he was, freshly healed in a miraculous one-week period, and now about to get bitten and mauled by this freakishly huge spider and die the same day.

"Doc!" Caleb called, his vocal cords straining to speak, and it was more of a hoarse whisper instead. With a start, he realised he'd backed against the counter and could retreat no further.

In the service, he'd known some men who were deathly afraid of water, fire, or dogs due to some previous trauma. Shaking his head in horror, Caleb wondered why his fear couldn't have been something like the other fellas, or maybe snakes, of which Ireland had exactly none.

Caleb's phobia-made-real scuttled along the edge of the wash tub, then dropped to the floor with a plop, its legs flexing to absorb the impact. It slowly stood, then crouched again, and repeated this several more times.

But then the spider paused at the bottom of its latest crouch, and remained there. It quivered briefly, preparing to launch itself across the short distance to where Caleb now stood.

Backed against the counter and frozen in place, Caleb was about to call for the doctor a third time, but he seemed rendered mute by fear. Without warning, another flash of recollection from his past overwhelmed him. Sadly, it wasn't from his recent past, something which would give him a helpful hint to the location of his cursed cavern of gold. No, instead, it was a flash of what had happened all those years ago, and his heart pounded in his chest, feeling like it might explode, as the details of that day suddenly came rushing back.

CHAPTER TWENTY-SEVEN

No Neck backed quickly away from the emerging ants. If his eyes could have opened any wider, they would have surely fallen from his head. "I never thought they was this big!"

Ants continued to emerge from the horse's mouth, a high-pitched keening coming from each and every one, their mandibles cracking and clacking as they began to spread out. They seemed inquisitive at the moment, and not threatening, appearing to be the forward guard only assessing the situation. By the time the last scout exited the horse, they were a little over two dozen strong.

Though not as troublesome as two hundred, Jesús suspected they could be just as deadly. Remembering what had happened to One Ear when he'd fired upon the ants, he called out to his new recruits, "These things are like angry hornets! Do not harm any of them, or they will attack!"

Bad Haircut seemed to take this advice to heart and was already moving his panicking horse away from the ants. He hadn't yet mounted it, perhaps worried a similar fate might befall it as had No Neck's horse.

And now, because No Neck had no ride, he also dashed toward Bad Haircut's horse, arriving just as his companion had begun to climb aboard the saddle. As No Neck attempted to scramble on behind his buddy, he got pushed back down.

"Get off, ya bastard! I don't need ya slowin' me down!"

"You can't leave me here!"

"You've got two good legs! Use 'em!"

A fresh contingent of ants suddenly pushed out of the horse's mouth—several more dozen from the looks of it. However, these creatures seemed not involved in scouting but rather in food transportation. They swarmed over the carcass with military-like precision, chewing and gnawing with their powerful pincers, dissecting the equine intruder into easily transportable chunks.

While the two men argued over the horse, the scouts continued to dart about the encampment, searching for other threats to their underground kingdom, sometimes coming dangerously close.

No Neck tried again to climb aboard the horse but was kicked away by Bad Haircut, now fully in the saddle.

The neckless man pinwheeled his arms to keep balance, stumbling backwards as he did. Unfortunately, his floundering feet couldn't see the ant approaching at his back, and he stepped on it with a moist, cracking crunch.

And that one misstep was all it took.

Whether it was the sound, the sight or the pheromones released when their compatriot got crushed, whatever it was, the other ants responded accordingly—all of them. The scouts stopped scouting, and the vivisection squad stopped dissecting. As one, they scuttled toward their downed comrade and the towering cause of its demise.

"Holy shit, holy shit!" No Neck exclaimed, currently

attempting to wipe the ant's remains off the bottom of his boot onto a patch of grass. "I didn't see it, honest!" Whether he was stating the obvious as an excuse to Jesús or perhaps to the ants themselves, it didn't matter, one of the colony had been killed, and its attacker must now pay the ultimate price.

The ants scuttered toward the interloping giant with surprising speed, looking to swarm it and do whatever it took to stop it from ever harming another of their own.

With a squeal, the panicked man spun around in a circle, flailing his arms ineffectually at a couple of eager ants which had scurried up his back and now tried to slice into him with their mandibles. Stomping and kicking briefly at other ants as they approached, No Neck disappeared into the forest, screaming like a banshee, his growing red entourage following close behind.

"I do not think they care it was an accident," Jesús said, shaking his head. He'd watched all this with horror and resignation. Here he was, just trying to go about his business, and once again, it was being interrupted, this time because of a stumble-footed buffoon and his horse. Well, at least he'd gotten what he came for, and everything else was now secondary, including that man's life.

Bad Haircut shot past on his horse, galloping down the trail toward town, shouting over his shoulder, "I don't care how much damned gold you promised me! I quit!"

Perhaps attracted by the thrumming hoofbeats above their heads, or maybe because they were already on their way, another brigade of ants poured forth from the dead horse's mouth.

Jesús swung up onto his horse, saying, "I think we should follow his lead."

Already in his saddle, that was all Antonio needed to hear.

213

"Adios Amigo," he called as he spurred his steed down the path after Bad Haircut, who was already rounding the bend at the far end.

The red devils needed something to remember him by, Jesús decided, something that would hopefully buy them some time as well. In his saddlebag next to the newly attached ammunition bag was some residual dynamite from the recent jailbreak, another bundle of a half-dozen sticks. Initially, he had mused using both bundles at the time and was now glad he hadn't in more ways than one. If he'd done so, he would most likely have more than just wounded and deafened his lackeys; no, he would have killed all of them and probably demolished the building in the process. And that would have been quite unfortunate, not that the men might have died, but because then he would have to find more minions.

Hefting the dynamite in one hand, Jesús reined in his horse to steady its panicked trotting at the approach of the ants. He took a long drag off the half-smoked cigarillo hanging from the corner of his mouth, then touched its glowing tip to the dynamite's short fuse.

With a scowl, Jesús said, "Do not eat members of the Hole-in-the-Wall Gang!" He tossed the hissing bundle to the ground just in front of the approaching insectoid mass, then spun his horse and galloped down the trail in pursuit of Antonio.

**

Bad haircut rode hard and fast with little heed to where he was going. A bend in the trail was fast approaching, and he kept glancing back, straining to see if anything red was coming down the path behind him, but nothing was in sight yet.

He was just at the bend when No Neck stumbled from the underbrush onto the trail in front of his horse. Several ants clung to his back, and he squealed like a stuck pig. The creatures were dug in deep and firmly attached, worrying their knife-like mandibles into the soft flesh between his shoulder blades.

The horse was going too fast to stop, and with a terrified whinny, it plowed into the ravaged man and sent him flying forward down the path.

Slow to react, Bad Haircut discovered he couldn't stop his speeding mount's trajectory. They continued briefly forward until his horse stumbled over No Neck's prone form, and they both crashed to the ground.

Joining his ride in the dirt, Bad Haircut looked up in horror at what covered him and seemingly everything else in sight.

Stretched across the trees and bushes on both sides of the trail, hundreds and hundreds of spider webs billowed like a silken shroud in the growing breeze.

The panicked horse struggled upright almost immediately, still whinnying in fright, its fear giving it the strength to buck and shake itself free of the thick, clingy webs. Once clear, it bolted down the path toward town.

But Bad Haircut and No Neck were not as lucky as the horse. The webbing was quite sticky and surprisingly strong, and they struggled to free themselves. The ants attempting to imbed themselves in No Neck's back had tried to scramble free, but they, too, found themselves entangled in the webs.

"What the hell is this shit?" Bad haircut shouted in surprise. He tried to sit upright but discovered he was stuck fast to the ground by thick webbing that limited his movement.

No-neck was on his knees, shaking his head and trying to clear it. His forehead had impacted the trail's hard dirt with some force when the horse hit him, and it appeared he was suffering some after-effects from the blow. He groaned in semi-lucid pain and tugged at the web stuck all over his bald head and face.

Bad Haircut lay on his back, staring up into the trees that arched over the path. He blinked several times and rubbed at his eyes with his one free arm as if unsure he saw what he thought he was seeing. However, he quickly realised his eyes were not deceiving him and exclaimed, "Sweet Mother of God."

No Neck paused his attempts at freeing himself from the webbing to follow the other man's line of sight. As he did, he began to shriek, joining his already screaming buddy in a chorus of terror that sounded like the devil himself had suddenly appeared and was now trying to drag them both down to hell.

Though not from hell itself, the monstrous, spikey-legged spiders seemed the next worst thing. Dozens and dozens of the freakish creatures scampered down their sturdy threads, eager to see what they'd caught in their silken trap. Some were as large as a man's hand, while others were the size of his head.

Unexpectedly, the sound of a huge explosion tore through the day somewhere behind them. Almost immediately, hoofbeats sounded nearby, further distracting the men from their recent spate of screaming.

Antonio came charging around the bend, not paying heed to where he was going after the recent blast. Fortunately, he was able to rein in his horse at the last moment, his eyes widening in horror as he saw what was blocking the path.

"Help me, Antonio!" Bad Haircut cried.

"And me!" No Neck exclaimed. The movements of the ants stuck in the web around him were now slowing, the insects having just received bites from numerous fist-sized spiders that scampered in the web around them. Several had crawled onto the neckless man and begun to bite him as he pleaded, "Please tr..." He collapsed and rolled onto his back.

Antonio cringed back, seeing it was already too late to help either of the men. One of the largest spiders he'd ever seen dropped onto No Neck's potato-like head and clamped itself onto his face. The man squealed and shrieked but couldn't move his head or use his hands to free himself from the monstrous creature. Soon, his cries turned to muted gags as the arachnid began stuffing a moist, glistening tube protruding from its abdomen into his mouth. Almost immediately, an equally large spider dropped onto Bad Haircut, who was still stuck to the ground, then began positioning itself over the now-paralysed man's shrieking mouth.

Aghast at what was occurring before him, Antonio asked in a small voice, "Help you? How can I help you?" More spiders streamed down from above onto the trapped men, and he could see they were well and truly doomed, and there seemed nothing he could do, save one.

Drawing his revolver, Antonio aimed unsteadily at the spider on Bad Haircut's face, then pulled the trigger.

***

The explosion had been enough to jar the golden fillings in Jesús's mouth and make his ears ring, just as when he'd freed his companions from the jail. He galloped away from the horrors of the encampment, glad to be done with the deadly ants and heading back toward the safety of town and the promise of gold.

A bend in the path up ahead was fast approaching, but Jesús took a moment to look back at the results of his little explosive surprise. The smoke and debris were still raining down, and he began to smile. Hopefully, he had blown most of the diablos rojo to kingdom come, and they would think twice about attacking him in the future.

Returning his attention to the trail, Jesús pulled his horse up short, seeing the back end of Antonio's horse stopped just up ahead on the path.

A gunshot rang out, and Antonio said, "Shit, my aim was off! Sorry, amigo."

Jesús edged his horse the rest of the way around the bend to see who Antonio was talking to, or rather, who he had been talking to. With surprise and revulsion, he discovered that Bad Haircut could no longer be called that, for he no longer had any hair.

Antonio's poorly aimed shot had not only hit the monstrous spider on Bad Haircut's face but had also blown off the top of the man's skull, his grey matter now lying exposed to the air. Dozens of smaller spiders continued to descend from the trees, with several dropping into the sticky mass that remained in the man's brain pan.

"This is madness!" Jesús exclaimed. Somehow, he'd gone from impossibly large ants to freakishly huge spiders in less than a mile. What sort of place, filled with such beauty, could hide such horrors, he wondered.

Antonio turned away, heaving like he was going to throw up. But Jesús could not look away, and he watched, both horrified and fascinated, his eyes wide and glistening.

A large spider was clamped around No Neck's head like he'd placed a mask shaped like a spider onto his face. And this 'mask' appeared to be pulsing, as if filling him up with...

Suddenly overcome with revulsion, Jesús drew his revolver, took aim and pulled the trigger. The spider, along with most of No Neck's head, exploded in a splash of red, green and black goo, which sprayed all over the surrounding spider webs.

Antonio wiped the back of his hand across his face to remove some errant vomit dribbling down his chin. He looked to Jesús with an expression of confusion and horror. "Wha-what is this place? Monster ants? Giant spiders? Are we in hell?"

Jesús shook his head and said, "No, compadre. This is merely hell on earth. But do not worry, we are like angels and will get our golden reward very soon."

Antonio laughed weakly at this, sounding a bit more like his regular self. Of course, the swig of brandy he'd taken from the half-pint Jesús had pulled from an inner pocket had also helped. Antonio returned the green glass bottle to Jesús, wiping his mouth on his vomit-stained shirt sleeve.

The men backed their horses away from the web-covered section of the path as some of the spiders began crawling across the hard-packed dirt toward them. Their handguns easily took out the larger ones since they were a bit slower, but the smaller, hand-sized spiders were the ones they had to watch out for—they were much quicker and much harder to shoot. Jesús now wished he had not thrown the last of his dynamite at the surging ants since it would have been good to blow these venomous freaks back to hell.

Once at a safe distance, Jesús resolved then and there that these creatures, like the ants, could not be allowed to live, especially not after killing members of the Hole-in-the-Wall Gang, even if they were new and useless. He took another short pull on the Napoleon brandy and offered it again to Antonio, who took a quick swig and handed it back.

Jesús took a yellowed handkerchief from his pocket. He rolled up one end, stuck it into the half-empty brandy bottle, and then held it upside down briefly so the alcohol could moisten the hanky. With that done, he puffed on his dwindling cigarillo until the end glowed bright orange, then touched it to the handkerchief. Flames sprouted from the soaked cotton, and Jesús casually lobbed the now-flaming bomb onto the ground beneath the spider's webs.

The green glass shattered on impact, and a 'whoosh' of red-orange flames greedily licked up the silken webbing, then rushed into the dry fir branches overhead. The searing fire scorched across the spiders, and they plopped to the ground, twisted and blackened. Greenish ooze seeped from fissures in their charred chitin, their insides still crackling and popping from the intense heat that had flash-cooked them.

Giving a satisfied nod, Jesús said, "Let us go collect what is owed to us in town while it is still standing."

With Antonio following behind, Jesús guided his horse into the underbrush so they could detour around the spiderweb-clogged bend in the trail. As the horses crunched through the dry brush, a high-pitched keening came from the direction of the river. They were perhaps a mile from the encampment. The fact they could still hear the ants so loudly meant they were still alive and coming this way, and even dynamite couldn't stop them, it seemed. Jesús continued through the brush as they approached the town, avoiding the path. Somebody would be coming down that trail pretty quick to see about the fire, and it would be best to avoid meeting them on the way.

Smoke rose into the cloud-filled sky at their backs. The dynamite and his recent torching of the spiders appeared to have set the forest on fire. Jesús shrugged at the thought, not overly concerned, even if that were the case since it worked to his advantage. Between the fire and the approaching ants, he may have just created the ultimate diversion, one which would greatly aid his quest for more gold. An added bonus was that anyone of importance would be much more busy trying to save their pathetic little town from annihilation than they would be looking for the Hole-in-the-wall-Gang.

CHAPTER TWENTY-EIGHT

Ezra Randall's undertaking business had been booming over the last little while. He'd recently moved from down near the Nugget to a new building a couple of blocks up the main street. Now located on the edge of town, he was just next door to the new police station. With sleeping quarters upstairs, the new funeral parlour had a separate display room for coffins in front and a small chapel off to one side. The preparation room and embalming table were in the back, right next to the receiving door.

Sandy now stood outside this door, the remains of Sam Shepherd slung over one shoulder. From what he recalled, Ezra kept the receiving door unlocked in the daytime while working. That had been the case last week when Sandy brought over Farley Jones's cadaver and also the next day when he'd come back to collect the pine coffin for burial. He hadn't seen the undertaker since, and today, for some reason, the door was locked. Was Ezra actually closed after all?

From what Sandy understood, Mr. Sinclair had sent the undertaker by the ice house to retrieve the body of Teddy Malone, but that had been a couple of days ago. As he pondered that, Sandy also recalled Ezra hadn't been into the Nugget for his usual roast beef, Yorkshire pudding and large glass of port this week. It had become a bit of a tradition on Friday evenings back when Ezra's office had been just a few doors down from the Nugget. Oh well, maybe the man was changing his routine a bit, being so busy and all.

A side door led to the chapel, and Sandy found it unlocked. He knocked, poked his head tentatively inside, and called, "Mr. Randall?" There was no response, and he moved across the threshold to explore the funeral parlour's further recesses. Calling out as he moved through the chapel, his voice echoed slightly off the walls, which were bare, save for a large crucifix over the pulpit.

Ezra lived here alone, apart from the cadavers he sometimes shared the space with. Just the thought gave Sandy the creeps and enough to have him not sleep for a week. It was bad enough having Sam's corpse draped over his shoulder, but at least it seemed more like a bundle of laundry than a man at the moment, thanks to Sam's now more compact size. He shook his head. How Ezra could sleep here each night after what he had to do here each day was beyond him. Calling out again, he moved to the back where the embalming table lay.

Sandy recalled the day he'd brought Farley over here. It had been just after hearing Caleb and Kitty's description of the man's demise and after the doctor had shown him the jarful of spiders he'd captured. That day, Sandy had transported the cadaver on a cart rather than over his shoulder, just in case. It had been well-wrapped in a thick layer of tarp, and the Doc had assured him the spiders were all gone. Nonetheless, he'd had a bad case of the heebie-jeebies the whole time. When he'd finally deposited Farley on the table, Ezra had remarked that even though he'd been in the business of death for so many years, he found the demise of Jones to be particularly disturbing.

With a sigh, Sandy placed the remains of Sam on the same table he'd placed Farley just the previous week. Ezra used the table for embalming, but only when requested or required. He'd told Sandy he generally didn't bother to do such a thing for people interred locally and reserved it for cadavers being transported over a distance. He'd added that the procedure was not without its risks to the undertakers themselves due to the toxicity of the chemicals used. On a shelf along one wall were several glass bottles labelled 'Arsenical Fluid', amongst others, which he used in the process.

Strangely, the undertaker also used this prep area as his kitchen. No matter how appealing the meal may be, Sandy couldn't imagine eating it in a room where someone's internal organs had been removed and their body cavity filled with sawdust only hours before. But maybe it was because the plumbing was already located here for the undertaking business, making it a convenient location for the kitchen as well.

This town was among the first in the West Kootenays to have indoor plumbing in many of its structures. A water supply and sewer system had been installed as the town had grown up around it, just after the Golden Nugget's construction. This system had been Mr. Sinclair's idea, who'd designed it to be similar to what Vancouver had installed almost a decade before, just after the great fire decimated that city in 1886. With a shake of his head, Sandy hoped such a thing never came to pass here.

"Mr. Randall? You here?" he called again. Not getting an answer, Sandy entered the front parlour of the house that also served as a showroom for several different models of caskets, depending on the deceased's level of wealth. There was maple with sturdy steel accoutrements for modest budgets, oak with elaborate brass fittings for the more well-heeled, and finally, for those of less fortunate financial standings, plain old pine. But apart from the coffins, the room was devoid of anyone living.

Clumping loudly in his heavy boots, Sandy climbed the flight of steep stairs to the finished loft but did so with difficulty. His boots were larger than the stair's narrow tread by several inches, and he had to climb on the pads of his feet.

Due to the steep angle of the surrounding roof, there were only two rooms in the loft. One was Ezra's bedroom, the bed made, neat and tidy, the other seemed for storage of various tools of the trade, and neither contained Ezra.

Stopping in the street-level display room one final time, Sandy thought of what Mr. Holmes would do. Though he was just getting into The Adventures of Sherlock Holmes, he had already learned that once a person rules out the impossible, whatever is left, however improbable, must be the truth. And now, looking about the room more critically, Sandy noted something out of place which he hadn't noticed when he'd first entered—something Mr. Holmes would have spotted right away.

A series of coffins stood open and leaning against one wall, almost upright as if inviting customers to come and check out their comfortable and luxurious silk-pillowed interiors. However, the oak coffin with the brass fittings was closed for some reason. What was the truth behind that, Sandy wondered.

There was something black hanging out of one side, halfway down. In fact, it looked like a coattail that belonged to the long, black jacket Mr. Randall wore. Was he storing his clothes inside one of the coffins now?

With a deep breath, Sandy steeled himself, then carefully opened the top half of the coffin where a person could view their loved one resting peacefully in their new eternal home.

Sandy staggered back, letting the coffin lid drop closed with a bang. He had found Ezra Randall, but unfortunately, it seemed that something had found Ezra as well.

Inside the coffin were hundreds and hundreds of spiderlings crawling all over his now withered corpse, encased from head to toe in spider silk. But why was he in this coffin?

Had someone put him there? Or had the man noticed something crawling up his leg, and as he tried to knock the venomous creature from his body, it had bitten him, and he'd tumbled into the coffin? Sandy could picture the coffin doors slamming shut as Ezra lay paralysed but alive inside, the spider now free to have its way with him. He shuddered heavily at the thought.

Had there been spiders still in Teddy Malone's corpse? Or perhaps left inside Farley Jones, which had somehow escaped the doctor's detection? Thinking of the man's drinking habits and volume he regularly consumed, Sandy realised it was quite possible.

As that thought filtered through his mind, Sandy spied a couple of spiderlings that had escaped when he'd lifted the lid. They scampered rapidly down the casket's side and hit the floor running. After a bit of cursing and stomping, Sandy eventually got them both. About to breathe a sigh of relief, he cried in horror instead when he discovered one spider he'd missed, now crawling up his bare forearm.

Sandy grunted in disgust and swatted at the creature, hoping to get it off his person before it could bite him, but he was too late. As he wicked the little beast from his skin, he felt its sting. It dropped to the floor with a soft plop, and he stomped on it like the others. However, the damage was done, and his right arm went suddenly numb, dropping limply to his side. Though the spider had been small, its toxic venom seemed nonetheless potent.

Hoping that the spider's bite wouldn't spread beyond his limp arm, Sandy hurried to the exit, looking everywhere at once and wondering if there were any more spiders loose in this place of death.

Sandy pressed the door closed with his back and breathed a momentary sigh of relief. He massaged his useless arm, feeling no sensation whatsoever like he had fallen asleep on it and just woken up. Though he'd witnessed Doc Brown's larger, caged spider bring down a man a little smaller than him with one bite, he wanted to make sure he was going to be okay and figured another visit to the Doc's office would be in order.

The already interesting day became a little bit more so when another explosion sounded in the distance, this time from the direction of the river. What was going on now, he wondered. Was it another blast set by the same outlaws that had demolished the jail? Whatever it was, he figured they would all find out soon enough.

CHAPTER TWENTY-NINE

Young Caleb kicked the can back to his friend, saying, "You've gotta do better than that, Paddy boy! There's no way you're gettin' another one past me!"

Patrick passed the tin can, currently substituting for a ball, to Sean, Caleb's other friend, who made a stumbling pass back to Patrick. Sean was arguably a worse football player than Caleb, which was saying something, and it was quite surprising how that Sunday afternoon in Dublin eventually turned out.

With the obligatory morning church service out of the way, the boys had been freed from their duties for the day. Feeling the need to burn off some energy, and since the afternoon was grey and rainy, the trio had ended up in a favourite spot, an abandoned warehouse a couple of blocks from where they lived.

Fading back, Patrick kicked the can behind himself, then tapped it over to Sean, who lashed out reflexively with one foot. It connected squarely, and the can flew straight and true toward Caleb, who dived toward it, stopping it with his head.

The evening stars suddenly appeared, and Caleb smashed into a dividing wall that separated the warehouse from the small suite of offices near the front door. Like the warehouse itself, the wall was old, its plaster crumbling like chalk, and it did nothing to hinder Caleb's velocity. And so, like a one-boy wrecking crew, he crashed into a narrow gap between the outer brick and mortar and the inner plaster and lath.

At that point, it became an afternoon of discovery for young Caleb. First, he found he couldn't move his arms or turn over and was, in fact, wedged in the wall. Patrick and Sean had thought this hilarious and ignored his pleas to pull him out. Arms pinned to his side, legs sticking out of the gap in the wall, Caleb had called to the boys for several minutes, thinking they were only pretending to be gone. But after a while, he discovered he was well and truly alone and that his so-called friends had abandoned him to his fate.

For the longest while, Caleb listened to the gentle rain of the late April afternoon ticking and tapping against the crumbling shingles overhead. It rushed along cracked gutters and into broken downspouts, finally draining into the River Liffey beyond. Soon, he began to feel a growing need to pee, no doubt aided by the sound of the running water.

It was then Caleb made his final discovery—that he was not alone.

At first, the noise had blended with the ticking and tapping of the rain, but then, as it had drawn closer, Caleb had been able to identify it better, much to his dismay. Wide-eyed, he watched a frighteningly large spider (at least what he'd thought of as frighteningly large back then) drop down onto a piece of broken lath near his head.

Never a fan of spiders to begin with, Caleb had screamed quite solidly for several long moments. Despite that, no one had come to his aid since the other buildings around the warehouse were long abandoned.

The long-legged arachnid had been unfazed by Caleb's histrionics and, when he'd finished, had still been crouched next to his head, staring at him with its multitude of black eyes.

But that hadn't even been the worst of it. No, that prize would have gone to the egg sacs Caleb prematurely ruptured with his untimely and blundering intrusion into the spider's world. The sacs in question were right next to his head, opposite from mama spider, and he'd broken them open during his thrashing fit of fear. Despite his further screams of protest, the spider scuttled its spiky-tipped legs across the tender young flesh of Caleb's face to greet the new arrivals into the world.

Hundreds and hundreds of tiny spiderlings now crawled out of the egg sacs torn asunder in his fall. They crept over his face, his neck, down his shirt collar, into his ears and up his nose. You name it, they went there, or so it felt. It was a complete violation of his being, a horrific experience he'd endured for what felt like days and weeks rather than the hours and minutes it was.

Ultimately, his mother had saved the day when she'd informed the mothers of both Patrick and Sean that Caleb hadn't shown up for Sunday dinner. Upon learning this, his 'friends' had returned to the warehouse to find Caleb still where they'd left him. Though they later told him of the relatively short time he'd spent stuck in the wall, to young Caleb's mind, he felt he'd been flung into perdition and destined to spend eternity in a straight-jacketed hell of damp, dark and spiders.

When they'd pulled Caleb out, he'd been uncommunicative and staring blankly. The trauma had so shaken him, it had taken several days for him to finally come back to himself. For the longest time afterwards, whenever he'd felt an innocent tickle or itch somewhere on his body, he would slap crazily at the spot and everywhere nearby, triggered by the mere thought of a spider anywhere on his person.

But fortunately, those spiders hadn't been venomous, and the baby spiders hadn't lain any eggs in Caleb's ear canals or sinuses because they couldn't, of course, as far as he knew. Unfortunately, the experience had left its mark. To this day, when he got a tickle in his nose or an itch in his ear, he sometimes wondered if there were spiderlings that had never found their way out of his head and were still crawling around somewhere inside.

And right now, all that came flooding back to Caleb as the monstrously large spider quivered before him, ready to release the tension in its legs and pounce upon him.

Doctor Brown came hurrying around the corner from the back room, saying, "Did you capture it?"

Caleb was rooted to the floor, the counter digging into his back. "I can't get to the net, Doc! It looks like it's goin' to leap if I move!" He was sure the spider would jump him and inject him with its venom if he made any sudden moves, and yet if he did nothing, it might still do the same. He stood frozen with indecision.

The doctor was too far from the long-handled net to utilise it but found a nearby alternative. Moving with surprising speed for a man of his advancing and unsober years, Brown scooped the green metal pail off the examination table and slapped it overtop the spider in one smooth motion, then said triumphantly, "Never fear, Brown is here!"

It turned out the spider was the one that needed to be fear-filled, or at least pain-filled. Many of the creature's legs had been outside the circumference of the pail's rim when the doctor slammed it down, and unfortunately, two were amputated in the process. They lay twitching on the dusty floor, green goo oozing from their wounded ends. The spider jiggled and jerked under the container, making noises as if it had a slow leak once again. The pail's handle rattled against its side as the spider scuttled its remaining legs about, dragging the bucket in small circles on the floor as it tried to escape. To Caleb, it looked for all the world like a monstrous hermit crab that had just found a new home. He gave an audible sigh and said, "Thanks, Doc."

"You're welcome, my boy." Brown retrieved the amputated legs from the floor and marvelled at them for a moment. "However, this is unfortunate. I wanted to keep our friend here in one piece." He placed the no longer twitching limbs onto the examination table.

"I'm sorry to disappoint you, Doc." Caleb was trying to sound more relaxed than he felt but was unsure if he was succeeding. His nerves still felt raw after his recent encounter with the eight-legged hellspawn.

"That's quite all right." Brown flattened one of the cardboard cracker cartons, then bent down and slid it under the pail's edge. After a brief bit of jiggling, he stood and transferred the wounded spider back to the bird cage, adding, "I suppose this will be a good opportunity to study the inner workings of our friend here."

Caleb had watched the doctor for a moment but then turned and looked out the front window. "Whatever floats your boat, Doc." He wasn't particularly interested in what was outside the window at the moment but rather wanted to avoid looking at the grotesque spider any more than he had to.

"And speaking of inner workings, before you go anywhere, I'm afraid you'll need some sutures, my boy."

Caleb turned back in surprise and said, "But I thought you said I was okay!"

Brown nodded toward Caleb's pant leg. "You might not want so much exposed skin with everything crawling around out there, not that a thin layer of cotton is much protection, but it's better than nothing."

Caleb's trouser leg had been cut halfway up to allow him to pull his dungarees over his cast. But now, they just flapped in the breeze, and he realised the doctor had a point. "Yes, if you could throw in a couple of quick stitches, that'd be great, Doc."

Within a couple of minutes, Caleb's trousers no longer flapped about his leg, and he sported a neatly stitched temporary seam made of suture silk. He stood and looked at it admiringly. "Thanks, Doc. Now I can go see what's happenin' around this town without flappin' in the breeze."

"Just take it easy until we can be more certain of your leg," Brown advised.

"It'll be at the forefront of my mind, Doc." His hand now on the door handle, Caleb paused and asked, "So what're you up to now?"

Brown gestured to the remains of the ant in the washtub and said, "I think I have a plan which I want to put into motion."

"A plan? What d'ya mean?"

"With this colony looking for new food sources, we'll no doubt be making more contact with these little red devils, and I want to be prepared because I feel we're going to be seeing more of them sooner rather than later."

"And what have you been up to?"

"Well, after receiving the captured ant from Sandy earlier this morning, I returned to the trash bin behind the Nugget's kitchen to look for samples of what may have attracted it in the first place. I retrieved several empty tins, a couple of waxed cardboard cracker cartons, and a piece of brown butcher paper used to wrap raw meat. And so, I tested these items and discovered some surprising results. Afterwards, I immediately enlisted the aid of a friend of ours, and I'm hoping things work out."

Caleb was going to ask for more clarification on the doctor's tests when another shuddering explosion ripped through the sweltering calm of the summer afternoon, sounding even louder than the previous one. He took a small step back in surprise and squinted through the half-glass in the door's upper half. "What in blue blazes is that?" He answered his own question almost immediately, saying, "Whatever the cause, it can't be good."

"Undoubtedly." Brown peered out the front window, noting the smoke rising from the forest. "I wonder if Angus will need me at the firehall soon."

In addition to working his practice, the doctor told Caleb that he was also part of the volunteer fire department, though he didn't actually fight the fires. Sandy had been the one that talked him into volunteering, saying the doctor's medical expertise might prove valuable at some of their callouts.

Caleb nodded, "I think I'm apt to agree with you, Doc. Maybe I'll head over with you to the smithy in case Angus needs another able-bodied hand."

"Actually, he does." Brown moved to the front door and joined Caleb. "Not only was Sam Shepherd a friend of mine, but he was also a volunteer firefighter." He opened the door and gestured for Caleb to go first, saying, "I need to top up my extinguisher and grab a couple more things. You go ahead, and I'll meet you there."

Moving out the door, Caleb said, "Guess I'm goin' to get a chance to test out my new leg sooner than I thought." In the back of his mind, a part of him wondered, in light of what had transpired so far, if he'd still be able to walk, let alone breathe, come this day's end.

CHAPTER THIRTY

Sandy hustled down the dusty street, his right arm limp and dangling. No matter how much he tried to will it to do something, it only hung there, useless. He had to hold it next to his body with his left hand to stop it from flopping around as he moved. The spider's bite had rendered him the same as a stroke victim. He'd had an uncle who'd suffered one and became paralysed down his entire right side and unable to speak. Uncle Mort had recovered from his stroke somewhat since, but he still wasn't quite what he used to be, and Sandy could now understand quite acutely what the man must have gone through.

Smoke drifted into the air from the direction of the river, and he could smell it faintly already. It had started just after the blast and had gotten worse only a few moments later. Sandy was in disbelief that some numbnut had decided to play with dynamite in the middle of a dry forest. As spring had waned in the valley, the start of summer had been hot and dry with little rain. A person had to be careful in the bush not to smoke or create a spark, or else there could be trouble. But judging by the amount of smoke, common sense seemed something the person with the dynamite hadn't possessed, and they were either careless, clueless or both.

When Sandy had left Ezra's, he'd thought of checking in with the Doc about his spider bite, but since the smoke was growing thicker by the minute, he'd decided he best head to the smithy instead. He didn't feel too bad at the moment. Despite his limited abilities, he figured he should still be able to volunteer and help out on the pumper wagon. He recalled how Chief Angus had marvelled at his being able to pump it all by himself when it normally required four sturdy men, two on each side. With his upper body now running at half-capacity, Sandy felt confident he could still do the work of at least two volunteers.

In addition to himself and Chief Angus, some of the other ragtag members of the town's volunteer firefighters included Police Chief Hildey Dugrodt, Doc Brown and, until recently, Sam Shepherd. Sandy shook his head sadly. In addition to being Doc's drinking buddy, Sam had also been a helpful team member. He'd shown up rain or shine whenever the alarm bell sounded at the firehall, though sometimes a little less sober than others.

No sooner had all these thoughts finished percolating through Sandy's mind when he heard the fire bell start ringing at the smithy. He hurried a bit faster down the dusty street, trying to run a little, but it seemed the spider bite had affected him more than he'd thought. When he went too fast, he felt like he might trip and fall, so instead, he stuck to what seemed to be working and continued walking as fast as he could.

Within a few minutes, he was nearing the smithy, only to discover Doc Brown arriving just ahead of him. The doctor clanged as he walked, now sporting dual extinguishers under each arm, his leather satchel slung across his shoulders. Angus was on the other side of the courtyard hooking mules Ester and Camille to the front of the pumper wagon. And Mr. Caleb was also there, walking around without any crutches or a cast! What kind of magic was this, Sandy wondered, and he called out, "Mr. Caleb! What happened to your foot plaster?"

Caleb looked down at his leg and shook his head. "I can't tell you, lad, and neither can the Doc. I got it wet and was going to have it replastered, but when the Doc checked it, he said it looked healed."

Brown nodded in agreement, saying, "It seems a miraculous recovery on our Irish friend's part, to be sure."

"How's it feeling?" Sandy inquired.

"Like I could run all the way back to Ireland."

"Gosh, that's a long way! You should pack a lunch first."

Caleb laughed and said, "And I'll make sure to bring some extra socks." With widening eyes, he noticed Sandy holding his arm and asked, "And what's happened to you, lad?"

"That's something I was comin' to tell ya, and the Doc, too."

"What is it, my boy?"

"I got bit!"

"By what?" Caleb wondered. "So many things around here could've done the job."

"More spiders!" Sandy said excitedly.

"Where?" Brown asked, and then his eyes grew large, and he answered his own question, saying, "The undertaker's?"

"Sure enough! I couldn't find Ezra anywhere until the very last."

"Where was he?" Caleb asked.

"In a coffin!"

"A coffin?" Caleb and the doctor both inquired

simultaneously.

"Who's in a coffin?" Angus asked, just finished with the mules.

"Ezra, the undertaker. I think he hid inside or fell into it, along with the spider that bit him. The inside of the coffin was swarming with them. And one of them bit me! Now my arm is sleepin'." He grasped his limp arm, held it out, and let it drop to his side to prove his point.

Caleb said nothing but shuddered involuntarily at the image Sandy had described.

"Well, we know where to go with these—after the fire, at least." The doctor patted twin fire extinguishers, one slung under each arm, filled with his acid mixture. He explained, "I borrowed an extra extinguisher from the Nugget earlier this morning when I finished picking through the trash out back."

From Sandy's paralysed side, Rufus suddenly appeared with a 'woof'. The wolfhound placed his paws on the boy's shoulder and gave him a quick but thorough face washing. "Hey, fella! How are you?" Sandy laughed and reached around with his good arm to give Rufus a combination pet and hug, then lowered the large dog back to the ground and scruffed his head some more.

"He's fine." Police Chief Hildey Dugrodt answered for the dog, joining the other volunteers. To Sandy, he said, "I tried to leave him at the station with VanDusen, but Rufus wouldn't have any of it. And on the walk here, once we got a half block away, he spotted you, and there was no stopping him."

With his head scruff complete, the dog trotted over and began licking the chief's hand as if apologising for deserting him partway through their walk to the smithy.

Dugrodt nodded toward the rising smoke cloud as he

petted the dog. "I see we got something going on near the river. Must have been the same blasted fool who blew a hole in my jail."

"I'd be prone to agree with you," Caleb said.

Hildey looked down at Caleb's leg and observed, "I see you're out of your cast."

"You've got a keen eye, Chief. Apparently, I'm a rapid healer."

"Well, that's good news then! You're hereby a duly deputised member of the local fire department," Angus proclaimed proudly.

"You didn't even give me a chance to volunteer!" Caleb said with half a laugh.

"Things move fast around this town. And besides, with the demise of Sam, we're one hand short now," Angus replied.

"The Doc and I were talking about that just a short while ago, and I hope I can fill in and do him proud," Caleb said with a slight nod.

"No disrespect to the dead, but at least you're sober, so that's a good start." Chief Hildey replied.

Angus tied Rufus to a hitching post in the shade of a willow tree. The lead was long enough that the dog could get a drink from the creek if he wished. He scruffed the dog's head and said, "We don't want you getting underfoot out there."

Caleb stood watching the chief tie the dog up. He was about to see if there was anything else he could do before departing for the fire when someone suddenly gave him a gentle but forceful shove in the back, sending him stumbling slightly forward. "What in the..." He whirled around and saw a friend he'd been neglecting standing behind him.

"Well, hello, Emily." He scruffed the mule's mane and she whinnied in delight. As he did, the animal nudged her nose at the pocket of his dungarees.

Shaking his head sadly, Caleb said, "No, I'm all out of sugar cubes. I've got to go and help the firemen right now, so you'll have to wait until I get back." Emily snorted at him as if disappointed. Continuing to pet the mule, Caleb led her back to the stable and closed the bottom half of the door so she couldn't wander away, but could still see outside. She whinnied again, staring dolefully at him with her big brown eyes as he walked away.

With the dog and mule secured and everything ready to go, the men climbed aboard the wagon. Angus flicked the reins, spurring the mule team into action. With a jolting start, they bumped down the rutted street toward the forest and the site of the billowing smoke.

***

Caleb held onto the side of the pumper wagon as it bounced along the narrow trail toward the river. One of the spots they'd just ridden over had caused such a jolt he'd bitten his lip. He tasted blood as he probed it with his tongue and grimaced. And because it was so dry, dust kicked up something fierce and seemed to go everywhere. He sneezed, then wiped his nose with the sleeve of his dusty shirt. The smoke hadn't been helping things either, and the closer they got to the river, the thicker it got—things didn't look good. Hints of yellow-orange flames shot above the trees on the smoky horizon, and the warmth of the summer day seemed amplified, thanks to the heat of the growing fire in the small valley.

Across the wagon from Caleb, hanging on for dear life, was Doc Brown. His acid-filled fire extinguishers rattled against the side of the pumper tank as they clattered along. Sandy was next to Caleb and clung tightly to one of the wagon's brass handles with his good arm. Fortunately, the spider bite hadn't spread and seemed only to have affected the right side of his upper body. Next to the doctor was Lucias, of all people. The man in black had arrived at the last moment and flagged them down in the street, saying Sinclair wanted him to help protect his interests and ensure the fire didn't get anywhere near town. Chief Hildey rode shotgun beside Chief Angus, currently guiding the mule team down the narrow trail.

As they came around a bend, things came to a sudden, juddering stop. The water inside the five-hundred-gallon tank sloshed back and forth, causing the pumper to rock forward and backwards several times as the men climbed down from the wagon.

"What in the hell happened here?" Chief Hildey wondered aloud.

A group of trees which straddled the path had been set alight for some reason. Fortunately, their initial blaze had burned toward the river rather than the town, thanks to the direction of a strengthening breeze. The clouds overhead were a tumultuous bruise of purple-grey, the remaining blue sky of earlier in the day now almost gone.

Intertwined in the centre of the trail lay the blackened remains of two men. One of the still smouldering corpses was missing its head, the other the top of its brain pan. Around them lay the curled, crispy remains of numerous spiders.

"I'd say we found the source of the fire," Angus said.

Caleb replied, "But this isn't the source of the explosion we heard earlier. There's no sign of a crater." From his days in the army, he knew what an impact crater looked like after a mortar or cannon had battered the landscape. The area near the trees was charred, but the ground around them still seemed intact. Whatever the reason for the explosion they'd heard, it had happened closer to the river.

"That's right," Sandy agreed. "Things are only burnt here."

"And whatever happened, ants were involved, too," Caleb noted. He flipped a piece of debris over with his foot. On the other side, one corner was a bright, fiery red. He stepped on the ant's shell with a crunch, giving his new leg a stretch.

"But it wasn't the spiders or the ants that killed these men." Brown pointed to the damage done to the heads of the immolated men and finished, "Someone put these men out of their misery, it would seem."

"Or killed them because they couldn't be bothered to save them," Caleb offered, recalling Jesús Oritz and what he knew of the gang leader.

"Either way, that's not good," Sandy said, alarm in his eyes as he scanned the immediate area, no doubt looking for anything creeping or crawling in their general direction.

Angus nodded, saying, "At least the wind was blowing away from town when this was lit."

"Well, I think it's headin' back this way!" Caleb coughed, his eyes watering from the thickening smoke now blowing in their direction.

The fire had burned away from the trail a short distance, going sideways as it did. But thanks to its growing size, the blaze had changed course again and now licked back toward the group of men and the direction of town. A separate fire burning closer to the river was also being driven toward them, thanks to the increasingly erratic breeze. Part of it seemed caused by the incoming storm front, but another part seemed driven by the fire itself. As the vegetation and trees burned all around, great volumes of air were drawn in to feed the ravenous flames. This created an updraft, and Caleb could see burning embers begin to blow high into the cloud-filled sky, making him worry about fires yet to come, depending on where the embers landed.

Caleb unfurled the hose while Sandy stayed beside the wagon, left hand on the pumper handle and ready to go. Though the muscular boy could likely work the pumper by himself with one hand, Lucias and Chief Hildey joined him, manning the handle on the other side. Sandy gave a nod, and together they began to pump.

Gathering up the nozzle, Chief Angus pulled the brass lever and began spraying everything he could, trying to knock back some of the approaching flames. But the heat was intense, and the pumper's short throw and small stream of water did little good against the ferocious fire.

After a moment, the fire chief shook his head and shouted, "It's no good! It's too far gone! We'll have to hope the wind changes. Nothing more can be done except head back toward town and wet whatever we can because if anything catches there, we're going to be in big trouble!"

Brown heard the sound first, his ears perhaps more attuned to it than the other men. He handed one of his extinguishers to Caleb, saying, "I think our trouble just got smaller and bigger both at the same time."

"What do you mean, Doc?" Caleb slung the extinguisher over his shoulder and heard what the doctor had been talking about as he did. A high-pitched keening, barely audible over the crackling of the approaching fire, was growing closer by the second.

The first handful of the colony's scouts had arrived, now only a dozen yards away. Caleb figured something had gotten them riled up—possibly the explosion they'd heard; otherwise, the creatures would have been underground and well away from the fire's heat.

Sandy was readying some rocks to throw, stacking them along the rear edge of the pumper's frame with his one good hand. To his side, Lucias had pulled his Winchester from the sling under his arm and now drew a bead on the advancing ants.

A flash of his time inside the cavern came back to Caleb, and he briefly relived the toss of his nitro-filled pack at the pursuing ants. Though the earlier blast near the river had been dynamite, it had the same effect as his nitro had and only further riled the creatures. Thinking of the angry ants, he suddenly recalled what had caused the animals to attack him in the first place—when he'd defensively lashed out his boot at the first scout. He called, "These are only the vanguard, and they really don't like it when you get aggressive with them. When I kicked one in the cavern, that's when they attacked me!"

The men paused their extermination efforts for a moment. Lucias reluctantly returned the Winchester to its sling. Sandy hefted a grapefruit-sized rock in his hand for a moment before placing it back on the edge of the pumper, saying, "Well, they better stay well away if'n they know what's good for them. I'm a great shot!"

With a nod to the boy, Lucias said, "Me, too, kid."

Behind the scouts, across a small meadow, ant after ant scuttled toward them in a red wave of death. Whether it was their appetite or the blazing forest at their back that provided the impetus, whatever the reason, the colony's arrival seemed imminent and inescapable. The vanguard seemed emboldened by their approaching comrades; keening and clacking, they now scuttled closer.

Brown said, "Let's see if the new formula works better on these little fellows." With that, Caleb and the doctor began pumping and spraying as the creatures approached.

Though it looked like water, when the extinguishers' spray splashed on several ants and the ground before them, the agitated animals stopped in their tracks and skittered back several feet. Their high-pitched chittering now had a different tone and oscillated slightly, perhaps warning those behind.

"A resounding success, I'd say!" Brown shouted in glee.

Caleb and the doctor continued to spray a defensive line of acid solution along the ground. Anywhere the spray hit, the oncoming ants refused to go, and it seemed the doctor was quite correct. However, the main complement was still advancing across the meadow, and there was no way they would have enough solution to keep the creatures at bay for long.

With that in mind and panic mounting in his voice, Caleb said, "There are just too many of them for the amount of spray we've got in these things, Doc!"

"I'm afraid you're right. Effective though it is, we're going to be soon overwhelmed."

Angus said, "You two keep spraying that stuff around here." He gestured in front of and around the wagon where the ants would soon arrive. Nodding his head toward the mules, the fire chief added, "I want to get Ester and Camille turned around before those things get here."

The doctor and Caleb began pumping their extinguishers for all they were worth. And though the fluid soaked into the dry ground, the ants still refused to cross over it toward them.

Sandy looked to the doctor, eyes wide, and said, "Do you think they'll keep comin' this way toward town? Or will that stop them and send them elsewhere?"

Brown shook his head and said, "I'm afraid not, my boy. They'll easily go around this with the fire burning at their backs and forcing them forward."

Caleb said, "Unless the wind changes, at the speed they're travelling, these buggers will probably reach the town within a half hour!"

With the scouts held at bay for the moment, he reached into the satchel across his shoulder, saying, "Let's see if we can slow them down a bit."

Brown withdrew a handful of small beige balls from the satchel and lobbed them, one by one, toward the remaining scouts on the other side of the defensive acid line on the ground.

"What're you doin', Doc?" Sandy said in surprise. "Feedin' them?"

Brown shook his head and said, "Hopefully, these are something that should give them a very bad case of indigestion."

They watched as the ants eagerly gobbled down the small balls, some taking the remains in their mandibles and retreating toward the advancing army.

"That's what I was hoping to see!" Brown cried.

The doctor withdrew another handful of balls and tossed them to the remaining scouts that hadn't yet had a taste.

Hildey shook his head as he watched the ants feast and said, "Your snacks don't seem to be slowing them down too much."

"Is that poison, Doc?" Caleb asked.

"In a way," Brown replied, then tossed the remaining bait to the ants. He turned the satchel upside down and shook it, saying, "But that's all I've got for now. We'll need to make more when we get back to town."

"Please tell me you have some of that cyanide in there that you were experimentin' with?"

"Heaven's no! That would be far too dangerous to the local ecology. Unfortunately, my hors-d'oeuvres might take a little while. They need to be shared amongst the colony."

"But how long, Doc?" Caleb inquired, his eyes growing large at the advancing wave of ants.

"If some of this compound makes it back to the colony's food stores, and they all partake, it could wipe out the colony, but it might take up to a week."

"A week! We might all be ant food by then," Caleb exclaimed with disbelief.

"Sadly, that is a possibility, yes," The doctor replied with a nod.

Fortunately, the coordinated spraying of the acetic acid had been effective long enough, and Angus had the wagon finally turned around. His voice horse from shouting, he commanded, "Let's get the hell out of here!"

There was no argument from the group of men, and they leapt onto the side of the wagon. The mules needed little encouragement when Angus flicked the reins, and they took off with a jolting start, the minimal water remaining in the pumper wagon sloshing hollowly.

Along the trail back to town, they encountered several men approaching on foot and horseback, coming to aid in the firefighting. Angus and Hildey waved them off and sent them back to town, telling them they had bigger problems than the fire.

Shaking his head as he bounced about, Caleb muttered, "Nothin' but more bad cess." He'd been hoping to easily get rid of the ants down at the river once the spider situation was under control, but that plan seemed to have gone out the window. And from what Sandy said, there were now more spiders to take care of in the undertaker's house and wherever else the damnable creatures had been laying their eggs.

It seemed the little town he was starting to grow fond of faced multiple perils. They would either succumb to a plague of giant ants, be impregnated by a horde of monstrous spiders, or get burned alive by a raging fire. If they were really unlucky, and that seemed the way of things at the moment, Caleb figured it would be an apocalyptic trifecta of all three.

No matter which way Caleb sliced it, it seemed all of their collective woes were caused by one thing, his greed. He thought once again of what might have been if only he'd bypassed this valley and headed over the pass toward Sproat's Landing. So much would be different if he'd never found that cavern. Several people would still be alive, and no fire would threaten the town because no outlaw gang would have come through this valley and encountered the horrors he'd unleashed. All in all, life would have continued as normal for almost everyone involved. But now, thanks to him, things in this valley might not be approaching normal or anything like it for a very long time to come.

CHAPTER THIRTY-ONE

The guillotine's blade dropped down, snipping the tip from the cigar Sinclair had offered. This brought a thin smile to Jesús's lips. He reached across the desk and took the cigar from his host with a nod, then grinned more broadly, saying, "That is a lovely little toy, Mister Sinclair. Something my boys would love to play with back home, though I am sure their mama would disagree."

Lighting a match with his fingernail, Oritz touched it to his cigar. He puffed for a moment, then angled his head toward the other toys in the man's glass and oak display case across the room. "And it looks like you have more than a passing interest in similar objects." Housing all manner of strange and interesting things: from books and photos to knives and swords, it seemed to have it all, including some obsidian gemstones so dark they seemed made of midnight.

Puffing on a fresh cigar he'd just decapitated for himself, Sinclair said, "Aye, but those are more than just toys, my friend. I am a collector of all things arcane." Sinclair blew a smoke ring and added somewhat snidely, "D'ya know anything of the subject?"

"I have seen many odd and mystifying things over the years, but one of the strangest I've seen are men who are unwavering in their belief in their God above. I find it mysterious that a grown man could believe a beneficent hand might reach down from the sky and pluck them to safety or save them from death." He shook his head and finished, saying, "Let me tell you, most of them were sorely mistaken."

Sinclair eyed Oritz for a long moment, peering over his crystal tumbler of scotch. "We two are a lot alike."

"Are we?" Jesús took a sip of his own scotch, enjoying the burn as it ran down his throat.

"Yes, we are. We're both immigrants to this country. And both have worked incredibly hard to get where we are."

Jesús nodded. "You are quite correct. Though I would say that we have approached things from different angles."

Sinclair shook his head and said, "I'd wager those angles were not so different after all."

Though Jesús wanted to keep things rolling along in case any of the diablos rojos made it into town before he finished his transaction, he wanted to ensure he got everything coming to him first. And one of the biggest things he craved at the moment, perhaps even more than the gold, was information. And so he said, "Regardless, one thing that I am, is baffled."

"Really?" Sinclair asked.

"Yes. Why were you willing to assume the Irishman's debt to us." Oritz gestured toward the eight sacks lined up along the wall near the office door. He and Antonio had already been shown their contents upon arrival by Lucias. All were filled with exactly what Sinclair had promised, pure gold.

Thomas studied him again, took another sip of scotch and said, "You shouldn't be baffled."

"Really? Why not?"

"You're askin' for the same reason I'm payin' you."

This did not make sense, and Jesús shook his head. "What? Why would you want to pay us off so we can go on our way? The only thing I can think is that there is something you do not want us to know about." He gestured toward Antonio as he spoke who was standing behind him. Oritz glanced to the other side of the room to the woman perched on the arm of a settee. Dark-haired and aristocratic, the woman stared at him, her hazel eyes glittering. She hadn't spoken during the entirety of the meeting so far and only stared at Jesús, making him somewhat uncomfortable for some reason.

Sinclair nodded. "You're a very astute man, Mr. Oritz."

Jesús returned his attention to the Scotsman and flashed his golden smile, saying, "I try not to miss much."

"Well, in this case, you're correct."

"Am I?" Jesús tilted his head inquisitively. He hadn't expected this man to so easily give up his hand.

"There is something more. Much much more."

Jesús leaned forward and said, "Tell me more."

"Our mutual friend not only made off with your gold, but as he looked for a place to hide from ya, he came across a very interestin' discovery up in the hills around our wee town."

Propping one hand under his chin, Jesús said, "Do tell."

"As you already know, Mr. Cantrill can't quite seem to remember where your gold is. Nor can he recall where his little discovery is located thanks to an unfortunate blow to his head."

"I can fix that," Antonio said, tapping a fist into his opposite palm.

Thomas shook his head and said, "That's not going to help. But I do have a means by which he may remember somethin' more. Somethin' that works by his own admission."

"And what is that."

"Before we go any further…" Sinclair leaned into the desk, his chair giving a slight squeak, and in a slightly conspiratorial tone, he continued, "I'd like to offer you a different deal."

Jesús nodded over his shoulder toward the gold and said, "Better than that?"

"Infinitely so."

This reminded Jesús of a game he'd played under various names, both back in Spain and the Americas, North and South—el juego de las cascaras, or the shell game. "Very well. We will forgo what was under shell number one and take the second shell in your little game."

"You have chosen wisely," Sinclair said. He waved a few of his stubby fingers at the scotch decanter on the desk, and the silent woman stood and topped up their glasses.

Taking a sip of the expensive alcohol, Jesús now studied Sinclair. Why was this man offering to cut him in? Did he trust the Hole-in-the-Wall Gang for some particular reason? Was it name recognition? Just as Wells Fargo was known for its delivery coaches and banks, maybe the Gang was known for its criminality, death dealing and debauchery. Perhaps Sinclair figured they were a known quantity and were at least something rather than an unknown. In any event, he decided to play along with things for now. Placing his glass upon a cork coaster on the gleaming desk, Jesús said, "And what did you have in mind?"

Sinclair creaked back in his padded leather chair and said, "I'd like to suggest a partnership between my interests and yours."

"Go on."

"If you can help locate what Mr. Cantrill can't recall, I'll give you a quarter of everything we walk away with, and you can do what you want with the Irishman after that."

Jesús shifted in his chair, pursed his lips for a moment, then said, "That last part is very interesting; however, it is not a very equal partnership."

"Very well. What would you suggest?"

"Make it half."

"What?!"

"You heard me, Mister Sinclair. I have a lot of mouths to feed back home."

Sinclair pondered this briefly, then, much to Jesús's surprise, gave a single nod and said, "Agreed."

Oritz reached across the desk and shook the Scotsman's hand, discovering the small man's digits were even more sausage-like than his own.

"I'm givin' you free rein to do anythin' you need to jar Mr. Cantrill's memory."

Wanting to verify this part, Jesús tilted his head and asked, "Anything?"

"Aye. Short of killin' him, at least at this point. As of the last update I received, the only thing he can recall is rock, trees and a flash of gold."

Narrowing his eyes, Jesús replied, "Do not worry. We will make sure he recalls more than just a flash."

"Very well." Sinclair stood and walked around the desk. When only inches from Jesús, he stopped and looked him in the eyes. They were almost the same height, but Sinclair had the advantage weight-wise. In a low voice, the Scotsman said, "Just so we're on the same page, if you try to cross me in any way, you'll be dealing with Mr. Lucias, who you've met previously. Unfortunately, he is otherwise occupied at the moment, but trust me when I say he is a man of few words."

Jesús grinned, his assortment of gold teeth sparkling in his new business partner's eyes. His smile widened further, and he added, "Of course, you can rest assured that when you make a deal with the Hole-in-the-Wall Gang, the reverse is also true."

Antonio moved toward the office door, opened it, and stood off to one side.

As Jesús approached the exit, Sinclair said at his back, "Oh, and you can take a couple of those sacks with you, just so you can see we're all on the up and up here."

Jesús turned and nodded toward Sinclair, saying, "Many thanks, my friend."

Once Antonio had grabbed a sack in each hand, they made their way out the same way they came in, through the back door, since they didn't want to attract attention. He doubted there was much chance Johnny Law was actively out and about looking for them, not with their wounded jail and approaching fire. He figured they stood a fairly good chance of going unnoticed since the police might not think to look so close to town in the midst of their emergency. They would be hiding in plain sight, as it were—his new bowler really helping him blend in with this crowd of crazy Canadians.

While Jesús waited for Antonio to fasten the gold sacks to his horse, he realised this was a fortuitous day for the Gang. Not only were they still being rewarded, but he may have made a deal that would support and benefit the Gang and its many members for years to come. As an added bonus, he could also move forward with his other little plan and indulge in one of his favourite criminal activities, something right up there with robbery, extortion and murder.

CHAPTER THIRTY-TWO

After leaving Caleb at Doctor Brown's, Kitty returned to the Nugget to collect herself. The shock of what had happened at the pools was still fresh in her mind, and she'd decided to lie down with a cool cloth across her forehead. However, when she closed her eyes, she kept seeing the remains of Sam Shepherd floating out from under the edge of the platform, his sightless white eyes seeming to burn into hers. And so, she'd decided to keep her eyes open instead and had wanted to find something to take her mind off things for a little while.

Carla, Monique, and Lucy were off enjoying the day as she had been since the second-floor girls were not required to work the holiday. There was a chance the other ladies might be back at the cabin, where she could speak with them about her trauma, but she didn't feel up to walking all that distance, just in case they weren't there. The last thing Kitty wanted was to be alone out in the forest at the moment, especially with all the creatures creeping and crawling around.

Several minutes later, Kitty found herself in the kitchen with Maggie. Surprisingly, she hadn't been hungry for a change, but she knew the reason why. Briefly closing her eyes again, she shuddered as Sam Shepherd suddenly floated past, his blind white pupils still staring at her accusingly. Blinking her eyes open, Kitty said, "And when I tried again just now, there he was!"

"Oh, that's horrible," Maggie commiserated with a shake of her head.

"I can hardly believe it," Kitty agreed.

"You poor thing." After a pause, Maggie added, "And that poor man as well, of course."

Kitty nodded and said, "I don't know if I'll ever go near the water again after that." She grabbed another handful of peanuts from the large bowl on the counter and began shelling them.

Upon arriving in the kitchen, Maggie informed Kitty that Doctor Brown had tasked her with making some 'homemade' peanut spread. He'd been by earlier in the morning, after the ant's capture, and confiscated the remaining tin of commercial peanut paste from her pantry. He'd said he needed it for scientific experimentation, which Mr. Sinclair had authorised. When Maggie asked exactly how much additional paste Brown had wanted her to make, she'd been floored by his response of, "Oh, another ten pounds or so should be good."

Between getting her baked pies and treats out of the way, Maggie had been shelling peanuts, then running them through her meat grinder for most of the morning. Though the kitchen was currently open, the hours and selection of meals were limited today. The bar and the kitchen would be closed by mid-afternoon to give Maggie and Muddy a bit of the holiday off.

The saloon was pretty much empty already, and the food orders had mostly stopped since most people were out and about taking in the events happening around town and down at the lake, so Maggie had been able to devote more of her time to peanut processing for the doctor.

When Kitty had walked through the doors, Maggie had

said, "Just who I was needing, another volunteer!" Her other peanut helpers, assistant cook Mike and waiter Ed had already left early, both having a shortened workday because of the holiday.

And so, for the last little while, Kitty had been shucking, or shelling the peanuts, as Maggie had corrected her, adding that people shuck corn and shell nuts. Kitty knew she would have to take Maggie's word for it. Until she'd come to North America, she'd never experienced a peanut in her life. And yet now, here she sat, helping shell a huge burlap sack of the nuts they normally reserved for the bar patrons.

With a substantial amount of nuts already ground, Maggie ran the latest batch through the grinder, and the chunky paste tumbled into a bowl already half-filled with the slightly oily spread.

"What's Doctor Brown doing with this anyway? Baking cookies?" Kitty wondered.

Maggie laughed, saying, "You'd think so. He said he has another ingredient he's going to add to the paste and that you wouldn't want to eat it when he's done." She gave a small shrug and scooped the peanut spread from the bowl into a large five-pound tin that, according to the label, at one time contained 'Johnson's Finest Lard'. Tamping the lid down, Maggie sighed and said, "There! That's the lot for now, except for one thing." A broad smile broke across her face, and she added, "Would you be a dear and do me a favour?"

"Of course, Maggie. What is it?"

Maggie placed the peanut spread tin beside another already on the counter and patted their tops. "Could you run these down to Doctor Brown's office? If he's off at the fire, just leave them on his back stoop." She began untying her apron and finished, saying, "But if he's there, ask him if he needs any more; otherwise, I'm done for the day."

With a small smile, Kitty said, "It'd be a pleasure to get some fresh air." The kitchen smelled of nothing but peanuts at the moment, and she found it quite overwhelming. Growing up without them, she discovered they were an acquired taste (and smell) and preferred hazelnuts, walnuts and almonds, which had been more readily available to her in Scotland.

Kitty picked the tins up and placed them in her new lidded basket. Delighted to receive such a thoughtful and useful gift, she'd been carrying the stylish basket everywhere since Caleb gave it to her this morning. Though the tins were rather large, she'd been able to fit them inside with the lid down, but just barely.

"Okay, Maggie, I'll be back in a few minutes."

"All right, dear. And if you're still bored when you return, I'm sure we can find something else for you to do."

Kitty gave a laugh and a wave as she pushed through the screen door to the alley. The afternoon was not as stifling as she'd expected, and a moderate breeze had sprung up. Unfortunately, it was accompanied by towering, dark clouds that now threatened to obscure the last of the blue sky above. At the bottom of the stoop, Kitty took a deep breath and grimaced. The growing breeze had also brought the smell of smoke with it, no doubt from the fire near the river.

Hoping for the best, Kitty strolled down the back alley toward the doctor's office, admiring her new basket as she went and thinking of her possible life with Caleb, her mind a million miles away.

Reality came crashing back when a man stepped out of the shadows next to the building, blocking her path just a few steps short of Doctor Brown's back door.

The man smiled at her, the white scar down the right side

of his face crinkling up as he did. "Watcha got in the basket, little missy?"

"Nothin' that concerns you."

"Oh, I wouldn't be too sure about that," said another voice at her back.

Kitty spun on one heel and discovered the gold-toothed man only a few feet behind her. He grinned broadly and said, "Everything about you concerns us, Miss Kitty; you should know that.

Scarface added, "Yeah, your good health is real important to us," then sniggered at his comment.

"What do you want?"

"Is it not obvious?" Gold-tooth inquired.

"Yeah, we want you," Scarface said as he lunged toward Kitty.

Kitty stepped back and brought her tin-filled basket upward and outward. It slammed with a solid thud into Scarface, connecting with his chin. His teeth cracked together, and he stumbled backwards, falling on his bottom with a surprised grunt.

"That was not nice." Gold-tooth placed a hand on Kitty's shoulder from behind.

"Neither is this." Kitty stepped backwards and drove one square bootheel down onto the top of the man's foot, and he let out a shrill squawk. As she stomped, she jammed her elbow backwards into his solar plexus, turning his squawk into an 'oof' as she knocked the air out of him.

Her attention still on Gold-tooth, Kitty realised too late

that she hadn't been keeping tabs on his scar-faced companion. Without warning, the man suddenly wrapped one grimy arm around her chest from behind and clamped his dust-covered hand across her mouth. He hissed in her ear, "That's enough of that for now, little missy."

Kitty struggled and tried to stomp on Scarface's feet as well, but the man had seen what she'd done to his companion and kept them well back and away from her solid boot heels.

Scarface briefly removed his hand from Kitty's mouth, and she prepared to scream. But Gold-tooth was right there and immediately tied a filthy rag across her lips to gag her, and it did so in more ways than one. She continued to struggle, but her hands and legs were soon bound, and she found herself slung over the back of Scarface's ride.

Flicking his horse's reins and leading them into the forest, Gold-tooth said, "Let us find out just how much Mr. Caleb Cantrill can actually remember."

End of Book 2

FINAL WORDS

We are now two-thirds of the way through this series, and I hope you are enjoying reading it as much as I am enjoying writing it. Monster novels, movies and comics have always held a special place in my heart, just as I am sure they do with you. I'll take something unknown skulking around in the dark over a maniac with a knife any day. And if that unknown thing is a monstrous horror from the past, well then, all the better.

Though I write Horror Thrillers, I have never written a Western Horror Thriller, and it has been an enjoyable challenge. I hope the world I have been constructing seems believable to some extent and, despite the monsters, is a place you might like to visit if it existed in the real world. This series has required a large amount of research, and I have tried to remain as historically accurate as possible while interweaving facts of the real world with my fictional characters and places in a seamless fashion. I hope I have succeeded and that you feel like you are there in each and every chapter you read.

With my challenges hopefully out of the way for now and no more hip replacements in my future (I've run out of bad hips) or animals to go missing (I've run out of pets), I am hoping the final book in this trilogy, CLAW Emergence: Return to Darkness, will make it into your hands a little more quickly than the six months it took to bring Into Daylight into the world. If you are already part of the Katie Berry Books Insiders, you will never miss a thing and know as soon as it's available. If you're not an Insider, you should subscribe to stay up to date and for your chance to win two great monthly prizes (see elsewhere in this novel with a link to subscribe or go to Katieberry.ca).

If this story entertained you and you would like to share your thoughts with others, please leave a review; they are critical to a book's success. To make things easier, here is a direct link to the Amazon review page for CLAW Emergence Book 1 so you can leave a few thoughts while everything is fresh in your memory:

Amazon.com/review/create-review?&asin=B0C9XQ9RT8

Please make sure to sign up for my newsletter, The Katie Berry Books Insider, for further novel updates, free short stories, chapter previews and giveaways. To join, click here:

https://katieberry.ca/become-a-katie-berry-books-insider-and-win/

Good health and great reads to you all,

-Katie Berry

CURRENT AND UPCOMING RELEASES

CLAW: A Canadian Thriller (November 28th, 2019)

CLAW Emergence Novelette – Caleb Cantrill (September 13th, 2020)

CLAW Emergence Novelette – Kitty Welch - (November 26th, 2020)

CLAW Resurgence (September 30th, 2021)

CLAW Emergence Book 1 (December 24th. 2022)

CLAW Emergence Book 2 (July 1st, 2023)

CLAW Emergence Book 3 (Fall 2023)

CLAW Resurrection (Fall/Winter 2023)

ABANDONED: A Lively Deadmarsh Novel Book 1 (February 26th, 2021)

ABANDONED: A Lively Deadmarsh Novel Book 2 (May 31st, 2021)

ABANDONED: A Lively Deadmarsh Novel Book 3 (December 23rd, 2021)

ABANDONED: A Lively Deadmarsh Novel Book 4 (July 15th, 2022)

BESIEGED: A Lively Deadmarsh Novel (Spring 2024)

CONNECTIONS

Email: katie@katieberry.ca
Website: https://katieberry.ca

SHOPPING LINKS

CLAW: A Canadian Thriller:
Amazon eBook: https://amzn.to/31QCw7x
Paperback Version: **https://amzn.to/31RYPK7**
Amazon Audible Audiobook: https://amzn.to/2Gj3j45
(Also available on all other major audiobook platforms)

CLAW Resurgence:
Amazon eBook: https://amzn.to/2YeDdZt
Paperback Version: https://amzn.to/31RYPK7
Amazon Audible Audiobook: https://amzn.to/36nLSgk
(Also available on all other major audiobook platforms)

CLAW Emergence: Tales from Lawless – Kitty Welch:
Amazon eBook: https://amzn.to/37aSnAn
Large Print Paperback Version: https://amzn.to/3tTs0a9
Audiobook on Audible: https://amzn.to/3szAmXM

CLAW Emergence: Tales from Lawless – Caleb Cantrill:
Amazon eBook: https://amzn.to/3ldYoC3
Large Print Paperback Version: https://amzn.to/3meDVg9
Audiobook on Audible: https://amzn.to/3qkKvUe

CLAW Emergence Book 1: From the Shadows:
Amazon eBook: https://amzn.to/3VnB6di
Paperback Version: https://amzn.to/3Xjv5Q1
Audiobook: August 29th, 2023
(Also available on all other major audiobook platforms)

CLAW EMERGENCE Book 2: Into Daylight
Amazon eBook: https://amzn.to/3JEC9Tf
Paperback Version: https://amzn.to/3NwKfhG
Audiobook Version: Coming Soon
(Also available on all other major audiobook platforms)

ABANDONED: A Lively Deadmarsh Novel Book 1 – Arrivals
and Awakenings
Amazon eBook: https://amzn.to/3jM3GDX
Paperback: https://amzn.to/3yruNLL
Audiobook: https://amzn.to/3yNot00
(Also available on all other major audiobook platforms)

ABANDONED: A Lively Deadmarsh Novel Book 2 –
Beginnings and Betrayals
Amazon eBook: https://amzn.to/3BTn4a9
Paperback: https://amzn.to/3BTneyh
Audiobook: https://amzn.to/3FrwcVF
(Also available on all other major audiobook platforms)

ABANDONED: A Lively Deadmarsh Novel Book 3 – Chaos
and Corruption
Amazon eBook: https://amzn.to/3HpBNMM
Paperback: https://amzn.to/3IOGTE7
Audiobook: https://amzn.to/3PtVyqr
(Also available on all other major audiobook platforms)

ABANDONED: A Lively Deadmarsh Novel Book 4 –
Deception and Deliverance
Amazon eBook: https://amzn.to/3w06XqF
Paperback: https://amzn.to/3Qh5t3m
Audiobook: https://amzn.to/3NVOdC9
(Also available on all other major audiobook platforms)

Made in the USA
Monee, IL
30 July 2023

40171756R00156